NOT

Until

HER

MIRANDA MELANIE

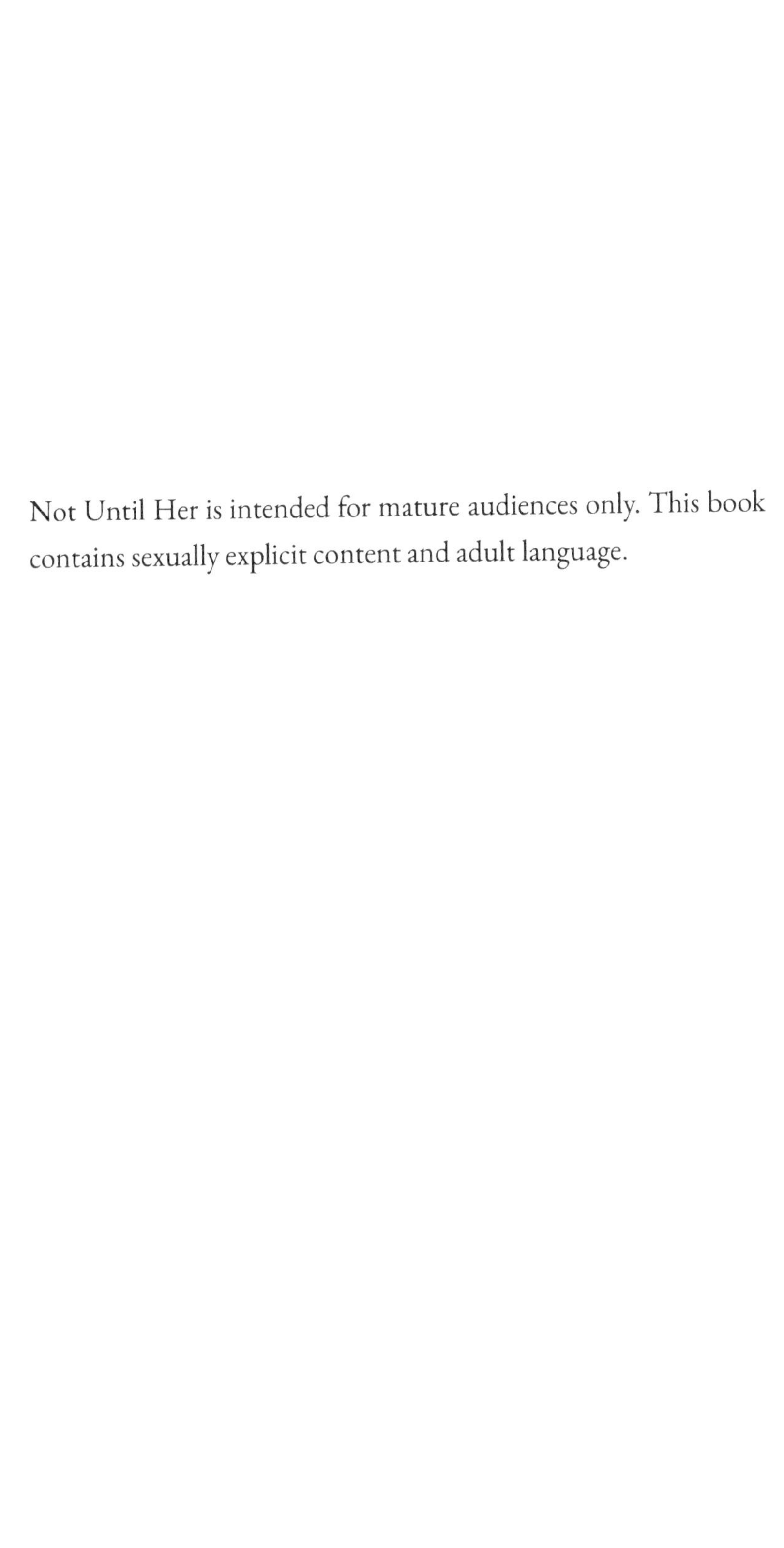

Not Until Her is intended for mature audiences only. This book contains sexually explicit content and adult language.

1

It's the best day of my life.

I might have said that before a few times, and might have thought I meant it.

This time is the real deal.

I have been living in the same apartment since my divorce was finalized almost five years ago. My six year old daughter has lived half of her life in this apartment with me, and the other half at her dad's house. Both places have their flaws, his being that *he* is there.

The problem with my apartment started about two years ago, when a couple of freshly eighteen year old boys moved in next door.

Sleeping through the night has not been something I'm very familiar with since that first day.

Neither has Dahlia, my poor, sweet child. At least not in her own bedroom, which shares a wall with the neighbors. So it's been the two of us in my bed. She sleeps better than I do, living in blissful ignorance of the problem. It's like the muffled sounds would reach my ears because I *knew* they were there.

They're gamers. Gamers shout *a lot*.

And always at two in the morning.

Today, a couple of moving trucks were parked on the curb. One of them was actually blocking my car in, preventing me from heading to work on time. It felt like a sign that I was meant to stay put, so that's exactly what I did.

I think the last time I pretended to be sick was at least a year ago, so it's not like I'm abusing the option.

I spend my day going back and forth between watching true crime documentaries, and watching from my front window as the two of them and their families head up and down the stairs with their arms full.

I watch them hug goodbye and go their separate ways.

They grow up so fast.

Thankfully.

I am so glad they're gone. I am so ready to sprawl out on my bed without worrying that I'll accidentally punch my daughter in the face while I sleep. I'm ready for her to get used to her own bed again. We had been doing so good before they happened, she almost always made it through the night.

I'm not foolish enough to think this will be the easiest adjustment, but it's still exciting to start. I sincerely hope whoever moves in next has some empathy for a single mother, and doesn't play video games with loud gun sound effects.

We can't move. We get such a deal on our rent.

Sweet Ted, the landlord. He's the type that seems grumpy and closed off, but he's got a great heart once you get to know him. He's quick to take care of any problems, and knows a guy for everything. We've never had a problem lasting more than a couple of days because if he can't get someone to come down in a timely manner, he does it himself. I'm guessing he was a plumber in his youth, but I have no confirmation on that.

Also... he doesn't let me pay rent in the month of December. It's the most generous anyone's ever been to us, we literally *can't ever move*. We're too spoiled.

There's a knock on the door that interrupts my thoughts. I know without checking that it's drop-off time. Caleb has been surprisingly on time for the last few weeks, which I will not be questioning. It's been nice to have Dahlia here before the sun goes down.

"There's my princess!" I greet her cheerfully as I open the door.

I really do miss her when she's gone. Our apartment is too quiet. I get bored. The three days go by so slowly.

"Mommy! We got you flowers!" She holds out some pink roses excitedly, waving them in front of me.

Of course he would let her go picking flowers from some stranger's yard, and he wouldn't think about thorns poking her fingers.

"Careful honey, those stems can hurt." I give him a pointed look, the first one he's received since I opened the door.

He has a few more in his own hands. I ignore them.

I go back to my daughter and accept the rose, careful not to let it slide in her grip. The last thing I want is to make her cry the second she gets home. I still have to feed her dinner, and start the long process of getting her to sleep in her own bed. It's going to be a long night.

I hold up the flower to examine it, and... it looks like the thorns were scraped off.

"I clipped them from the bushes, and I cut off the thorns before she touched them. No need to worry," he tells me.

I guess I can throw a couple of dad points his way for that. I don't give them out often.

"Thanks," I say tightly. "How was your weekend?"

She had Monday off of school for a holiday, so it really was a weekend for them. A rare occasion with our custody arrangement that usually only allows both of us a single day without getting her ready for school in the morning.

"It was great. Took her down to Grandma and Grampa's house, and we got to spend some time with aunt Catherine. You swam the weekend away in the pool, didn't you?" He looks down at her with the last sentence and she nods vigorously.

I miss that house. That indoor pool. His parents. His sister. I miss everything about my old life except for him. I'm glad Dahlia gets to enjoy it, and still sees all of her family often. His sister is incredible and Dahlia adores her. She's kind, attentive, and fun without being reckless. Catherine is the best aunt to her that I could possibly ask for.

The same goes for his parents. I don't know how he came out of that family.

"Are you tired, bug?" She nods some more, and I know it's true. She'd be talking my ear off if she had any energy to spare. "We better get to relaxing then. Have a good night, Caleb."

"Actually, do you have a minute? To talk?"

Not for you.

But I always make it a point to be nice to him in front of Dahlia.

"Can you set your bag in your room, and I'll be right there?" I give her a kiss on her forehead as she goes, agreeing without words. She should sleep very well tonight, from the looks of it.

"These are for you, by the way."

He hands me the rest of the flowers.

"You can't just go clipping flowers off of people's rose bushes."

"I didn't. They're *my* rose bushes."

He looks so smug. I don't show him the reaction he wants, which is for me to be shocked. Maybe he's even hoping I'm impressed.

I am both shocked and impressed.

Where the hell did he find the time to plant rose bushes?

Actually, scratch that. I'm sure he didn't have to do it himself.

"Why are you giving me flowers?"

"I thought it would be a nice thing to do, Reya. I don't even get a thank you?" he asks.

"You never do nice things for me. There's an ulterior motive here."

"I don't want anything from you," he says.

"Good," I say.

He sighs, then pauses.

"I just have to tell you something."

I groan.

"Oh no, what did you do?"

"Whatever terrible thing you're assuming, can you stop?"

I offend him so easily that I can already see his ears turning red.

"Just tell me! If it's not a terrible thing, then I'll be able to stop assuming."

He moves to sit on one of the chairs I have by the front door. We don't have a back patio, so I take advantage of the space up here. It doesn't bother me that it isn't private, the most I do out here is sit on my phone, or pretend I know how to crochet.

I don't. But trying makes me feel like I have my shit together.

And it's very therapeutic, even if the only result is a bunch of tangled yarn thrown in the back of my closet. Vic has been waiting for the day I successfully finish the headband I promised her for years. I don't think that day will ever come.

Caleb motions for me to sit down, looking impatient. Not a new trait when it comes to me.

I sit, hoping it will make this go faster. I need to feed my daughter before she passes out.

"She already ate, by the way. One of those toasted subs from the shop down the road."

I can't help but roll my eyes. That might be convenient, but it's not part of our agreement. On his drop off days, I always do dinner. When I drop her off, he does dinner. It's how this has always worked.

"What if I had already started cooking? You could have let me know beforehand."

It's a seriously rude oversight.

He nods.

"You're right, I should have. I just thought I was doing you a favor."

"I don't need favors from you," I tell him.

"I know you don't."

We sit there in silence while I fume, and he pretends he's calm. I know it's pretending because of all the years he's been in my life. He's not capable of fooling me.

"Well, spit it out. What do you want to tell me?"

He clasps his hands together, looking way too serious for my liking.

Shit, this better not be about custody. I can not afford to change my life around again for his convenience.

"You know that I've been seeing Raquel for a few months."

I nod. Sure, he mentioned he was dating a girl he'd met at work. He also told me I didn't have to worry about him introducing her to Dahlia, because it was too soon.

Is it not too soon anymore? I guess that was a couple months ago.

"It's going well," he tells me with a smile. *Barf.* "Really well, actually. I wanted to invite her this weekend, but I hadn't had a chance to talk to you."

"Thanks for waiting to talk to me."

"Of course," he says. As if he's always been *so reasonable*.

Spoiler alert: he has not.

"Anyway, I think the best way to move forward would be for you to meet her."

I pause. I think about this.

I know it's probably true. I should meet her, I just don't really *want* to meet her. Nothing against her, but how awkward would that be?

Great to meet you, I gave birth to your boyfriend's kid.

I shudder.

"You want me to meet her?" I repeat.

"It was her idea, actually. It's important to her that you know she's around for the right reasons."

I'll give her points for that.

"And you have no arguments? You're not worried about me threatening your new girlfriend?" I ask.

"No arguments," he replies. "She comes in peace."

"How will this work? I'm stuck third wheeling?"

"You don't have to be. It could just be the two of you."

"Yes," I answer quickly. The less time around him, the better.

We discuss a date, a night next week when he'll have Dahlia. It's probably going to be the most awkward dinner of both of our lives, but I'm not really nervous.

Having terrible taste in boyfriends doesn't make or break a person. I *married* Caleb, and I'm the coolest person I know. Hopefully there's a pattern there.

2

"I don't know if I'm up for it."

"Did Reya Barry really just say she isn't up for something? Where are the flying pigs?"

I snort.

"Dahlia hasn't been sleeping well the last few nights. I don't think exhausted is even an adequate word for how I feel."

I can picture her pouting. A combination of feeling sorry for me, and feeling sorry for herself to miss out on my presence.

"She won't sleep in her own bed?" Vic asks.

"I knew it would be difficult, but I might give up. I'd rather sacrifice space in my own bed forever," I admit. That would be better than the heartbreaking sound of my daughter crying when I know I'm what's causing it.

"Don't do that. Have you tried laying with her until she falls asleep?"

"Of course I have!" I snap.

"Well, don't take it out on me," she admonishes. "I sleep just fine in my own bed."

"You know how irritable I get without sleep. I'm going on night four."

I grab a Pepsi out of my fridge, one of my only vices these days. I stopped drinking alcohol over a year ago, after I was responsible for a really uncomfortable situation involving our friend Autumn, her boyfriend, and her ex.

Then I fell asleep while the good stuff was happening. That's the worst part. What's the point in drama if I don't get to watch it unfold?

"But she'll be at Caleb's." I can hear that pout in her voice. "You can drink a couple of your sodas, put on something sexy, come to karaoke night with me, and then sleep! Peacefully! I really, *really* don't want to go alone, babe."

And the entire thing is Autumn's worst nightmare, so Vic can't exactly ask her. Otherwise that's exactly what I'd suggest. Why does it have to be karaoke, and not a trip to the library?

"Why do you have to go at all?"

"Because I see this woman at yoga twice a week, and I promised her I'd be there to support her business. I really don't want to hear the disappointment in her voice while my ass is in the air, Reya." She pauses for emphasis. "Amanda *always* catches me off guard when my ass is in the air."

Okay, I do understand. I don't want Vic to suffer through that. She has to go.

"Plus, I want to hear your beautiful voice," she adds, really pulling all the stops she's got.

"It would be cruel of me to deprive you of my talent."

"It would!" She yells it so loudly that I wince and pull the phone away from my ear.

"Okay, calm down over there. What are you wearing?" I ask.

"You know that blueish green dress? It's the only one that fits me at the moment."

I gasp. "Not the one with the tassels."

"Yes, that very one. I refuse to go shopping for clothes that won't fit me in a couple weeks."

It's a boho-chic nightmare. I fully believe Vic can pull off anything she wears, but... does anyone really pull off any clothing with tassels?"But you still have that black one from when you were pregnant with Eli, don't you?"

I switch the phone to my other ear, grimacing. When you're too stubborn to hold your phone in your hands, it kind of hurts to smush it against your ear with your shoulder. I find my common sense somewhere, shaking my head at myself and pressing the speaker button before setting it down on the counter.

"I wish I could still fit into it, but I never got this big with Eli. I'm honestly worried this girl is going to come out weighing fifteen pounds."

I shudder at the thought. Dahlia was a little less than nine, and even that seemed impossible at the time.

"Then there goes any chance of us coordinating our outfits. What time am I picking you up?" I ask defeatedly.

I end up in a pair of emerald green woven pants, and a long sleeve black top with lace around the collar. One thing about me is that it's always one or the other: big pants and a tight shirt or tight pants and a big shirt. Another thing about me is that I will religiously coordinate my outfits with whoever I'm with. I'm grateful that this is the outfit I came up with tonight, because I'm incredibly comfortable, *and* Vic and I look super cute standing next to each other.

It better be warm inside this bar, because neither of us are dressed like we know it's the middle of winter.

I've never been here before, which is surprising. Not that I make a habit of visiting many bars, but my girls and I had a phase. When Autumn was freshly twenty-one, we made sure she had the full experience. There wasn't a single weekend for months where we weren't getting drunk together.

Tall Glass is technically a town over, but that means very little when the towns are this small. We arrive less than ten minutes after I pick up Vic, to a brick building with an edgy blue neon sign.

"There are a lot of pregnant people here," I whisper once we're inside.

"She did invite everyone."

"Is everyone in your yoga class pregnant?" I ask with a chuckle. She looks at me sideways.

"That's the whole point, babe. Prenatal yoga?"

Wow, okay. I missed that fact, but it makes sense.

"Then why the hell is this happening at a *ba*r of all places?" She fully turns to look at me, a disbelieving look on her face.

"Where else would you host a karaoke night? Starbucks?"

I don't think that's a terrible idea. Why make it strictly a night-time thing? Get my iced tea in the morning, a cake pop, and a show. All before work? Someone should make that happen.

I think a lot less people would complain about Monday mornings.

Or a lot more, depending on who's doing the singing...

Okay, scratch that idea.

A woman approaches us with a smile that takes up most of her face. Her outfit actually looks eerily similar to my own, colors and all, except hers is complimented by a very large, round belly.

"Thanks for coming, cute stuff!" She wraps her arms around Vic and squeezes tight. "This is the best turn out we've gotten at one of these."

"Of course! I love that for you!" She points to me. "This is my best friend, Reya. Reya, this is Amanda from my yoga class. We actually have the same due date."

"March first?" I ask cautiously, because I might not be so sure that's the date. Vic has told me a hundred times at this point.

It's a leap year, so the odds are good that one of these children isn't going to have another birthday for the next three years if I'm right.

"Initially, yep." She nods. "It's looking like little Caleb is going to be ready sooner than that now."

I quickly look at Vic and she smirks.

What are the odds? Why can't I escape?

"Caleb?" I ask, gesturing towards her belly. She puts her hand over it.

"After his grandpa." That huge smile is back on her face, despite the fact that I'm sure I look ill.

There are too many Caleb's in the world. I'll never escape.

"How exciting," I manage to say. "It was nice to meet you, but I am desperately in need of a soda."

Maybe even something a little stronger, given the hoarse voice currently belting out the wrong words over the speakers. My eyes land on the bar.

"Great to meet you, too! I'll see you both up there!"

She gives Vic a friendly pat on the shoulder before turning away.

Vic bursts into laughter as soon as we start walking.

"Yikes."

"I thought you might feel that way."

"That reminds me," I tell her as we sit on a couple of stools. The bartender looks overwhelmed, so it's a good thing we're patient people. Actually, Vic is the patient one, and it makes me want to do better whenever I'm around her. I try not to let my leg shake too aggressively while we wait. "I have a date with his new girlfriend coming up."

She shakes her head.

"I know you hate the guy, but you can't go stealing his girlfriend. You're supposed to be peacefully co-parenting."

My jaw drops.

"Not a *date* date, wow Vic. I'm going to pretend you don't think I would stoop that low."

"You called it a date, what else am I supposed to think?"

"I call everything a date. This is a date right now," I say, pointing between us.

"Don't tell my husband that."

I tilt my head to look at her through my lashes.

"Your husband loves me, he'd be happy for us."

"Maybe," she admits with a shrug. "But he'd still be a little jealous."

I notice the woman working finally make her way down to us and I give her my best smile. The kind that says, *I also work in customer service, and I know your pain, and we will be the easiest customers you have to deal with all night.'*

"What are we drinking tonight?" she asks us in a husky voice. The kind of voice I bet makes her lots of tips. The kind of voice I wouldn't mind bossing me around.

She's attractive. Blonde hair in a messy bun, tattoos covering her arms, shoulders, and chest. She's probably out of my league. Probably straight, even though I mentally slap myself for making the assumption. I hate when it's done to me.

"We'll do a Pepsi and a Sierra Mist please."

"I've got Coke and Sprite," she offers. My heart sinks.

"Sprite is fine for me," Vic quickly responds. When she looks to me, there's concern on her face. I am a picky, particular person. I would choose not to be if I could, because I hate this feeling right here. Like a normal person would decide on a different drink, but I can't be normal.

"Nothing for me then, thanks." I try not to sound disappointed.

A small frown forms on the woman's face, before she turns to look at the other customers sitting at her bar. None of them are looking her way, needing her attention. Instead of turning back towards us, or to grab Vic's drink, she ducks down and out of sight.

We share a confused look.

When she appears again, standing, there's a can in her hand. One of those mini ones that isn't ever enough to curb the craving.

But I don't care, I am so happy to see it. There's practically a heavenly, glowing light illuminating it before me.

"I keep these hidden for a regular of mine, but I can spare one or two." She cracks it open, and it's the most beautiful sound I've ever heard. I watch as she pours it into a glass filled with ice.

I must have been so transfixed by the miracle she performed for me, that I didn't realize she'd already poured Vic's as well, until she was placing both drinks in front of us.

"You're my hero," I tell her. I'm in awe.

"Do you guys have mozzarella sticks?" Vic asks.

My stomach growls at the last two words. I haven't eaten enough as it is today, but there's something about the dim lighting of a crowded bar that makes fried food sound so much better than it actually is.

"We do. Just one order? Comes with six."

"Probably two, just to be on the safe side."

Okay, so maybe we aren't the easiest customers, but she doesn't seem to mind.

I give Vic a high-five, ecstatic that we're on the same page. Neither of us need to eat that much cheese and bread in one sitting, but life is all about the small things that bring you joy, right? Eating all six mozzarella sticks will bring me joy, despite the inevitable tummy ache.

The woman behind Vic taps her shoulder, and it's obvious when she turns around that they also know each other from their class.

And the woman on the other side, apparently. The three of them get caught up in what looks to be a very exciting conversation. I wouldn't know for sure, I can't hear it over the sudden sound of another terrible singer on the stage.

I watch their performance for a beat, but I'm just not entertained by sober karaoke. They either try way too hard, or they're too reserved. Either way, not fun.

Given the amount of women here that can't consume any alcoholic beverages tonight, I think I'm in for a lot of it.

I glance at the bartender again to find her expression probably matches my own. I don't know how I'd last, having to listen to this every week.

I say as much the next time she's close enough to hear me.

"It's not always so bad. The drunk ones are usually pretty entertaining."

"I was just thinking the same thing."

"Are you going to get up there and give us a song, pinky?"

Oh, no.

I loathe that nickname, but I manage not to cringe.

"It's Reya," I put my hand out for her to shake and she does just that. "And maybe, but it won't be nearly as fun considering–" I point to the Pepsi.

"I'm Bailey. You sober?"

I nod, and then realize her question probably goes deeper than this current moment.

"I mean, it's not like I *can't* drink. I don't need to stay sober or anything, I've just taken a long hiatus at this point."

She smirks at me.

"So it doesn't make me a terrible person to offer you a shot or two? For entertainment purposes."

She suddenly nods at someone to the left of me, and starts pouring their drink without saying a word. She's clearly a natural, her movements fluid and confident.

I wait until she's done and handed off whatever whiskey-filled monstrosity she just created. Not that I doubt what she's doing, I just don't like whiskey.

"Sure," I say when her hands stop moving for a few seconds. "I'll take a shot, whatever you recommend."

Vic hears enough that she looks over her shoulder to raise a brow at me, but she goes right back to talking, like she just *had* to pause and do that mid-sentence. She's adorable.

But Bailey? Bailey is hot. The more I watch her, the more I want to keep watching her. Anyone would feel the same if they paid attention to how she works in her space. I bet she's been at this bar for years, knows every inch of it like the back of her hand.

When she hands me the intimidating sized shot glass–*did they start making these bigger or something?*–I ask her.

"How long have you worked here?"

And then I down the shot. It's smooth enough that the burn doesn't make my eyes water, and I allow a few seconds before taking a sip of my soda.

"A few years. My uncle owns the place."

"I take it you enjoy this?" I point towards her busy hands.

She smiles at someone else, grabbing their empty glass.

"It has its good and bad days, but it's what I know how to do. And I make decent tips, so that's a good enough reason for me to stick with it. I feel bad for anyone who has to live paycheck to paycheck."

I tilt my drink at her.

"Thanks for your pity," I say.

"What do you do?" she asks.

"I manage a store."

"That sounds like quite a workload."

"It's all I know how to do," I say, repeating her earlier words. "There are worse things than selling band t-shirts to angsty teenagers."

Bailey's nose crinkles.

"There are much better things."

I look around the bar exaggeratedly. The way she can't let her focus stay in one place for too long, because there's always someone else that needs a drink, or has something to say. It looks like utter chaos.

And I'm probably her worst nightmare, the kind of person getting her caught in a conversation when she has other things to do.

It's too bad I don't really care.

"I couldn't imagine doing what you're doing. I'd lose my mind."

She smirks.

"I lost my mind a long time ago, pinky."

She's seriously going to need to not call me that again.

I'm spared at least for the moment when she walks away, answering to a raised hand on the opposite end. I get irritated with customers as it is, she's practically a saint for dealing with drunk, obnoxious ones.

Vic is finally done with her own conversation, seeming to come back to the real world when she looks at me.

"How long does it take to get mozzarella sticks made? They just fry them in oil, right?"

I nod. "Might be my fault. I'm quite distracting."

"Are you flirting with the bartender?"

"Not yet, I'm not."

3

I'm not the most attractive I've ever been as I scarf down mozzarella sticks, but I'm not the *least* attractive. I know that because Bailey keeps glancing sideways over at me, no matter what she's doing. I know what someone who's interested looks like, and it's exactly what I'm seeing.

At some point, a guy walked behind the bar and started making drinks. I watch as they make their way through a rush, moving around each other perfectly. Not an elbow bumped or a drop spilled.

Vic asks me to sing a song with her and another one of the women from her class, but I'm not a fan of the song. I know what my voice is meant for and what it's not.

She glares daggers into me as she's dragged onto the stage without me. I'll make it up to her, she'll just have to be patient.

Vic has always been a fan of my singing voice, swears she could listen to it all day.

She doesn't believe me when I say the same thing back to her. She has the voice of a damn angel, and she hits notes that I could only dream of. It's obvious that as soon as the first words leave her mouth, the entire place is enraptured. People around me, ones that were uninterested and involved in their own stories, have shut up to pay attention.

She still won't believe me after this, despite all of this clear evidence. Her friend is good, but her voice shakes with nerves, and she could really raise the volume a bit. All in all, they're the least embarrassing act of the night.

So far.

I watch as the applause quiets, and the next duo takes their place in front of the mics.

"Do you ever come out from behind there and take a stab at it?"

Bailey chuckles and shakes her head.

"Not usually, but no one has gone out of their way to convince me."

"I have to go out of my way. Got it." My ears are filled with giggles from the next two girls trying to sing. Given their nerves, I doubt they're going to stay up there for the whole song, something by Rihanna I think. I raise a brow at Bailey. "Does that mean I have to reach back there and pull you out?"

She laughs loudly, gaining the surprised attention from her coworker.

"Dave," she calls to him, before holding up the same bottle she'd used to pour my shot. "Mind if I..." Then she points to the stage area.

He shakes his head in disbelief, but seems amused. I must be special, because something tells me no one really has gotten her out here.

"Have a blast, hon'."

"I'm going to need this first," she tells me before throwing back a shot of her own. I watch her throat move as she swallows and it's one of the single hottest things I've witnessed. I've never found necks to be particularly attractive, but there is a first time for everything.

"I'll take another one, too. Fuck it."

Only after we've both taken our second shot, do my eyes track her as she walks around the bar to stand next to me. She smells strongly of vanilla, enough to remind me of the days I only ever bought the cheapest, sweetest body spray I could get my hands on.

It's honestly a little off-putting, but not enough that I reject her outstretched hand.

"I won't do Taylor Swift. Anything else is on the table."

I gasp, a look of horror filling my face. There goes my game plan.

"What's wrong with Taylor Swift?"

"What's not?" She smiles, completely oblivious to the fact that I'm actually horrified. "But we'll start with how overplayed she is. I can't count the amount of times I've been forced to listen to people squeal the words to *Shake It Off*. Grown men think that choice is hilarious."

I'll let that slide. Any song is annoying if you hear it too much, and I can go the rest of this night pretending that's her only problem with one of my favorite artists. My normal, overzealous defense will just dampen the mood.

We sweet-talk our way to be up next, mostly because Vic was signed up multiple times. I get a little sass from her for choosing Bailey as my first partner, but again I tell her I'll make it up to her.

Bailey chooses *Mr. Brightside*, and I somehow manage to refrain from making a comment. It's not a bad choice, but she wanted to talk about songs that are overplayed?

It's a cute moment, when the music starts. We look at each other and smile, feeling the rush of a bunch of random, pregnant womens' eyes on us.

Not that being pregnant is a relevant fact about our audience, but I haven't been able to forget it.

The second Bailey starts singing, I look away from her and hold back a cringe. She's one of *those*. She's trying really hard, not matching the pitch for a single second. You know when you can tell someone was told they had a beautiful voice as a child? And then they roll with it for the rest of their lives, and sing like they have to prove that's still true? Even when it isn't?

Yeah.

I sing louder than I normally would, just enough to fill my own ears. To keep everything else out.

It only works half the time.

I still enjoy myself, and when all is done I can't stop smiling.

"Holy shit," Bailey yells. "You're a literal star."

I wave her off.

"Yeah, right. I'm just having fun."

"Everyone in the world wishes that their version of *just having fun* sounded that good."

"Reya!" Vic's voice reaches me before her hand wraps around my arm. "It's our turn. Get back up there."

I give Bailey an apologetic smile, but I'm not that sorry. This is going to be good.

I made out with Bailey. A lot.

It was almost more, but I thought that would've really upset the Uber driver.

More than we already had. The poor thing was so uncomfortable.

I insisted that Vic should head home without me, and that was her compromise. She would only leave without me if she could get me an Uber. Bailey was already planning to take one home, so there was an added stop.

Her apartment was much closer to the bar, and I pouted when we reached it. She tried convincing me to go inside with her, but I found some scrap of self control to tell her I couldn't.

We exchanged numbers. We'll see how things go.

I had fun, but I know we're not a love match or anything. A couple hours of talking quickly let me know that we don't have anything in common. They say opposites attract and all that, but there's no way I could show serious interest in someone who hates Taylor Swift that much.

It goes way deeper than the cringey old men at karaoke night. She's really got something against her, and I think hating on successful women for no good reason is a red flag. That's all.

I don't think I got drunk, I don't have a hangover. Then again, I always chug a glass of water before bed so that probably helped. All I woke up with was the need to pee, which is exactly why I got into the habit. If my full bladder isn't going to pull me out of bed, nothing is.

I pull a t-shirt over my head as I walk out of my bathroom, and head for my kitchen.

If I could survive on drinking Pepsi all day long, that's what I would reach for in my fridge. Unfortunately, the amount of caffeine does nothing to energize me these days, which is the downside of my little addiction. I remember when one can would make me wired and jittery. I miss it.

I'm not the biggest coffee fan, I only drink it when I have no other options. Although tea doesn't exactly taste the best, it does the trick when I throw in three bags at a time. Sometimes I spice it up with sugar, or honey, or fruit flavored syrup.

It's a cold morning, so I fill my electric kettle and pull out a box of tea that smells like cinnamon and vanilla. Maybe it's a controversial opinion to have, but I think smelling tea is always better than drinking it.

If only that gave me the boost I require.

My chilly hardwood floors have the cold seeping through my fuzzy rainbow socks. What I miss most about living with another adult is that there was a chance they could turn the heater on before I got out of bed. Caleb usually did, and despite his many faults, it was appreciated.

It would help if I had Amelia pick out some rugs for the space, but I always forget how necessary they are until I'm actually standing in my kitchen and making my hot tea.

Which means I remember every day, just not for very long.

It takes a few seconds for me to realize that my usual silent morning isn't silent. The sound of footsteps from outside the door reaches my ears. Low, mumbling voices, and the occasional laugh. It's not only the fact that people exist out there that takes me by surprise, but the time of day. These were prime sleeping hours for the kids that used to live next door.

My curiosity leads me to my window, the one overlooking the large front patio that connects the two apartments. I push the curtain aside, just the smallest crack to avoid being spotted. I want to have the one up on my new neighbor, by knowing what to expect from them before they get their first impression of me. I tend to get very mixed reactions when people meet me for the first time. They either think I'm the most adorable teenager they've ever seen, or way too immature for my grown age.

I can't even blame them. Being mature is overrated.

The first thing I see is the back of a man's head. His hair is a mix of differing shades of gray. There's someone sitting in a chair–my chair, actually–whose face I can't see either, because they're facing away from me. Long, shimmering, golden blonde hair falls over their shoulder, and I see the side of what appears to be black sunglasses. I'm led to believe there's someone facing *them*, but the man must be perfectly blocking them from my view. I back away, not feeling like being a total creep today. I'm sure I'll have a chance to introduce myself soon. I usually wouldn't care about doing it right this moment, but I haven't fixed the bedhead I no doubt have, and I'm still feeling grumpy about the cold.

If they're still checking things out, or moving things, or whatever they're doing this afternoon, then I'll introduce myself on my way out to work.

My phone chirps on the kitchen counter, and I jump like I've been caught. I huff a breath, hating how easily sounds do it to me.

Destiny: *I have a headache. Can't come in today.*

I scowl at the screen. Destiny has a headache every other week. I want to ask if she's heard of Excedrin, but I'm a nice boss. A cool boss. I'm the manager they actually want to work with most of the time.

Funny how that results in more of them calling out on my days. I don't get it. Jenna, my co-manager, is terrifying. I can tell that working with her makes our employees nervous, but telling her that they can't make it at all must be scarier somehow.

Reya: *Did you ask Macy or Paige if they could take your shift?*

I already know she didn't. She's going to say she did, but Paige will confirm for me tonight that she didn't hear from her.

Every. Other. Week. We play this game.

Destiny: *They said they can't.*

Reya: *Feel better.*

But what I really mean, underneath those two words, is that I hope she quits soon so I can play a different game. I'm bored of this one.

Working a thirteen hour day instead of my usual eight or nine means nothing for my paycheck. Coming in early to cover someone's shift doesn't benefit me in any way. Making a set salary has its ups and downs for that reason. I get paid enough to typically make up for moments like these, but it's hard not to dwell when it happens.

And it feels like a waste. One of our employees could use the extra money, but none of them ever want to come in on their days off. Not that I can blame them for that. I'm wholly unavailable to them when Dahlia is here and not at school. When she's with me, that place is the least of my concerns. Hence the reason Jenna is my co-manager instead of the Assistant Manager. She needs to be able to take care of every last detail in my absence.

In case of an emergency, when the two of us have something going on, or we get sick at the same time, there's a part time guy. Henry can mostly hold the fort down, but I've definitely had to run over to the store in my pajamas and a face mask to assist him once or twice.

I sigh, frustrated with the lack of time I'll now have to get my day started. Her shift starts in less than an hour.

I attempt to sip on my tea as I walk right back to my bedroom in search of an outfit to wear. It's a bad idea, because more of it sloshes into my mouth than I intended, and the hot liquid burns my tongue and my chin as it drips down.

This is great.

This is fine.

I set the mug down on my dresser, fully knowing it might leave a ring on the wood and I'll be whining about that later. Right now, I don't have time to care.

I rummage through my dresser drawer, full of bottoms that are all the same color: black. In theory it's a good idea to keep similar things in the same drawer, but not when I want to locate one particular tiny pair of leggings and *everything* gets yanked out and unfolded in my search to do so. Again, it's future Reya's problem.

I do this a lot, so future Reya tends to not like me very much.

I throw a long t-shirt over them, a faded yellow with some band's logo that I haven't listened to since middle school. It's cute enough, and it hides the fact that I'm not exactly supposed to be wearing leggings at work. My girls and I have a mutual understanding, I don't say a word to them about their own dress code deviations, and all's fair. I can't be expected to survive a long day like today without an elastic waistband. It's far too much to ask of a person.

On a good day, I love to play around with my makeup. As a rule, I won't be caught in public without winged eyeliner, and I prefer to make it bold. I've got every color of the rainbow and more in my collection.

If I wasn't about to stop at a drive-through on my way to work to grab a breakfast burrito, I'd do a smokey eye look with yellow or pink liner. Some days I can't decide if I want to match my hair or my clothes, but I *will* always be matching. The lack of time on my end allows me to put an unhealthy amount of blush on my cheeks and nose– actually, it's going all over my eyelids too. It kind of makes me feel like a fairy. I add black eyeliner, black mascara, and I'm left with just enough time to put on some deodorant and a spritz of my favorite perfume.

I have Vans the same shade as my shirt that I pull on over no-show socks. A glimpse past my curtain again tells me that there is no longer anyone out there, and it's started to rain.

Perfect.

I just hope the few seconds it takes to find my coat aren't going to make me late for work, because that drive-through is always packed this time of day, and I'm not going to survive my shift if I don't sit through it.

4

A moving truck is blocking my car. Again.

Except this time, I have a dinner date with my ex-husband's girlfriend, and I really don't want to be late.

I don't see anyone sitting in it, and there isn't anyone outside. I look to the front door of the apartment next to me and grimace. Odds are good that the culprit is in there, and I'm going to have to meet my new neighbors right now. I'm not thrilled to start out our relationship by asking them for a favor.

I have no choice, there's no way I can squeeze my car out of the lot without causing tens of thousands of dollars in damage. I did think about it for a split second, and decided it's not worth it.

I knock on the door and wait. I don't hear any voices or footsteps. It's not a good sign, because if no one's here then I don't know how the hell I'm going to find the person responsible for keeping me trapped.

The parking space is located in a very inconvenient spot. It's pretty ridiculous that this has happened twice now. Maybe I should ask Ted if I could swap. The woman below me doesn't even own a car. She rides a bike that she locks up in her backyard.

Yeah, the downstairs neighbors are lucky enough to have yards. I freaking wish.

I turn and stomp away, mentally preparing to ask someone for a ride. Either of my friends would say yes in a heartbeat, but I'm always hesitant to ask. Vic, because her hands are so full with two kids, and another on the way. Autumn, because she is also very pregnant, and she's not having an easy go of it. Her morning sickness missed the memo that it's supposed to end after the first trimester.

And that it's only supposed to happen in the morning.

Before I can become desperate enough to reach out to my parents for a ride, the door opens behind me.

I spin so fast it's dizzying, with a huge smile plastered to my face.

"Can I help you?" The older man asks, eyeing my bright pink hair with a curious expression. I realize he's the same one that was standing out here the other day.

"Hi! My name is Reya, I live next door."

I put a hand out for him to shake and he thankfully goes right for it.

"Pierre. My kid is moving in here."

He nods to the doorway behind him, but makes no move to go find this kid and introduce me. As long as they're not a teenage boy, we should be good.

"It's so great to meet you! That's so exciting." I give him finger guns, because why? I actually don't know, I'm thinking too hard. "I hate to bother you on such a big day, but the moving truck down there is blocking my car in."

I point down to where we can see the back end of my little black car. And the back end of the big truck blocking it.

"Goodness, that won't do," he says. I don't know which part won't do, but I hope it's the one where I'm unable to leave. I *will* be late to this dinner, my time management already wasn't great. I gave myself a whole thirty seconds to spare, and that's been used up.

"Let me grab those keys so you can get on your way."

I breathe a sigh of relief.

"That would be awesome. Thank you so much."

I awkwardly follow him when he comes back out and heads down the stairs. He gets in the truck and moves it without a word, and I get in my car without waiting for one. I send a friendly wave in his direction as I pass, but I can't tell if he saw me.

Hopefully by tomorrow I'll uncover the mystery of who his child is, and have my chance to make a good first impression.

⁓ℓℓ⁓

I recognize her immediately.

Of course I've looked at her Instagram. She doesn't post her face much, but a selfie taken approximately six months ago with the tiniest orange kitten I've ever seen gave me enough to search for. The rest of her pictures are of sunsets, and waterfalls, and destinations I wouldn't go to the effort to get to.

Do not get me wrong, I love a nice view. I love nature. I went camping all the time as a kid.

But as a single mom in my late-twenties, that works full-time: I don't exercise. Which means if someone tried to drag me on a hike, I'd probably collapse within minutes.

Even the stairs going up to my apartment are a challenge for me most days.

"You must be Raquel," I say as I approach. I don't always feel as confident as everyone thinks I am, but I hope *she* thinks I am. It's not natural to have to meet the person who's currently banging your ex. We as humans aren't meant to put ourselves through things like this.

I'd put myself through a lot more for my daughter, but I really want to seem like I have my shit together while I do it.

"And you must be Reya." She doesn't stand, or offer to shake my hand. Her smile is polite enough, but I'm still taking away points.

Which means she is in the negative right off the bat.

I can't help but start comparing the two of us, our appearances, as terrible as that is. I examine her for any signs of similarities between us, but I don't think there's a single one. From what I can see of her upper half, she's fit. No surprise there. Her shoulders are tan, her jewelry is thick and gold. Her hair is dark and long. We could not look more different.

I find that I'm glad of it. How much worse would this be if the woman across from me also had cotton candy pink hair? It would be very weird.

"Thanks for meeting me like this. I think it's so important that we're all on the same page with Lia involved."

"Lia?" I ask before thinking as I sit down across from her.

"Dahlia?" Her tone makes me feel like I'm a total moron for not knowing that.

I tilt my head.

Maybe I'm overreacting, but I'm already annoyed. I'm throwing on negative points like I have a million to spare.

Because I do. It's a fictional point system that exists strictly in my head. I've thought of buying a white board, but I don't want to stress out my friends.

It feels condescending. Almost as if this woman is trying to assume that I'm not interested in being on the same page. Like she is some savior for asking for this dinner, and I'm the difficult child that wouldn't *want* to eagerly agree to this.

Maybe I didn't, but not for any reason other than how uncomfortable I knew it would be. Even though there is zero chance of me feeling any kind of romantically about Caleb again, it's weird to sit face to face with how he's finally moving on.

And I'm already not a fan, and I don't care if it's because I'm overreacting to the first sentence she's ever said to me.

"It's interesting that you have a nickname for my daughter before you've even met her," I say.

I know Caleb doesn't use it, or at least he never has to me.

Her eyes widen a fraction, but I watch as she attempts to play it off and nods.

Yeah. No.

My ex-husband has lied to me so many times, and I refuse to let Raquel fall into the habit, too.

"So, you *have* met her," I say in a tone that leaves no room for argument.

"Once," she answers quickly. "Briefly. I had to grab something and didn't realize you had already dropped her off—"

I fold my hands, and I must look quite menacing, because she quickly closes her mouth. I didn't know I still had it in me.

"Can you do me a favor? Can you be fully honest from this point forward? For my daughter's sake."

I'm not a fool. These two will regret trying to make me feel like one.

"I'm sorry," she whispers. "Caleb was fine with sneaking me around, but I really didn't want to, I swear. That's why I pushed for this. You deserve to know what's going on when she's not with you."

"Has he asked her to lie to me?"

She hesitates for a few brief seconds, but nods.

I'm so filled with rage that I start shaking.

How dare he? Not only convincing my baby to lie to me, but making it seem like it's okay? She's too young to have it in her head that there are some things she has to keep from her mom. I'm not supposed to be dealing with the secret keeping until her preteen years, which are *so* far away.

I thought I had more time.

Now I'm sitting across from a woman I don't know, in a restaurant I don't like, mentally berating myself for not being the kind of mom she would immediately run home and tell all of this to.

I don't blame her for a second. I'm not upset with her. She's young and impressionable, and I know she loves her dad so much.

I'm beyond upset with the adults here, and my feelings are so big and unwieldy at the moment that there's plenty left to be upset with myself, too.

"Look, you have a great kid. One who loves you so much, and gets so excited when it's time for Caleb to drop her off that it hurts his feelings. He's expressed to me that he doesn't–" she stops for a moment, shaking her head. "Maybe I shouldn't be telling you this, but I want you to understand. Nothing about this is okay, but he knows you're her favorite. He knows he doesn't have what two have."

"His jealousy is no good reason to convince our child that it's okay to lie to her mom."

She nods. "I agree with that. I've tried telling him the same thing, I swear."

"But that didn't stop you from coming around."

Her gaze falls to her hands where she fidgets with the rings she's wearing. There are a lot of them. Her hands must get tired of carrying all that weight.

"At first it didn't. I don't expect you to forgive me for this reason, but maybe you'll get it? Our relationship was new. I was a girl with a crush, trying to impress a guy that I was still getting to know. It didn't seem like my place to question him, but it does now. It's different now."

"Why now?"

"Because I know him very well. I know Lia well. I know a lot more about you than I did. All three of you deserve better than this, and he realizes that, too."

If she's right and he has come to his senses, it makes sense that she was the convincing factor. He wouldn't have gotten there on his own.

"What has he told you about me?"

"Not a lot. Just that you were both young, and life moved too fast for either of you to slow down and figure out what wasn't working." *How insightful of him.* "And he told me that you're a...lesbian."

She studies my face after saying the word. I can't tell if it's to check if I'm offended by it, or if she's worried I might tell her he was lying.

If only she knew how little she had to worry about. I'm the least threatening ex-wife on the planet, at least in the way that you couldn't pay me any amount of money to be interested in him again.

"Yep," I confirm. "One of the few things I can thank him for helping me realize."

In reality, it was much more complicated than that. It took me a long time after things ended between us to find myself.

I love being a mom. I let that become my only personality trait for the first couple years of Dahlia's life.

When I found myself ready to date again, I didn't know what I was even looking for. I thought I was bisexual for most of my life. I dated girls and boys in highschool, but none of those relationships were deep enough to make me wonder if I preferred one over the other.

I know now that the problem was *dating in high school.* We were all just kids. I had friends who seemed confident and sure of who they were, but I wasn't self aware enough to even notice that I *wasn't* sure. I never thought to question it until I started dating as an adult.

Sure, there are cute men out there. Some of them are really nice, and have much more exciting personalities than Caleb. I know that because I experienced it.

But *women.*

I just feel more connected to them, even the worst of them. I'm more attracted to their bodies and minds in every way. I felt more in the most casual of flings with women than I have with any man, despite the circumstances. The conversations are always deeper, the walls are always easier to knock down.

I know love and attraction are a spectrum. I don't rule out the *entire* possibility of a man sweeping me off my feet, but I'd have to see it to believe it. And I absolutely won't be waiting around for it to happen, when I am finally sure of who I am and what I feel. I picture my next love, my forever love, and I know deep down that it's not going to be with a man.

"I actually don't want to sit here and bash him. Enough time has passed, and I've wanted to see him move forward for a while now. Maybe I feel that way a little less at the moment with the information you've given me today, but still." I look around for a second, hoping there's a waiter nearby that could bring me a glass of water. There isn't. This place has terrible service. "You'll both have to sit down with Dahlia and explain that what you did was wrong. Apologize to her. Then we can go from there."

"We will," Raquel says. "Consider it done. And you deserve an apology too, I really am sorry."

I shrug.

"I'm not ready to say it's okay. Talk to her first."

She nods, and I can tell she's disappointed that I'm not relieving her of her guilt right this second.

With that, I give her a tight smile and grab my bag from the seat beside me.

"You're going? You're not going to eat?" she asks.

"The food here sucks. Have you had it?" Raquel shakes her head. "Great. Get out while you still can."

She pauses, looking around the restaurant. She's probably just now noticing the same thing: that no one's appeared to get her drink order yet. When she stands, taking my advice, I clear my throat.

"Do you have kids?" I ask, not having considered that possibility.

"No," she draws the word out like she's confused.

"You don't sound sure."

She lets out a nervous laugh.

"Sorry, no. I really don't."

I nod, believing her.

"I want kids," she adds. "At least two. We've talked about it being a possibility someday."

I didn't need to know that much, although Dahlia will absolutely love being a big sister.

"Ah," I say uncomfortably. "That's cool."

Raquel frowns, and then she surprises me by cautiously putting her arms out, like she's hoping I'll be willing to hug. I'm not feeling very willing, but I am merciful. I don't want to embarrass her.

I hug her. It's weird. She says she hopes to talk soon, that she wants to know me better, and I mutter some noncommittal response.

My reaction to her is mixed. Complicated. This whole thing could be a big performance on her end, and she doesn't actually care about any of it. Spending more time with her would probably help clear that up, but today's not the day I'm going to agree to it.

5

The few quiet nights I had were nice while they lasted.

I'm thrown from a deep sleep at two in the morning by a shaking, vibrating feeling I do not understand. I refuse to open my eyes right away, listening and feeling for an explanation. There's a pattern to it, a rhythm. Something that makes the muscles in my neck want to nod along to it.

It's music.

I rip out an earplug to an *attack* of it. A loud, bass heavy song, with deep and guttural screaming. If I were hearing it in any other context, I'd probably try to figure out what the song is so I can listen to it when I'm feeling angsty in my car later.

In this context, it makes me want to rip my hair out. Or someone else's hair, preferably.

Like the monster who thought this was a good time to be playing it.

It's so loud that the speaker might as well be right inside my room. It's impressive considering there is a hallway and another bedroom between me and the wall I share with the guilty apartment.

I'm in disbelief that this is happening after having just gotten rid of my problem. I don't want to move out of this apartment, but I might have to. What choice do I have? I'm obviously cursed to be kept up at all hours of the night if I stay here.

I sit up, my eyes wide and vacant. I honestly feel so absolutely out of my mind, the desire to sleep through the night weighing on me so heavily. The desire to will away what's happening again engulfs my every cell.

No. This is not how this is going to go. I will not let it.

I throw a robe over my half naked body, and storm out of my front door. I don't have the ability to think better of it with the music pushing away any possible rational thought.

My fist raps into the door, as heavy as I can make it. My foot taps impatiently while I wait.

I think I can see said door actually vibrating with the volume. It's both impressive and infuriating.

I knock again. I can't hear anything else inside, no evidence of humans, for obvious reasons. I hate that it means *Pierre's* kid won't hear me out here, no matter how long I stand my ground and wait.

I knock one final time, just hard enough to let out a tiny bit of my frustration. The *tiniest* bit.

I stomp back into my apartment, wishing I had a better outlet.

My head is starting to throb, and the early hour has tears filling my eyes. I want to be asleep. I want to never deal without another stupid loud neighbor. It's not fair.

It's completely fucked.

I aggressively pull open my junk drawer, where I find a pen and a pad of paper. While the stationary with Disney characters on it might dull the effect of my very serious words, I know it's all I have. There's no point in looking anywhere else.

To whom it may concern,

The music coming from your apartment is extremely loud for the time of night (or should I say morning) you choose to play it.

It would be lovely if you could keep it between the hours of 9am and 10pm as our rental agreement suggests. Thanks!

Sincerely,

Your very tired neighbor.

In the same drawer, I find an almost-empty roll of tape and rip off a small piece. Just enough to allow me to stick it right where they'll see it tomorrow. I think I did my best to keep my current mood out of it, so I'm hoping they'll be reasonable in the morning. I'm hoping they appreciate that I wrote a letter instead of immediately reporting them to Tim.

Or calling the cops, do people do that? It feels extreme, but not more so than my foul mood.

When I end up back in bed, the loud music still blaring, my eyes start to water. With frustrated, ragged breaths shaking my entire body, I put my earplugs back in, and bury myself under my pillows.

As you clearly said, those hours are a suggestion.

I will continue to play my music when it best suits me.

While we're looking over the rental agreement, I thought I might add that it also says to keep the outside of the building free of debris. You're one to talk with the cemetery of plants I have to stare at every time I come home.

Sincerely,
Your neighbor who doesn't care.

Okay, what a *bitch*. I could've been so much meaner in my letter.

Who would be that stubborn? That rude? Especially when they've been made aware that they're keeping their neighbor up at night? Their neighbor with a kid, might I add. It's so inconsiderate and selfish, and has me thinking maybe she's eighteen too. I can't imagine a grown adult writing these words.

Also, my plants aren't dead. Sure they look a little sad when I forget to water them for a few days, but they're going to perk back up now that they're rehydrated. She's going to eat her words.

On my way out for work, I stick another note on her door.

Maybe this is your first time living on your own, but a signed rental agreement isn't just a suggestion. Especially when your neighbors have children, and/or jobs, and require sleep at night. Which we all do.

Also, see plants. Not dead. They were taking a nap.

I can not live without adequate sleep. I become an entirely different, very irritable and upset person. On those work days I'm not the cool manager. I'm not the cool anything. I keep my mouth shut, and my movements slow, and hope no one does anything to piss me off.

I hate being that person. I hate being angry or grumpy or anything of the sort. Most people around me would describe me as upbeat and full of energy. That's what my standard setting looks like, and I like my standard.

As I lay in bed for the fourth night in a row with screaming ringing in my ears through my foam earplugs, I start crying. *Hard*. I tried knocking on their door again last night, but it was no use.

I'm so angry at the world. I'm so *unbelievably* angry at my new neighbor. I'm even angry at Tim for being so terrible at picking which people live next to me. I'm angry that if nothing changes, I have to move.

It's going to be so overwhelming to figure out, but so necessary. I can't live like this.

I keep thinking there's no way they'll keep this up, surely someone else will complain and get them to stop, but then they don't. I don't know exactly what's keeping me from filing a noise complaint. Maybe the fact that the last neighbors were just kids, and I didn't want to traumatize them by having the cops show up at their door. I still have no idea who I'm dealing with here, I don't think I'd be so hesitant if I did.

The worst nights when the boys lived there would send me to sleep at my parents house, or even in my car. The latter only worked when Dahlia wasn't home, and the weather wasn't freezing. But it helped. I slept, despite the pain I'd be in when I woke up. They obviously don't make backseats with comfortable sleeping in mind.

Yet still, I preferred to inconvenience myself rather than them. I did vent to Tim a few times, and I know he had some conversations, but he's a big softie. He didn't change anything.

I hate that my girl's not even here on a night she should be because of this crap, I hate that I'm inconveniencing *her*. The next thing I know, she's going to start preferring it over at her dad's house because she gets to sleep peacefully.

The boy's noise was one thing, but this wouldn't work. There's no way she could ignore this volume.

I wouldn't be able to blame her. I'd be sad, but I'd get it. Hell, even I would sleep at *Caleb's* house if it meant nothing interrupted me from the hours of ten to eight.

When I focus on my heartrate in hopes to calm it down, I just remind myself why I'm so worked up, and it works me up even more.

I'll talk to Tim in the morning, the guy loves me. If he sees just how upset I am, he'll do something about it. I think. I hope.

If he doesn't, then I'll start apartment hunting. I wish I could say I'd house hunt, it would get rid of the noise problems, but the market is ridiculous right now. I don't stand a chance.

I make a game plan while I'm lying there, because what else can I do? My heart is racing so aggressively fast that sleep is impossible. I'll tell my parents I'm staying with them in the meantime. They won't mind, because they're always complaining they don't see us enough. Maybe I could even move back in for a while, as defeating as that would feel. It would take some of the stress off.

And it's not like a ton is going on in my life that I need my own private space for. I'd just go from being unfortunately single, to circumstantially single.

I start to text Caleb, not caring about the late hour, to ask if he can keep Dahlia another night. My teeth grind the entire time I type, and when I realize just how badly, I erase the message.

No. We'll stay with my parents tomorrow night. That way, regardless of what happens, we both get our sleep, and I don't have to miss her anymore.

My mind full of possibilities keeps on chugging until finally the music stops. I open my eyes to see morning light spilling into my bedroom, and tears build up in my eyes. An entire wasted night is about to turn into an entire wasted day.

I do decide to text Caleb now, but only to ask him what time I should pick up Dahlia. When he doesn't respond within the first two minutes, I roll over while pulling my blanket over my head. Might as well take advantage of a morning nap if that's all I'm going to be able to get.

2:37 PM

I blink down at my blurry phone, and the locked screen full of notification banners. That was some *nap* I just took.

But such a necessary one, I think as I let out a huge yawn.

I missed my Tim window, because he never hangs around here this late. Sometimes I wonder why he works from his office here at all, when he only has a few units and we're all fairly low mainte-nance.

Not that I understand everything his job entails.

Most of the notifications are from Caleb, and I sigh as I open up our messages.

I quickly close them again when I realize he's berating me for not getting back to him after my previous message. If only he knew how lucky he was to live in a *house* his parents paid for. To never have to deal with shared walls, or worry about where to go next.

He's entitled and clueless, and probably won't ever understand that. Not that it's completely his fault, but it irks me just the same.

"I was supposed to work today, Reya." That's how he greets me when he answers the phone.

"I thought you would have taken care of that when I first asked if she could stay with you last night."

"I had," he grumbles. "Then you asked when you could pick her up, and I thought you were saying it was up to me to decide. I decided. I gave them a time I'd be in, and it's now three hours past that."

I roll my eyes, enjoying it less than when he can actually see it.

"I fell asleep after not getting a single minute of it last night. Forgive me for requiring that."

"Then you shouldn't have asked at all until you knew you'd be up," he says.

"And then you'd complain about not hearing from me all day. I wouldn't have done anything right either way. I'll be there in twenty to pick her up."

I go to hang up, but his next words stop me.

"Maybe you should make yourself comfortable with the idea of Raquel watching her sometimes. It would make things like this so much easier."

My protective mom instincts lurch to the surface, and I practically growl into the phone like a wild animal.

"I'm never going to be comfortable with some random woman being responsible for my daughter, just like you wouldn't if the roles were reversed here."

"She's not random," he says with a raised voice, exposing his frustration. "Her and Lia get along great. The two of them would be just fine for a few hours."

Oh, that stupid nickname they've come up with for her is *not* my favorite thing.

"You've probably already done it before, right? Just another thing I'm being lied to about?"

"Jesus, no. I haven't. You act like I'm keeping all these secrets from you, but believe it or not, I want things to be smooth between us. I'm not trying to start an argument."

"If you didn't want to argue, you shouldn't have convinced Dahlia to be a part of your scheming," I tell him.

"It wasn't scheming. It was two days!" he shouts.

The amount of time is news to me, but it's irrelevant. It could've been two hours. He still lied.

"You'd lose your shit if I had her around some girlfriend you've never met, even if it was just for *two days*."

"I'd trust your judgment," he says, lowering his voice.

"Yeah, okay," I say dismissively. I don't believe a word that comes out of his mouth. "I'll be there in twenty."

I get my electric kettle started, so I can make a cup of tea on my way out the door. I brush through my hair with my fingers, which is longer than it's been in years. I've always kept my curly mop of hair nice and short. I suppose it's still considered short, but I canceled a haircut appointment a while back and never rescheduled. Now it's almost down to my shoulders, and I'm liking it more and more every day. Especially now that I can put half of it up in a messy little bun, which is the look I go for today to hide the part that has fallen flat thanks to its time against my pillow.

I throw on some black pants that are just as loose and comfy as sweats, but look slightly less lazy. I pair it with a purple, skin tight, long sleeve tee. I'll throw a coat over my arm, but I probably won't wear it. I've become used to the bite of the cold on days like today.

Coats are strictly for wet weather.

6

"Look here, princess. This one is blue." My dad points out another ice cream flavor while he holds Dahlia in his arms so she can see them all. "Oh, and they have bubble gum! You like bubble gum, don't you?"

"But it's not pink." She tilts her head to the side. "Isn't it supposed to be pink?" she asks me.

I lean forward to look at the flavor in question. It's definitely usually pink, but the tub in front of the *Bubblegum* label is solid white.

"You're right. It should be pink."

We had come to this exact shop at least once a week last summer, we would know what color the flavors should be. The girl working behind the freezer is staring off into space, facing the large window that overlooks the parking lot. She didn't work here last summer. The girls who did are always so excited to see us, and they know us by name.

Okay, I'm a talker. They know the names of my entire family, all of my friends, and all of their hobbies.

I know when to read a room so I don't ask this one about the mysterious, colorless ice cream.

I follow her gaze to find that it's started raining out there. I'm feeling a small percentage of regret for leaving my coat in the car, and a small percentage of pity for this girl that's going to have a slow day for customers.

"I don't want that one," Dahlia tells us. "I want a pink one."

"Okay baby girl, there's strawberry." I walk down, inspecting all of the colors. "Cherry pie. Watermelon sorbet. Circus cookie." I wasn't really in the mood for ice cream when we got here, but that last one just put me in exactly the right mood. I know what flavor *I'm* going with.

Dahlia tastes every single one of those, and I can tell *Carly*–as her name tag reads–is over it, but how else is a kid supposed to make a decision? She should know that by now.

I order for myself, and my dad, while we wait on her to decide. One scoop in a cup of the bright pink circus cookie, and two scoops in a waffle cone of the neon green pistachio. I look at his longingly when it's handed over, second guessing my own decision. I'm a sucker for pistachio, but I try to mix it up.

"I want the blue one," Dahlia finally announces. What a plot twist.

When she's given her own cone covered in rainbow sprinkles, we sit down. I delay their eating by insisting on some pictures of the two of them, and then flip my phone camera around to capture a big smiling selfie of all of us. Only when I dive into my own dessert do I look down at my screen and notice Dahlia's nose has a stripe of blue on it. I laugh and hand her a napkin so she can clean herself up.

My dad chats about tearing down the fence in their backyard to build a new one. Their dogs, two huge golden retrievers named

Sunny and Rainy, were very sad to find out that most of their outside time will take place on a leash until further notice. I offer to take them over to Autumn's house, which is equipped with enough space for the girls to run around. I'm sure her dog, Freddy, would love the company if I brought them over there.

My own ice cream is almost gone when the bell above the door sounds, and another customer walks in. I glance up, knowing what an avid people watcher I am, and having no shame about it.

It's a beautiful woman, probably around my age. Her long, deep red hair looks like it was meant to be tucked behind her back, under the safety of her hood, but stubborn strands fall down the front of her chest anyway. It's an impressive amount of hair.

She doesn't look our way, or remove her hood when she walks up to the counter. Carly appears from the back, having heard the bell that probably drives her mad and haunts her dreams.

"What can I get you?"

"Four gift cards. Twenty dollars each."

"Perfect, we have a couple options–"

"That one," she interrupts.

I watch Carly's face drop, her mood determined by the attitude of her customer. I can't blame her, being interrupted makes me want to rage. I stare as the cards are scanned, and the customer taps her card on the reader.

"Have a good day," Carly says quietly as she hands out a receipt.

Understandable, considering the woman snatches it and heads toward the door without a word. Someone's either having a really bad day, or never learned to respect customer service workers.

Poor Carly.

I don't stop watching when the woman leaves, thankful for a glass door, and the giant glass window.

My heart stops when I spot the car she unlocks.

"You've got to be fucking kidding me."

"Reya Renee," dad scolds me.

I turn back to my company with a frown.

"Sorry sweetness, I shouldn't have said that word."

"It's okay. I won't say it."

I kiss her temple. "You're the best."

"Who was that?" my dad asks. His displeased tone tells me he noticed the same details I did.

"Well," I look back to the familiar car to find it quickly pulling out of the parking lot. I'm not surprised she'd go snatching receipts and speeding in an area with heavy foot traffic. "I think that's the reason I haven't gotten any sleep this week."

Because that forest green Subaru has been parked in our designated parking lot for the last few days.

Dahlia and I spend two nights with my parents, which works out great. Their house is close enough to her school that my mother walked her down there yesterday, and she keeps telling me she wants to do it every morning. It won't be happening from *our* place, because I'm not much of a walker as it is and we live about ten miles away. My mother was very vocal about how fine she'd be with us staying over more, and it's extra nice to have that reassurance given our current situation.

I help my dad whip up some pancakes with fresh fruit on top. He's the reason I fell in love with baking, always inviting me into the kitchen to help with whatever he was creating. It started as dumping things into a bowl, and he gave me more responsibility as time went on. Measuring, mixing, poking with a toothpick to make sure things were done in the middle.

I try to include Dahlia the way he did with me, but she isn't a fan of following a recipe or splitting the tasks with me. She wants to do it all, and she wants to do it her way. One of these days I'm going to let her, I just know she's going to be so disappointed when the glob that goes into the oven is going to turn into nothing but a hot glob after forty minutes.

Or I could replace it with my own when she's not looking so she thinks she's a genius.

I watch as she sits at the table, and picks through the mixed berries on her plate for the strawberries. She not only neglects the rest of them, but the pancakes themselves.

I chuckle.

"Do you want more strawberries?"

"Yes, please," she replies with wide eyes.

"Okay, I'll get you more strawberries if you take two big bites of your pancakes."

She doesn't hesitate, filling her face before she's even finished what was in her mouth.

Both of my parents shake their heads in disbelief, and I know exactly what they're about to say.

"She listens way too well to be your kid," my dad says with an amused smile.

"Seriously sunshine, how'd you manage that? We went to war to convince you to do anything at her age."

"Yeah, yeah. I was a difficult child, let's move on from that same old song, huh?"

They're just teasing, of course, but they do it *a lot.* In reality, I think I just wanted to run around without shoes on all the time.

And I *may* have had a habit of trying to walk out the front door when no one was watching, but I never went further than the neighbors house. I just liked that they had so many flowers in their front yard. After the alarm of the first couple times, they even started helping me pick some to bring back to my parents. It was cute.

I kiss Dahlia's head before setting a couple more sliced strawberries onto her plate.

"But I sure did get lucky." I poke her cheek, so she knows she's the reason.

Dahlia smiles and looks down as if the attention makes her shy, but I know it's an act. She's just too aware of how cute she is. She has a mom who will never let her forget it.

"What's the plan tonight? Staying over again?"

I look to my mom with a frown.

"I think we're going to head home and hope for the best, but don't panic if you happen to hear someone unlocking the door in the middle of the night."

"Noted," they say at the same time. My parents are adorable.

I feel briefly relieved when I pull into my parking lot and find that the green Subaru isn't in it. If I'm really lucky, it'll stay gone all night.

Dahlia and I ran errands most of the day, and I finished it out by taking her to the mall so we could walk around, and ride every single one of their little coin operated rides. It was all an attempt to make sure she'd be extra tired tonight. When she lets out a big yawn as we walk up the steps, I feel like it was a mission accomplished.

My jaw clenches when I spot a piece of paper taped to my door.

None of those things are my problem. I haven't received any other complaints, so maybe you just need to invest in melatonin and earplugs. :)

(Hydrated corpses are still corpses.)

This note is written on the back of my previous one, and is wrinkled where spots of rain must have hit it yesterday.

"What did you get?" Dahlia asks.

I crumple the paper in my hand, and try to hide the scalding anger that rises in me.

"Junk mail."

No one draws me a passive aggressive smiley face and gets away with it.

7

I slam the note down on Tim's desk. It looks rough, considering I'd rescued it from the trash after realizing it might come in handy to have the physical proof.

"My new neighbor is killing me. You've got to help me."

His eyes widen in alarm. "What is she doing? Are you okay?"

"Do I look okay?" I ask with a dramatic hand to my forehead. I'm aware of what he sees, especially the dark circles under my eyes. "She needs to be stopped."

"What happened, Reya? Here, sit down." He pulls out a seat at the small desk he's sitting at. It's small enough that he does so just by reaching over from his side.

I plop down into it.

"I haven't been able to sleep because of her blasting music. I might have to let my daughter stay an extra night at her dad's place, for the *second week in a row*. It's killing me, Tim. I can't do it. Please help me."

I'm aware that I seem a little crazy, as I spew the words out so fast and frantically.

He just looks at me for a few seconds. His blank expression makes me nervous, until I wave a hand in front of his face.

He chuckles, blinking a few times.

"I can see how that's stressful. Is it really that loud?"

"I wouldn't have bothered you if it wasn't. Have I ever complained before?" I absolutely have, but he shakes his head as if he's forgotten. "It really is that loud."

He scratches his head, looking confused or conflicted, or something.

"What?" I ask.

"I guess I'm just surprised no one else has complained."

I throw my arms up in the air.

"So am I! I was hoping you were going to tell me someone had."

Tim shakes his head.

"Not a peep from anyone."

"Does Mrs. Sheppard have a hearing problem?"

She's in the apartment below the culprit, and I would think she's affected even more than I am. That woman hates noise, she once complained that I walked down the stairs loudly and it echoed through her whole apartment.

Actually, not once. Three times. It was a whole thing.

"Not that I've noticed. Look, I can see how upsetting it is to lose sleep, and to worry about your daughter losing sleep, but..." He sighs. "I won't get into any details with you, but I spoke with her dad when she applied for the place. He says she's going through a rough time, dealing with some mental health concerns. Maybe the music is helping clear her mind, you know?"

Of course he's going to be patient and understanding when it comes to mental health concerns. He deals with it very closely every day.

I feel selfish for saying it's not fair, but it isn't. Why do I have to suffer in order for someone else to feel better? Not that I am at all convinced that this particular thing is helping her in any way.

"It's not a mind clearing volume, Tim!" I yell. "My bed shakes like it's possessed by a demon, which doesn't even seem like the biggest stretch because she plays the most *aggressive* songs." Never mind that I like aggressive songs at the right time of day.

Well, maybe not anymore. She might have ruined heavy metal for me.

"I get that, but I don't want to trouble her when she's just moved in. She's probably still getting settled. You get that, right? If it continues over the next couple weeks, I'll say something. How does that sound? Can you last that long?"

No.

"I really thought you were going to take my side here. I thought we had something special," I whine.

He laughs heartily, causing me to smile for the first time since walking into his office.

"Tell you what, I'll knock a couple hundred off of your rent next month for the inconvenience."

My jaw drops.

"I'm not going to let you do that. You do so much to help us already."

"Try and stop me," he says with a wink. "I am really sorry, dear. We'll figure it out, just give it some time."

"I guess I have to." I gesture towards the door. "I've got to go get ready for work."

"Have a good one today. Oh, and I've been meaning to ask what you used for the pumpkin bread you gave us for Christmas. The wife hasn't shut up about it since."

I beam, relieved to change the subject onto something that makes me so happy.

"I can jot down the recipe, that's an easy one. You'll have to let me know how it goes," I tell him.

"Of course. I'll even bring you some."

He says he'll be the one to bring it, because Tricia doesn't leave the house. From what I've heard, it's been years since she's stepped outside. I'm happy to help keep her occupied with a little recipe, and having a conversation through Tim. For a long time, I'd hoped a miracle would happen and allow me to meet her, but now I realize that's not how this goes. Not everyone can be changed, especially the ones that are content with their circumstances. Tricia is content, and I do what I can to make her even more so. Everyone needs friends.

"I'll give her my zucchini bread recipe, too. I'm telling you: so easy" I stand from my seat. "Let her know I said hello, and I'll have those for you sometime this week."

8

I shouldn't have to give my young child melatonin in order for her to sleep. It's cruel of you to think I should just so you can carry on with your noise pollution.

I quickly run out the front door so I can tape the note up before Dahlia comes out behind me and asks what I'm doing. I barely have time to step away before she appears in the doorway, ready to go.

"Did you want to bring your backpack?" I ask her before I move to pull our front door closed.

She goes through phases, gets attached to certain objects, and lately it's been a little purple backpack purse that she picked out at the mall.

"My backpack!" she yells, flabbergasted that she could've possibly forgotten it.

"Go grab it, bug. I'm not going to leave without you." I give her a reassuring smile, and she rushes past me to retrieve it.

I listen as she talks to herself, trying to pinpoint the location she last saw it. Toys are thrown around, that much is also obvious. That'll be a fun group effort to clean up later.

She announces when she finds it, running back out to me with the most victorious grin on her face, and holding the straps up in one hand.

"Do you have everything you need now?" I ask.

"I think so," she says, and turns to head for the car.

"Dahlia Anne, do not go down those stairs without holding my hand."

"I wasn't! I was going to wait right here."

She stands by the railing right before the stairs and does one little hop to show me that it's exactly where she was going to wait.

There's a fifty-fifty chance that's true.

I lock my front door, and then I check my little table to grab the travel cup I inevitably sat down there. It's a windy day today, and I don't want to admit how many cups I've set on that table and never saw again. Today's choice is a glass tumbler with cute little mushroom design, and I'd be devastated if it was knocked over and shattered.

As I turn with my cup in hand, ready to grab Dahlia's hand with my other, I see a small flash of movement. The black curtains in the next door apartment are swaying as if they'd been pushed aside and then dropped.

So, she's curious about me. That's good to know.

I pick up Sunny and Rainy from my parents house, along with their minivan. We could technically fit in my car just fine, but it wouldn't be nearly as comfortable.

Dahlia giggles and squeals the whole time. Either because one of the dogs is licking her face, drooling on her, or sticking their butt in her face when they turn to put their heads out the window.

It's fun to listen to, and I smile to myself the whole way there. It doesn't mean that I would ever get a dog of my own, because this could easily become too much with their high energy every day. I know myself, I'd be overstimulated and cranky after a few hours of it.

It also doesn't mean I love these two any less.

The excitement in the van increases when we pull up to Autumn and Miles' house. It's like Sunny and Rainy know what waits for them despite never being here before. But Dahlia, she knows exactly where we are. She's clapping her hands excitedly when I open the side door to let everyone out.

"Are you excited to see Mimi and Eli today?"

The exaggerated scream she lets out is a sharp pain in my ears. It even startles the dogs, and they freeze to assess any nearby danger. I stroke Sunny's back to calm her down.

"Oof, sweet girl. That volume was not necessary."

"Yes it was! Mimi!" she yells. "Mimi! Mimi!"

The way she loves Amira, Vic's oldest, warms my heart.

"I know, I know!" I tell her.

I leash the dogs, just to get them inside without worrying they'll run off.

"Can you get your seatbelt?" I ask her.

I've never seen her unclip the thing so fast before.

"Alright, let's go have some fun!"

It's still winter, and the wind is chilly, but I'm just glad it's not raining. Today is the nicest weather we'll probably have for a couple more months, so it's a good thing we're soaking it up while we can.

"Dahlia!" Autumn smiles wide when she opens her door, and my girl runs up to hug her.

I put a hand on her shoulder to decrease her momentum.

"Careful," I say. When they do collide, it's not as concerning as it would've been. Autumn doesn't even flinch.

Freddy barks from behind her, and I see him in Miles' arms, eager to get down and find out what all the fuss is about.

We step inside, and I guide my two animals towards the back yard.

"You do not want me to let them loose in here. You guys have too many expensive decorations."

The three dogs are set free, and they immediately run around and jump all over each other. Miles hangs back out there to throw them tennis balls, and the rest of us head inside where it's warmer.

"Where's Mimi?" Dahlia asks with a pout.

"She's going to be here any second, her mama just called me from the car," Autumn explains.

She claps her hands some more, and runs over to the toy kitchen in the corner of the room. They keep lots of toys around for whenever they babysit Miles' niece and nephew. I think it's the sweetest thing, considering that only happens once or twice a month.

Autumn and I catch up for a couple minutes, talking about work and how she's feeling. The answer is very, very pregnant, and sore, and tired, unfortunately. Miles has been working less to be there for her when she needs, which I'm grateful for. He gets a hundred extra points. It's more than I usually give out at a time, but Autumn is worth a million. Anyone that treats her the way she deserves is pretty high in my ranking.

I make a note to come over more often and check on her these next few months. The more support, the merrier, and I don't have so much going on in my life that I can't make time to do that.

There's a lot of screaming, jumping, laughing, and hugging when Vic's family walks in. Her husband greets us all with a polite smile and a nod, and then Autumn points to the backdoor. He goes for it quickly, leaving the girls to their chaos. He and Miles were fast friends, which is extremely convenient for us on days like today.

It's too bad for them that I won't be adding a third guy to their little group someday.

Dahlia drags them over to said kitchen to show them how to properly cook chicken apparently, and they both watch her with rapt attention as she adds a plastic bottle of ketchup straight into the plastic frying pan.

I hug Vic, and give her a quick peck on the cheek. She pulls on a strand of my hair.

"Girl, I swear this is even longer than it was the other week. Who are you?"

"I don't know, but I really like it."

"So do I," Autumn adds. "You have the prettiest curls."

"We all know you have a thing for curly hair," I tell her and I swear she blushes.

It's not news anymore!

Gosh, she's cute.

I look at Vic and laugh, but I notice something that shuts me up.

At least for a second.

"*Victoria*! Are those hickeys?" I gasp.

Then all three of us glance over at the children to make sure none of them heard me. I could have thought that one through before saying it so loudly. Oops.

"I'm a married woman, don't act so scandalized." She pulls up her shirt to hide the purple marks above her breasts. "My parents had the kids last night and we used our time wisely."

"Wise would've been making those a little further down, you know? Was he expecting you to wear nothing but turtlenecks for a while?"

She laughs, and we follow her to sit down at the barstools in the kitchen. There are snacks laid out for everyone, and a box of Pepsi.

Have I mentioned how much I love Autumn?

I help myself as I listen to the other two continue chatting.

"You might be right, there wasn't much wisdom involved. My legs are so sore today, I can barely walk. I should've thought that one through a little better."

"Good for you guys," Autumn says. "Glad you're still able to find the time."

"And you? How watered is your garden?" Vic asks.

There she goes blushing again, being all sweet and shy about it. She's not a prude by any means, but Vic and I are definitely the vocal ones in this group.

"Very. I thought..." She clears her throat. "I thought that a lot less would be possible at this stage, but he's very creative."

I sip on my soda loudly.

"And *very* generous," she adds.

"I need to get laid," I whisper, thinking out loud.

"Oh! Speaking of, you never told me how it went with the bartender."

"Bartender?" Autumn asks.

Vic looks at her as she pats me on the shoulder.

"*Pinky* over here had her tongue down her throat when I left for the night."

I hide behind the can of soda.

"First of all, do not call me that ever again. It was painful, and I was dying to correct her. Second, I don't do any tongue shoving in public." I sip my drink. "We waited until we got into the Uber for that."

They burst out laughing.

Our day goes on with more of that. There are a couple meltdowns amongst the children, either because someone doesn't want to share something, or because they're hungry and upset they can't eat the plastic cake. Eli tried. It went as well as one would think.

The men come inside, and I pray that the dogs have let out enough of their energy when they follow. I would feel so bad if they were at fault for knocking something over or chewing on something they shouldn't.

Miles starts an early dinner for all of us, and while I wasn't planning on staying to eat, I can't say no to free food. I'm especially not going to turn down tacos, when the spread of toppings is being laid out and the entire house smells like seasoned meat. It's heaven.

And Miles is a good cook.

"This is one of the last times we'll all be together without an extra person," Vic says. "There's my baby shower, and then..." she trails off, but we get what she means.

It hits me like a truck that she's right. In one month, she'll have Angeline. In three, Autumn will have her baby boy. Our chosen families just keep getting bigger.

"I love all of you so much," Autumn says, her voice full of emotion.

"I love you too, babe."

We all take turns with hugs, and saying goodbye. The kids are impatient and tired, so it's rushed, but it's also really special.

Everything's about to change.

The green Subaru isn't in the parking lot when I get off work, which I think means that monster of a woman won't be home tonight. I breathe out a sigh of relief, and hope I'm not getting my hopes up for nothing. It's already ten, and the last time she was gone at this hour, I got to sleep through the night.

I carry Dahlia up the steps, even though it is a struggle the entire time. She's getting too big for this. I try not to think too much about that, or I'm going to get even more emotional. I think there's been enough of it tonight.

There's a response on my door. Shocker.

I pull it off without reading it, and focus on unlocking the door. Dahlia is so tired she can barely keep her eyes open.

"More mail?" she asks. I don't know how she even noticed, but I nod.

"Nothing important," I say. "Can you go brush your teeth, and I'll be there in a minute?"

She nods and I set her on her feet, making sure she's steady before letting go. She sluggishly heads towards the bathroom, and I quietly chuckle to myself about how much she reminds me of me.

I didn't know you had a kid.

I flip the note over, confused. There's nothing else, just the one sentence.

What does that mean?

I can't read the tone on this piece of paper. It's not even a piece of paper, it's a purple sticky note. Surely this isn't an attempt to start a conversation. Or apologize? I mean, it's definitely not an apology, but...

I'm probably thinking about it a little too hard. She just didn't know I had a kid. That's all.

Ugh, there could be so many reasons she wrote that. How am I supposed to respond when I don't know?

I have no choice but to sit on it. I'm too tired after the long day we had to figure it out.

9

Before I can blink, it's Wednesday night again.

Caleb appears at my front door, and Dahlia runs to hug me like usual. I splatter kisses all over her face until she's a giggling mess and has to push me away.

She says goodbye to her dad with a quick hug and a promise to see him in a few days, as if he doesn't know that already.

"Can we chat?" Caleb asks once Dahlia goes running to her bedroom.

"What do you need?" I ask with a sigh. It's never anything good. He seemed eager to have Dahlia for that extra night, but if he thinks he deserves something in return for stepping up as a dad? He has another thing coming. It's been a lot less often recently, but things were rough when we first agreed to our custody schedule. Caleb had something come up every other week. I missed so much work. I depended on my parents for more than they should have had to give.

Which is why I'll never understand how much they still love the guy.

He gestures to the chairs next to us.

"The last time you asked me to sit down, you wanted me to meet your girlfriend," I say.

"I know you didn't love that, and you're probably not going to love this," he admits.

Shit.

I sit down anyway, just willing this interaction to be over. I shouldn't have to see him for more than a few seconds at a time.

"It's a big ask," he starts.

"Then don't ask it."

A cold wind attacks the space on my porch then, hitting my bare ankles with a sting. I wince, and mentally blame my ex-husband for the discomfort. I wouldn't be out here if it weren't for him.

"Do you want to go inside?"

"Alone, yes."

He shakes his head, but just pulls up his sweatshirt to cover his neck. His shoulders stay lifted to keep it in place.

"You know how my brother lives in Manitoba?"

I slowly nod.

"Turns out Raquel also has family there. A couple of aunts that she hasn't seen in a few years."

"And?" I press.

"And we want to go visit them. Spend some time with family for the summer," he explains.

I roll my eyes.

"So you need me to keep Dahlia for a couple weeks? Sure. Whatever. Text me the dates."

I stand from my seat, but he reaches out to grab my arm. I flinch away from him, falling back into the chair. He could've expressed himself without putting his hands on me, but I shake it off.

"That's not it. We..." He clears his throat. "We want to bring her with us. I want him to meet his niece. He has kids, a couple of them around her age so that she would have friends to play with. It wouldn't just be–"

"When?" I interrupt.

"May."

"How long."

"Uh... we were, uh–"

"Spit it out, Caleb. The dates."

He looks so panicked that it rubs off on me a little.

"Her last day of school is the twenty-fourth. We were thinking of leaving that next week." I watch him suck in an anticipatory breath before his next words. "And being there for a few weeks."

I do what feels right in the moment. I laugh in his face.

"Reya–" I interrupt him by laughing even louder, my volume intentionally obnoxious. I see how ridiculous it is that he even asked, but I want *him* to see how ridiculous. I want him to go home with his tail tucked between his legs and never think to ask me any such thing again.

I'm not unreasonable. I'm not a grinch that doesn't want my daughter to meet her distant family.

What's unreasonable is asking me to let her leave for what? An entire month or more, of which her *birthday* falls in. She's never spent a birthday without me, she's not starting now.

"Get out of here," I tell him, still laughing. I wipe a tear out from under my eye for extra measure.

"You're being really immature, Reya. Why can't we just have a conversation? Why do you have to laugh in my face?"

"Because it's hilarious that you asked me that!"

His head shakes adamantly.

"It isn't funny. I'm being serious. It could be a really good experience for her."

"She could have a *good experience* in a couple of years, when she's old enough to actually remember it," I speculate. "*Or* you could go for a few *days*, like normal people do on a normal vacation, and be back before her birthday."

I think those are both very fair options, but he doesn't look reassured by them. No, his face is stony and determined, and I don't want to hear about this anymore.

"I haven't seen them in years. They've never even met her," he pleads with me.

"Okay?"

"I want to spend time with them. Significant time."

"A week can be significant."

"You're being unreasonable."

I scoff. "I'm the epitome of reason. I gave you options when all I really want is for you to stop bothering me with this and go on your merry way home."

But of course, he's not leaving yet. That would be too easy.

"We both have to be there to get her passport. I can't do this without you being on board."

This time when I abruptly stand, I have no intention of letting him stop me.

"I'm surprised you didn't find a way to get it done without me, considering how much you like doing things behind my back."

He stands too, not looking nearly defeated as I want him to.

"You can't control what goes on when you're not around. I don't have to tell you anything unless it puts our daughter in danger, and guess what? Not once has she been. We have our issues.

You don't trust me. Whatever. But I'm a good dad, and I make all of my decisions with her in mind. I wouldn't have brought Raquel into the equation if I had even the slightest doubt about our relationship, or who she is as a person."

I walk to my door, grateful to hide my eye roll as I'm facing away from him. If there was someone from the outside looking in, I would look like the bad guy. I would look like the most unreasonable mom on the planet.

I don't think I'll ever get over the amount of conversations we've had where he was inconsiderate, and rude, and put me in a bad position. There are too many to count. So maybe he's finally grown up a bit, but I don't have to give in to what he wants just to be the nice guy.

"That all sounds very noble of you, but this act is a little too late. You're right, I barely trust you to look out for her when she's ten minutes away. It stresses me out *constantly*," I tell him. "You can learn how to compromise if you're so set on this, but even then... I just really don't want it to happen, honestly. At all. I don't expect you to care what I'd go through in the time you'd have her away, but it wouldn't be pretty."

"I do care. I'm not this twisted villain you make me out to be. I've been compromising with you for years now."

I shake my head, turning back to face him one last time before I know I'll be ending the conversation.

"I'm sure you'll probably always feel guilty for the way you treated me when Dahlia was born, but that doesn't make it *go away* for me. Seems like you're ignoring it pretty well, out of self preservation, I'm guessing. I can't. I worry every day that you'll shut down on her too. You haven't done nearly enough for either of us to prove to me otherwise. I *am* reasonable, dude. I look at it as a possibility, but it hasn't happened yet. I don't think it'll happen for a long time."

"How have I not done enough? She's taken care of—"

"Under *your* roof! I spent years struggling to pay my rent, and all that was for you was a chance to fight the custody arrangement. You never thought about the fact that my daughter and I needed each other, and maybe could've used a little help. But little, spoiled Caleb would think of every single possibility in the world before doing anything to help the mother of his child."

He starts to respond heatedly, but I put a hand up.

"I have dinner in the oven, I'm done with this conversation."

I open my door, and then I close it softly behind me. I'm angry, but never angry enough to frighten Dahlia. I take a few seconds to breathe, and push that interaction from my mind.

He's crazy if he thinks he's getting his way here.

The music is back. I thought that finding out about Dahlia would've been the thing to change her ways, but of course that would've been too easy.

I even managed to get her into her own bed, after hours of her fighting it. I sat on the floor next to her, and I read her books. I put all of her favorite toys around her, and I tucked her in so nicely. She cried a lot, and it was so hard, but we eventually got there. She was out and snoring, and I snuck away to my own bedroom to enjoy a full night of sleep.

I slept for an hour. I heard Dahlia crying first, and I ran to her in a panic before realizing what else I was hearing. That damned music woke her up, and terrified her. Who wouldn't be terrified in this situation?

"Shh, it's okay baby. It's okay, sweet girl."

She's gasping out words in between her sobs, but I can't make all of it out. Something about being tired and scared.

This is not okay. This is what I've been dreading more than anything about our current situation. I didn't want it to hurt *her*.

I move around the apartment, grabbing a couple things we'll need in the morning. Toothbrushes, a pair of leggings and a t-shirt for each of us, Dahlia's favorite stuffed animal and her blanket. She dozes off at one point, until a new song starts up with even more thumping bass and she resumes crying.

I feel like crying right here with her.

I load her into the car with promises of sleep, and quiet, and getting to see grandma and grandpa in the morning. It barely calms her down, but two minutes in the car and she's out again.

We shouldn't be in the car right now. We shouldn't have to flee the home that we pay for and have lived in a lot longer than that rude, inconsiderate, piece of–

I blow out a long exhale, not wanting to work myself up anymore than I already am. I need to focus on getting to our destination safely.

It is a challenge to get Dahlia out without waking her, and to not move her around too much as I unlock the door and get us inside.

To my surprise, I see my dad standing at his kitchen counter with a glass of water in hand. He looks less surprised to see me here. We smile at each other, but I go put Dahlia down in a bed before I even attempt to say a word. He must know better too, because he waits quietly while I walk down the hall.

"Bad night?" he asks when I'm back in the kitchen with empty arms.

"So bad."

I hug him tightly, and we just stand like that for a minute. I feel like I'm a little kid again, being comforted after a bad dream. This time I only wish it was a bad dream, instead of my painful reality.

"You've got to do something about it, sunshine. You can't let them drive you out of your house."

"I tried," I whine. "Tim isn't going to do anything. I guess her dad told him she was depressed, so he doesn't want to bother her for the foreseeable future."

I finally let go, and jump up to sit on the counter. Another thing that makes me feel like a little kid again. If my mom was awake, she'd yell at me to get my butt down. She always did back then. My dad just chuckles like he's also remembering all those years ago. Little Reya with her bright blonde hair, and big attitude.

"You have other options. You haven't talked to her about it, have you?"

"She's like, impossible to talk to. I've never even run into her coming and going from her apartment. The only proof I have of her existence, other than seeing her drive that car, is the music and the notes."

"If you don't want to call the police on her, you're going to have to put your foot down a little harder. Have you even knocked on her door during the day?" he asks.

"Well... no."

"Why is that? Are you scared of her?"

Am I? For some reason I don't feel completely set on saying no to that question.

"I don't think so," I answer.

"Why do you have to think about it? You are or you're not."

"I'm too tired."

He pats my shoulder a couple times, and gives me a smile that looks too pitiful for my liking.

"You're not helpless. Stop worrying about inconveniencing her, when she's obviously not worried about doing the same to you and Dahlia. If you don't stop this now, it's not going to stop."

"You say that like it's easy."

"You forget that I raised you. It is easy. You have more fire and determination in your pinky than most people have in their entire bodies. Use it."

My heart could burst. I'm so lucky to have such amazing parents that believe in me so much.

"I love you, dad."

"I love you too, sunshine. Get some rest."

Clearly you don't care that my daughter exists, because you so rudely woke her up late last night with your music, and she cried her head off. Messing with my life was one thing, but messing with hers is going to be a problem.

I'd LOVE to discuss things in person with you, but you've done a really good job at avoiding me. Want to drop the stubborn crap and do a single mom a favor? I'm sure we can compromise here.

Unless of course you're actually a ghost, in which case I kindly ask that you haunt a different building.

Thanks.

I don't want to disrupt Dahlia's schedule too much, so I let her take the bus home for the rest of the week. We hang out there, make dinner, watch some of her favorite shows, and play with her favorite toys. As soon as the sun sets, we head back to my parents to sleep. She hasn't complained for a second, and I could cry at how relieved I am to have such a good kid. She's a lot more patient and gracious than I am, because I am *pissed* about not being able to sleep in my own bed. I want to throw all kinds of fits about it. Stomping my feet and screaming my head off sounds so good right about now, and it makes me all the more grateful that I don't have to handle it from her.

Maybe that's why she is the way she is. The universe knew that there was only room for one big baby in our lives, and it was never an option for me to give up that title.

I expect to finally find a response to my previous note when we leave the house on Friday, but there's nothing. She took my note and didn't bother to answer because I was right.

She's avoiding me.

10

With a mug of hot tea that smells like a warm hug and tastes like dirt, I curl up in the chair on my front porch. The sun has already set, and I shiver the second I sit down. I could be better prepared with warmer clothes, but I stay put out of pure stubbornness. At least my hands are warmed by the drink I'm holding, not that it would help if it starts to snow like the forecast mentions.

Tonight's agenda is to watch enough videos on crocheting that I might feel inspired to pick up the ridiculous collection of supplies that has been rotting in my closet. This isn't my first attempt at this technique, but who's to say it won't be the last? Maybe today's the day.

I pull up a video I'd previously started, feeling good about the friendly face on the screen. Or... maybe she doesn't look that friendly, but her hair happens to also be pink. I take it as a good sign.

I immediately struggle with being bored out of my mind. I know what a slip knot is. I know how to hold the hook. I yawn, and set the phone down anyway, propped up with the stand that's built into my phone case.

I sit there, sipping, shivering, and struggling. There are mosquitos out here too, and I haven't done anything to protect myself from those pesky little monsters. Why did I think this was a good idea tonight? I haven't been home all that much lately, and I could be enjoying my couch or my bed. I could be soaking up quality time with those places while I actually can. There's no saying I'll be safe here tonight, I might still have to evacuate. I'm hopeful at the moment because her car is gone.

I know better than to assume that hope will last.

A text message pings on my phone, and I sigh as I close out of the video to open it. I'm not giving up, but I know how unlikely my chances are of going back to it now that I have something else to distract me.

It's from Caleb, and the message consists of a group of photos. It's Dahlia, sleeping on his couch. She's sprawled out on her back with an arm above her head and the other around an orange blob of fur that's resting its head on her stomach. I swipe to the next photo, a close up of the... cat. I do the math, and assume that this is Raquel's kitten. I guess cats grow pretty fast, because this thing is huge compared to the photos on her Instagram.

Caleb: *Meet Gouda. He's obsessed with Lia*

I chuckle at the name. Then I smile to myself. It's pretty darn cute, the two of them curled up on the couch. I'm sad I'm missing it in person. The only other cat she's met is Autumn's cat, Elaine, but she hardly counts. Especially since moving in with Miles and Freddy, she's a bit insane.

Reya: *Thanks for sharing*

Caleb: *Of course*

It's the most civil we've been over text in a long time, and maybe I'm just tired, but I soften towards him a small amount. I give him two points before the moment has passed and I change my mind.

I need more of this. I want him to include me in more things, and give me more reasons to trust him. If this was our new norm, maybe I wouldn't freak out over the idea of him taking her out of the country.

Maybe that's the only reason he sent the photos in the first place.

I shut my eyes tight, ridding that thought from my brain. I don't have to assume. I don't have to think the worst of him. It's just so hard sometimes.

I'm so invested in my line of thinking, that my brain lags when trying to process a new sound in the background. A thumping sound? Or a banging? Someone downstairs being noisy?

Only when it gets closer do I realize it's the stairs. *Feet* on the stairs.

Oh crap, oh crap, *oh crap.*

I don't have time to move, or feel less vulnerable, when a hooded figure appears a few feet away.

She freezes. I'm also frozen.

This is *weird.* Weeks have gone by without us running into each other, and here she suddenly is? It doesn't really feel real.

"You," I say, fueled by my surprise. It practically comes out as a shout.

Her eyes widen, but I have a feeling the reaction has more to do with my chaotic energy than her being affected by us meeting face to face. She looks around the space of our front porch, like there might possibly be an explanation–or an escape–but her eyes land back on me.

"Yeah?"

Her voice is higher pitched than I'd imagined. Almost sweet. Almost innocent. Her face is covered in darkness, thanks to the hood over her head. She's smarter and significantly warmer than I am right now.

"You're not a ghost," I blurt out.

"Sure I am," she replies quickly. "It's dark out here, you don't know what you're seeing."

Her gaze flits towards her front door. I see the disappointment on her face that she isn't walking through it at the moment.

I make a show of looking her up and down. As if she doesn't care that I want to see more of her, she sighs and removes her hood. Lots of deep, red hair falls down and takes up most of my attention at first. It's bouncy. It looks soft. I'm almost envious of it, wishing my own hair would grow out faster.

I should probably invest in some fancy shampoo or something, too. I bet her shampoo costs a fortune.

And then I look at her face.

And I'm left even more stunned. I don't even worry about the repercussions of standing from my seat to walk closer to her. She takes a step back when I'm only a couple away, so that's where I plant my feet and hope my legs don't wobble. I don't trust them, or really any part of my body at the moment. Whatever's happening to me isn't normal.

I thought she was pretty that day at the ice cream shop, but seeing her up close like this changes everything. She's *unreal.* Every small detail from the curl of her lashes to the shape of her nose is perfect. I'd think she was some kind of angel sent here just for me if she hadn't been making my life a living hell lately.

"No, I'm pretty sure I'm right," I mumble.

"Really makes no difference to me what you believe."

This time when she moves away from me, it's a couple of side steps that bring her closer to her front door.

"Wait, stop." I frown, not sure why I want to be in her presence. I must be a masochist. "You're just going to go inside?"

She scoffs like I'm unbelievable.

I am. It's fair. I asked her to talk, and I should take the hint that was her ignoring it.

"Um, yeah. Usually that's the first thing I do when I get home."

I take another step closer to her, and then stop when I notice her actually *wince* at the fact that there's nowhere for her to escape to.

"You've lived *right* there for three weeks and this is the first time we're seeing each other. I feel like it's a bigger deal than you're making it out to be," I say.

"I think it's a much smaller deal than you're making it out to be."

"I know you've had to be curious about me," I tell her.

She pauses before answering, probably wishing she didn't have to.

"I really haven't," she finally answers. "You seem rather irritating, and I was hoping to avoid you a lot longer than *this*."

I shouldn't be surprised by her words, but I am. And they hurt. They dig under my skin for a reason I can't explain, and sting like salt on a wound.

"I don't think you mean that. You don't even know me. I'm a delight."

She laughs, but there's no amusement in the sound.

"Whatever you say."

"I'm serious. I'm a damn ray of sunshine."

Pun intended, but she doesn't know that. I give my parents some mental points for coming up with that one, because it's good. Classic.

Her presence distracted me long enough that I forgot about the mosquitos trying to attack my ankles. I'm only reminded by the tickling sensation of them landing on me now, and I bend down to swat them away. I should've known better, this is the entire reason I own so many pairs of thick, fuzzy socks. They're my version of battle armor, and I walked right into this fight half naked.

"Well, *sunshine*, I'm done with this little... chat."

By the time I can think to ask what her problem is, I look up to see her gone, and her front door slams behind her.

I should feel a lot of things, but I wasn't expecting to feel so let down.

I like the hair.

I read the small sentence again. And again.

And again.

Can you say whiplash?

She blared her music all night again, so I barely slept. And she was so mean last night, wasn't she? I don't think I imagined it. I'm not in the habit of getting my feelings hurt so easily, but our interaction is somewhat of a blur. Most of what I remember is just her *face.* I can't *stop* remembering her face, even when I try really hard to distract myself with other things.

I pulled out the yarn today. I even got a couple of rows done on Vic's headband. I don't know how the hell that happened, but it was therapeutic. Maybe I just haven't truly needed to keep my hands and mind busy until now.

Are you joking?

I place that simple note on her door before I run to the grocery store. I'm not thrilled about it, but I know I need to take advantage of the free time I have.

Another sticky note is waiting on my door when I return with my arms weighed down by bags full of food. I didn't need to struggle as much as I did, but I feel like I'm winning something when it only takes me one trip.

Nope.

What does it say about her that she's been home all day and still saw my note. Is she checking? Or did I make that much noise when I left earlier?

I want someone to vent to about this whole situation. I may have talked my parent's ears off when I was staying over there, but they're *parents*. They want to offer solutions, and insight, and I don't really want to go as far as to tell them that I think she's the hottest woman I've ever seen and that her stupid little note gave me butterflies.

Butterflies. At my big age. I didn't know that could happen anymore, it's been so long.

She is infuriating. Clearly incapable of empathy. Someone I could never see myself being around without wanting to strangle them.

So why the hell did those four little written words elicit this kind of reaction from me? It makes no sense.

11

I'm sitting on my couch, listening to a podcast Autumn was excited about the other day. These two girls chat about books they love, and this particular episode was all about her most recent novel. They seriously gush about it for an entire hour, and I'm loving every second. It's so cool to have watched her go through the process of writing, and stressing, and doubting, and now there's no lack of proof out there that she's good at what she does.

I love it for her so much, and I can't wait to text her when I've finished listening to this.

I play some random puzzle game on my phone while the episode plays. I've never found it easy to get into podcasts or audiobooks, because I get distracted. I feel as though I need to be watching what's going on, or it can't hold my attention.

This little system has been working pretty well for me, though. I don't get the science behind it, but mindlessly moving these blocks has really helped me focus.

I line up yellow with yellow, blue with blue; I get jumpscared by one of the girls shrieking when they bring up a spicy bathtub scene and laugh to myself. That scene was hot as hell, and I can't help but wonder how much of it was inspired by true events.

There are a *lot* of details.

Somewhere outside, I hear a noise and instinctively pause the episode. Of course I'm curious, especially when the closeness of the sound can only be explained by one person. The only person in the vicinity who would be out on the front porch area, because it's also *their* front porch area.

Keys jingle, and a door closes. I'm almost tempted to look through the window, but I'd die of embarrassment if she saw me snooping now.

I glance over to my kitchen counter where I know her note is still sitting.

"No, I'm not." I'm guessing she's on the phone. *"I have school that day."*

Her footsteps sound loudly across the wooden boards.

"Yeah, yeah. I think ninety-nine percent of your daily activities are a waste of time, but I'm kind enough to keep it to myself."

Kind, yeah right. It is nice to know that her bad attitude appears to be the standard.

Her voice gets quieter as she walks down the stairs and it irritates me. I want to keep eavesdropping.

"Honestly Colleen, fuck off."

With that tone, I am *so* glad I'm not Colleen.

She must make it down to the parking lot, because along with her voice, the sound of her footsteps also disappears.

Now that she's gone, and my chances of having another awkward interaction are also gone, I move my activity to my favorite seat outside. This little set cost more money than I'm willing to admit, not even including the cushions.

Outdoor seat cushions are made from pure gold, apparently.

They're comfortable. They look nice. I'm glad I have them, but I'd be even happier if I wasn't still paying off the credit card I put it all on."

Time begins to slip away as I watch the sunset behind the buildings in my neighborhood. My podcast ends, so I put on another: some true crime story the app recommended to me. I'm a couple hundred levels deep in this silly little game. The weather is a bit better than the night before, and I am dressed appropriately. My rainbow fuzzy socks come halfway up my shin, and my oversized sweater is practically a blanket. It's the least stressed I've been in weeks, and I forget how nice it is to just sit around doing nothing. Sure I feel good after a nice, long, productive day, but downtime is important too. I need more of it.

I must doze off without realizing, because I open my eyes when I hear footsteps on the stairs again. Falling asleep outside with my front door unlocked is not the smartest thing I've ever done, but I can't say I'm surprised that my body is still trying to catch up on sleep whenever and wherever it can.

She appears at the top, hair in the messiest bun I've seen, looking grumpy and in a hurry.

"I really don't have time to talk," she mumbles without looking at me.

Actually, that's not completely true. She looks at my socks. There's an unmistakable few seconds where she doesn't look away from them. Her expression gives nothing else away, not how she might feel about them or anything. She doesn't stop moving towards her destination.

"Okay?"

I wasn't going to make her talk, I'm hardly even conscious. I don't say that though, I just watch as she lets herself into her apartment.

She slams the door behind her.

I'm looking down at two giant dishes of lasagna. I wasn't initially expected at dinner, so I have no idea what army Amelia was cooking for tonight. As far as I know, it was just supposed to be her, Sam, Autumn, and Miles. None of which typically eat very much anyway. At least, not compared to how much food I can put away.

"Is this one dairy free?"

I know one of them is. Amelia never forgets to make special accommodations for Autumn. Fake cheese is starting to look so real these days, because they are identical. I'd have no way to tell.

"Yes," she responds. As soon as she looks away, she looks back again. Her eyes dart back and forth. "Wait, maybe. Miles!"

His head instantly pokes into the kitchen.

"Yeah?"

"Can you try a bit of the cheese on top and tell me which one is which? I can't remember."

He rounds the corner, his shoes loud on the kitchen tile. He must have rushed here after work, because he's still wearing scrubs. That's the only indicator, considering he looks wide awake and ready to tackle anything.

That energy level is going to be really nice when they have a newborn soon.

Grabbing a fork from the drawer below, he takes a small bite of the one I suspect to be fake. I'm going off of zero evidence, just a hunch. When I raise my brows in question, his scrunch together. Without a word, he goes for the next one.

A few seconds pass, and he appears to really be thinking about it.

"Well?"

"Oh, it's definitely that one," he says, pointing.

I lift my heels, raising up and down in silent celebration that I was right.

Probably one of the more useless reasons I've given out points, but he gets some for confirming my hunch without even knowing it. Just a few, nothing too crazy.

"I think that's the one I want tonight," he turns to tell his mother. "I don't even like cashews, but they really did something here."

"Cashews? What does that have to do with anything?" I ask.

"Fake cheese," he offers.

"What do cashews have to do with fake cheese?"

He blinks, seeming confused at my question.

Autumn walks in, interrupting whatever he might have said. Her head falls on my shoulder when she reaches me.

"Where's Dahlia?" she asks.

I pout at the reminder that my daughter should be here, and isn't. Stupid, annoying neighbors that want to ruin my life, as if ruining my sleep schedule isn't enough.

"She's with Caleb." I put a hand up when I feel her mouth drop open. "It's a story for another time. I'm too angry to tell it right now."

Her hand comes up to my back and rubs a couple of soothing circles.

"I'm sorry, babe."

I shrug, and then feel bad because it pushes her off of me.

"You didn't have to move."

She laughs.

"I know you weren't shoving me off, but my back can't take much more of that."

She leans back a little, attempting to stretch it out. Miles instantly takes notice and steps behind her, placing his hands on her shoulders and massaging.

I need that kind of devotion in my life. These shoulders have needed massaging for years now.

"Can we go back to the peanuts and cheese?"

"Not peanuts. Cashews," he says.

"Aren't they the same thing?" The laughter stops, and silence fills the kitchen. "What?"

"No," Amelia says softly. "Peanuts are legumes, and cashews are nuts."

"That only answers my second question."

Or, technically, it *would*. If I knew what a legume was.

"What do you think fake cheese is made out of?" Autumn asks.

I shrug. "I've never really thought about it."

She walks over to the fridge, and her eyes scan the contents when she pulls it open.

"Aha! Here we go." Turning it over in her hands so the ingredients face up, she brings it to me.

I scan the list and my eyes bulge.

"What the hell? It's practically peanut butter."

"Still not correct," Miles says with a laugh. "*Cashew* butter."

"I'm never going to change," I say. "I think I want the dairy *full* cheese tonight."

"You and me both," Amelia says, and pats me on the shoulder. "And Sam. He'll never get used to the other stuff."

We all help ourselves to the pasta and bread, and settle at Amelia's large dining table. We chat about lots of nothing: my parents renovations, Autumn's current projects, Miles' utterly hilarious patients at work. The sarcasm and wit in some of his stories is next level.

I love old people. I think I went into the wrong line of work.

Amelia's finally moving her business into a bigger office, and it's taking longer than she'd hoped. Her and Sam complain about the construction company they went through, and he lists off all the things he'd be doing differently if he had the time to take it on himself.

It's all so natural, and I can't help but feel a little awe when I'm in the middle of moments like these. The perfectly normal ones, where we really are just family. It doesn't matter that I'm some random girl Autumn brought around that keeps showing up to these dinners. It doesn't matter that Autumn had a complicated history with Amelia and her younger son. It doesn't matter that Sam is the newest member of this table after deciding he wanted to marry Amelia after only a few months of knowing her.

It works. Your people are your people no matter how they got to be there.

And just like any family does, I have my quarrels with some of them. Amelia in particular.

She does her best, and I see how much she loves Autumn. It's obvious how hard she tries every single day to make her feel welcome.

But it was downright stupid that she ever made her feel *un*welcome. As Autumn's best friend, I can't let it go as easily as she does. Neither can Vic, and we've had our talks about it. We're protective. Autumn came into our lives as someone who was really hurt and vulnerable, and I can't forget what the reason for it was.

It's a good thing that Justin and I aren't usually here at the same time, I'll say that much. And it's an even better thing that none of us will ever have to interact with Miles' ex-wife, because I'd have more than words for her.

Conversation turns to Autumn's due date, inevitably.

"I love you guys, but I don't know if I want anyone else in the room when I'm delivering him," Autumn says.

Miles chokes on the bite of food he was attempting to eat, and coughs a few times to sort himself out. I try to help with a couple pats on the back, but he waves me away.

"I'm good. I'm fine." He turns to his girlfriend. "*Anyone?*"

"Of course I'm not talking about you, silly."

"Oh good. Great," he whispers.

Most people might assume that she wasn't talking about the father of her child, but Autumn struggles so much with her anxiety that you never know. It wouldn't be the most surprising thing.

I wish I could've forced Caleb out of the room when I was giving birth, he was so unhelpful. At one point he actually put on headphones because he was *uncomfortable* with all the noises I was making. I remember just how judgmental his words had felt, as if anyone could silently push a child out of their body.

I can't make this crap up.

"You definitely have to hold my hand the entire time," she tells him.

"Even if she crushes the bones until they're unrepairable," I add.

He looks her in the eye and smiles.

"If there's anyone I'd let break my hand, it's you."

"That's disgustingly sweet," I say. "Enough of that."

"I want you all there after," she goes on. "To meet him first and get pictures of all of us together at the hospital."

"Of course," Amelia answers. "Whatever you want, we're there."

I nod in agreement.

We discuss around the table, who will be where. Who needs to be in charge of what. Every little detail and possibility is discussed, in order to put her mind at ease. Autumn doesn't need to worry about a single thing when the day comes.

Vic and Julian are on their own dinner date night, but they're a part of this conversation too. One of us will just fill them in and give them their assignments in our group chat later.

Autumn clears her throat and gives me a pointed look.

"I'll forgive you for being late as long as you have Dahlia with you."

"Without question. I'll give Caleb a heads up just in case it's one of his days." I reach in front of Miles to squeeze her hand. "*If* I'm somehow late, which sounds *nothing* like me, it'll be because I'm tracking her down."

Note to self: Do not let Caleb take her to his parents house that week. That's three hours of driving that I do not want to do at the drop of a hat during any hour of the night.

Autumn squeezes me back with a big smile on her face.

I'm so excited for that day to come.

12

"Don't have time," she grumbles for the millionth time.

When the shock wears off from seeing her, *yet again*, I decide I don't believe her today.

"What are you in such a hurry to do at home on a Tuesday night?" I ask out of plain curiosity.

She stops for a single beat, so fast that I almost doubt if I saw the hesitation at all.

"Nothing that's your business."

That's fair.

"Feeling gracious enough to let me sleep through the night tonight? Maybe you could turn the volume down for once?"

"No," she simply replies.

"Sounds about right," I sigh.

When her back is fully facing me, I let my eyes linger on every detail they can. Her hair is split into two ponytails that fall down her back. She's wearing a cropped crewneck sweater, and a pair of black skinny jeans. I'm not proud of checking out her ass, but I can't bring myself to look away until she's gone inside. I've never seen one so perky.

I bet she does squats for fun.

Her next note shows up the morning after.

Can you stop cornering me when I get home at night? It's getting creepy.

Cornering her? I barely even talk to the woman, so it is beyond me why that's the conclusion she's come to. For the most part, I've minded my business and barely even looked her way. It's not my fault that I don't have a back porch to utilize for my fresh air.

Creepy?! I live here. This is my front porch. I've been sitting on it since long before you showed up.

When I go to put it in the usual place, I'm startled by the door opening in front of me. How in the world did we go weeks without seeing each other, and now she won't stop popping up? I'm over it.

I think it's the first time I'm seeing her without any makeup, and it changes nothing about my attraction to her. It softens up her face, making her look nicer.

Well, it would if she wasn't scowling. She looks disgusted to see me here, so that's a *great* feeling.

"What are you doing?" she snaps.

I wave the note in front of her face, pretending I'm not affected by her attitude.

"How else am I supposed to get this to you? I don't have an assistant to do my bidding for me."

"Your bidding?" she asks. Then she shakes her head, not wanting to know apparently. "Leave me alone."

My jaw drops.

"It takes two to tango, I'm not the only one with a pen and paper here."

"You started it, and I'm ending it. Stay away from me," she demands.

If this little wrench hadn't been thrown in my plan, she would've read my note and known that I'm not going to cower in my apartment just because she doesn't want to see me.

"Stop playing music at night."

She rolls her eyes.

"Nope."

Then she shoulder checks me– more like shoulder *slams* me– to get me out of her way. I stumble back and watch and she pulls her front door closed and locks it.

I don't even know what to do other than stare at her in shock. Why is she so horrible? Seriously, what did I ever do to deserve this? She doesn't even know me.

"Would you rather I call the police? Because you can't keep this up. My daughter is *six*. She goes to school, she needs sleep."

With a sigh that says she can't be bothered, she walks away from me.

"You don't always have her here, and you can clearly leave whenever you do."

My blood begins boiling. It's obvious to me that this woman doesn't have any children of her own, or have regular contact with any. Who could say that with their whole chest, and simply not care about the inconvenience?

That isn't even a good enough word for it. It's not inconvenient, it's cruel. All a six year old should worry about is learning how to read, not whether or not she's going to be woken up in the middle of the night by terrifying sounds. She's at an age where those things will stick with her for a lot longer than the current moment. Am I going to end up with a teenager that wakes up in a cold sweat every night because she expects to hear growling on the other side of the wall? Is she going to be a grown adult living in her own home with that fear, when I won't be there to make her feel better? The thought of it makes me feel sick.

"I shouldn't have to take her from her home in the middle of the night to make sure she can sleep!"

She starts down the stairs, not even raising her voice to answer. Not caring if I even hear what she says.

"But you do have somewhere to go. Sounds like a problem solved."

"You are unbelievable," I gasp.

"Believe it." She turns back to give me the bitchiest smirk I've ever seen. "And stay away from my door."

I'm left standing by that front door, contemplating my entire life for an embarrassingly long time after she leaves. When the sound of a downstairs neighbor's door slamming snaps me out of my trance, I stare down at the note in my hand. It's a little wrinkled now, barely surviving that interaction.

Much like me. Like some silly metaphor.

I slap it on her door anyway, unsure if I want the adhesive to do its job and stay adhered until she gets back. Seems fair to put it in fate's hands, and if the wind blows it away? So be it.

Remove hanger. Scan item. Bag item.

Remove hanger. Scan item. Bag item.

Remove hanger. Remove security tag. Scan item. Bag item.

Repeat approximately three hundred times, until you feel like you're absolutely losing your mind.

Oh, but sometimes people spice it up for you. Sometimes they have a coupon that they swear they should be able to use, even when I read aloud the clearly stated line on it that says, *"This coupon can not be combined with in-store promotions or other discount offers."*

It feels self-explanatory, but I'm always surprised by how wrong people can be. Do I have the option as the manager to override it and give them what they want? Sure, and it happens pretty often to the ones that are nice about it.

But when they demand that I do it, and question my intelligence because they aren't getting their way? It feels good to smile and say no.

It feels even better when they ask for the manager and I get to tell them they're currently speaking to her.

My store always has a big sale for the anniversary of the store's opening. This year things were kicked up a notch to celebrate ten years, and now ten locations across four states.

This week has knocked Black Friday out of the water. I've never seen us so busy before, to the point where I've felt the need to sacrifice most of my down time. Every second that Dahlia has been at school or with her dad, I've lived here. At night when I'd normally be at home, stressed and tired, I'm here. I replenish everything on the sales floor, and make sure it all looks perfect for the next morning when I'm coming right back in.

I've done it *every* night Dahlia hasn't been home. I leave eventually, but I go straight to my parents just to sleep for five hours, then wake up and repeat. It could be worse. If I went home and had to see that awful woman, that would be much worse. I'm too angry to be anywhere near her. I'm *also* angry that I'm letting her win at the moment, and making her disruptive life all too easy, but I need to have my priorities straight.

When I finally do go home, there are only a couple more days left of the chaos at work. It feels weird to walk inside, like I can tell it's been empty for a while. The air is too stagnant, and everything is too quiet.

For now, of course. I'm sure that'll change.

I turn on the television, just to have some background noise. I open up the windows, despite the cold night outside. I get some water going on my electric kettle, and preheat the oven for tonight's dinner. I could do better than frozen enchilada's, but I could also do a lot worse. At least Dahlia loves them.

The second I think about how much I miss her, there's a knock on my door. Perfect timing.

"Hi, my sweet girl!" She hugs my legs, and I smooth down the back of her blonde hair that's sticking straight up. "Caleb."

"Reya." He nods in greeting. "How's it going?"

"It's okay. You?"

"Good," he says.

Then there's an uncomfortable silence, because we don't know how to talk to each other.

"Smells good in there. Dinner?" he asks. I nod. "She tried fish and chips for the first time. She destroyed the plate, and then asked for more."

I wrinkle my nose and look down at her.

"Fish? Really?"

"Yeah. I like the crunchy part on the outside."

"Fair enough," I tell her. "I thought kids were supposed to be picky eaters."

"Right?" Caleb asks with a chuckle. "I don't think she's turned down anything I've fed her."

"*Is* there anything you don't like?" I know she isn't the biggest fan of some things, but she eats most of it anyway. The blueberries on her plate the other morning come to mind.

"Hmm," she starts. Her eyes move between us as she thinks. "Green beans."

We both nod in sync.

"Yeah, that's–" I lose my train of thought when I hear the familiar sound of footsteps on the stairs.

We do this every Wednesday night, and *she's* never come home this early. I've never been worried she'd meet Caleb and piss him off, too.

Dahlia doesn't register the noise, and she thankfully runs to her room like she remembered something important in there. That's one bonus of having two homes, it keeps things exciting when she gets the chance to miss her belongings. I'm sure it's saving me money.

Caleb looks confused when I stop talking, until he peeks over his shoulder. There's my neighbor, looking... *ugh.*

She looks so good that I forget to breathe.

I mean, I'm so *angry* that I forget to breathe.

Because I *don't* like her. I might even hate her a little.

She glances in our direction for a brief second, but otherwise ignores us.

"Hi," Caleb calls out, putting a friendly hand up. She doesn't respond, and then she disappears through her front door. Like a ghost.

I know ghosts don't need keys or to bother with turning door knobs, but I'm paying so little attention to the specifics that she might as well have walked right through it without doing a thing.

"She seems nice," he mutters.

"She might be the devil."

He scoffs.

"That's dramatic."

Every muscle in my body tenses when he says it, that particular word momentarily transporting me back to a time I worked my ass off to heal from.

"Oh, Caleb." I tisk putting on a brave face. "You lost the privilege of calling me dramatic a long time ago."

He takes a step back, his eyes widening as he realizes his mistake.

"Sorry. I shouldn't have said that."

"Correct. Have a good night," I say.

To his credit, he does look like he regrets it. He knows that all the times he's said that before have stuck with me like super glue.

I think he tries to reply, but I close the door before he can. That's enough for tonight.

I let out a strong, steady exhale, preparing myself to quickly shift gears.

Now I have to make heading to my parents house sound like the most exciting thing in the world to Dahlia, despite how often we've been forced to go over there lately.

13

More scanning. More bagging. More fake smiles.

I can't wait for this sale to end. I don't have the energy for this week that feels never ending.

A huge pile is placed on the counter before me, and I start on it before I even look up.

"Do you need any gift receipts today?"

I slide a security tag into the magnet that removes it, and of course it doesn't just fall off like it's supposed to. Some of these things can be so stubborn. I wiggle it a little, even give it a tug, but it's fully stuck. I set it to the side, and decide to worry about it last.

Two more beeps of my scanner and I realize this person never answered my question.

"Shopping for yourself or someone else to–"

I lock eyes with a piercing green gaze. Instead of the harsh glare I'm used to seeing in them, there's surprise. They're the wide eyes of someone really taken aback.

I wouldn't expect to see her here either, but it can't be that shocking that I exist outside of my little apartment. She has to have noticed I've barely been there as it is lately.

"Myself," she finally answers.

That *voice*. It's such a contrast to her actions.

I press my mouth into a line to keep from saying anything, and I start to scan faster. When I get to the last item, the one that has a tricky security tag, I grab a rubber band. It's a trick that comes in handy in situations like this, but I try to be sly about it. I can't go around letting just anyone see it, because I know there are ones that would attempt it in the fitting room.

When I crouch down to hide what my hands are doing, Paige laughs at me.

I hear my neighbor's muffled voice talking to her. She asks her what I'm doing, and Paige explains.

"Do you have to do that often?" my neighbor asks.

"Yeah. Those tags really suck sometimes," Paige says.

Another customer must walk up, because my coworker breaks into her customer greeting, and I hear more hangers being thrown on the counter.

The tag pops off, and I take a deep breath before standing to face her again.

"Your total is two-hundred and eighty-seven dollars, and ninety-one cents."

I wonder what she does for a living as I watch her reach into a little black purse and pull out a matching wallet. I can't imagine it's customer service that's responsible for the funds on the debit card she finds there.

I try to peek at her name as she taps it on the screen. I'm absolutely not going to ask, she doesn't need to know I care at all what it is. I don't see it though, as if she intentionally held it to cover that information.

Whatever.

I don't care that much.

She goes to grab her bag of items at the same time I do, and our hands collide with a little electric zap. I wince, and pull away quickly. That happens all the time when I'm at work, so I assume I'm the one at fault.

"Sorry," I mutter.

I rip her receipt off the printer with my other hand and hold it out, but she doesn't notice.

She's too busy staring at me.

She doesn't stop, even when I'm looking right back at her. I see her eyes move slightly, like they're outlining the shape of every feature, every detail. I'm too stunned to move. It's weird, right? I should think she's being weird, but I actually, stupidly like that she's looking at me. I feel cute today, and I did my makeup to my highest standards. My bright pink eyeliner matches my hair perfectly, and I'm wearing flowery earrings that are the exact same shade.

And I *really* like that I get to look at her. I scan more details. Her feathered brows, her pouty lips, the piercings lining her ears. Her makeup is flawless, her red lipstick is bold. She looks like the kind of person that really has herself figured out. She knows what works, and she runs with it.

Because it *is* working. I have every reason to find her flaws, and to pick her apart, because I know her personality sucks. I just can't find anything.

She's so beautiful it makes my chest hurt.

I don't get to keep trying to find anything, because she suddenly looks down. Before I realize what's happening, she snatches the receipt out of my hand and heads for the exit.

I'm at a loss, as usual.

"You know her?" Paige asks. "She's like, *really* pretty."

Isn't she?

"No," I grumble.

But I spend the rest of my shift thinking of nothing other than how *pretty* she is.

—ele—

Dahlia falls asleep early, and I'm nervous about it. I'm always nervous being in my own home these days. I was planning to take her to my parents again, but I don't have the heart to move her now.

With my front door cracked open so I can hear if she wakes up and needs me, I plant myself on my usual seat outside. I'll get on my knees and beg if I have to, but I'm hoping my neighbor doesn't show up at all. I deserve that much: one easy, problem free night. Just one.

For now. At some point I'll let my dreams reach further.

I grab my hook and my unfinished crochet project, and pick up where I left off. My nerves are on fire, so it's nice to keep my hands busy. I go without listening to anything, enjoying actual silence while I've got it. I don't usually stop long enough to listen to the small things in the world around me. The rustling of leaves being jostled in the wind. Birds, bugs, distant cars. It's peaceful.

It doesn't take long at all tonight for my peace to be disrupted. This time I'm on such high alert that I recognize the sound of tires crunching on the gravel of our little parking lot. It wouldn't be anyone else, not at this time of night.

It's about to be game time, and I am seriously underprepared. I should've ran lines with my mom, or even myself in the mirror. That would've been better than nothing. What do I even say? Should I try to cry? Maybe if I lay it on really thick, she'll finally feel bad enough. I haven't exactly come to her with anything but an attitude before.

Zero attitude, Reya. Stay cool.

She must hustle up the stairs because it feels like I barely blink and there she is, wearing an all black tracksuit. She wears it too well, and I foolishly can't keep myself from admiring her curves.

"What are you doing?" she asks.

I jolt in surprise, not expecting her to have said the first word. Or said anything really, she's always so set on getting away from me.

I cautiously hold up the unfinished headband in my hands.

"Hanging out on my front porch. What are you doing?"

"Wishing I didn't have to share a front porch," she mumbles. It's not quiet enough to evade my ears if that's what she was hoping. I roll my eyes. "Were you waiting for me again?"

"I wasn't waiting for you," I insist. At least I wasn't all of the other times. I'm not going to admit that tonight happens to be one time I was, she's full enough of herself.

"Sure you weren't," she says with all the sarcasm in the world.

"We've hardly said two sentences to each other, which is not enough for you to so boldly call me a liar."

"It's not enough for me to think you're telling the truth either."

"I live here," I say slowly.

"Yeah, right in that exact spot apparently."

"I like this chair."

She looks at the other chair, the one across from me that I'm not occupying. Looking at it now that she is too makes me view it with fresh eyes. That thing looks brand new despite going through all the weather of all the seasons.

And then I forget how to think thoughts, because she comes over and sits down in it. Too close for my comfort, that's for sure.

"It's alright. The cushions are a little stiff," she says. "You can't be very comfortable."

I can't wrap my head around her talking to me like a normal person. I didn't know she was even capable.

All I can do is gape at her.

She raises her brows.

"Hello?"

I set the yarn down on the table, and place my hands in my lap to hide their shaking.

"No one ever sits in that one. Mine has an imprint of my ass at this point."

She fucking *smiles* at that. Maybe she has a twin, a much nicer one that showed up in her place. The real woman is probably driving recklessly through a school zone or something. Something that seems more like her than this.

Or I've fallen asleep outside again, and none of this is actually happening. It has to be one of those two things.

"Your guy friend sits here," she says.

I gasp in shock.

"You have been watching me!"

She raises her hands.

"Calm down, I look out my window every once in a while."

I know that much, I've caught her already.

"He's not my friend. He's my ex-husband," I correct. Not that she deserves to know anything about me, but I don't like the idea of anyone in the world thinking he and I are closer than we are.

"Huh." Not a question, just a way of acknowledging my statement. "Your kid's dad?"

"Why are you suddenly interested in talking to me?" I ask bluntly.

"I'm not. I just don't have homework tonight."

As if that's a reasonable explanation.

"You're a student?" I knew that much from my own eavesdropping, but I don't know what else to say.

She nods, that's it.

We have another one of those weird moments, where I know she's staring at my face, and she *knows* that I know. She's not being subtle.

"Stop looking at me like that," I say in a low voice. It's kind of like she doesn't know if she wants to throw something at my head or...

Well, I don't know what else it could be. Maybe it is just the throwing thing and I'm delusional. Maybe I'm completely imagining the way her eyes linger on my mouth.

"I don't want to be looking at you at all, but you're the one that keeps intercepting my walk to my front door."

I shake my head slowly, thoughtfully.

"I don't believe that."

"Believe it. You've done it so many times now."

"I don't believe that you don't want to be looking at me," I admit sharply.

Her brows raise, disbelief filling her expression.

"Are you that vain?"

"You said you liked my hair," I say with a shrug.

"I should've never written that," she mumbles, just to herself. "It's hair. It's pink. Get over yourself."

Her tone is back to being sharp and annoyed, so I'm not surprised when she stands up.

I follow suit.

"Please don't do it tonight," I begin to plead. "I'll beg. I'll stoop as low as bribing you. My daughter is sound asleep in there, and I need her to stay that way. *Please*."

"What would you bribe me with?" she asks calmly.

I look over to the row of pots filled with plants that are beyond saving at this point. They *have* turned into somewhat of a cemetery, I've been neglecting them for too long now.

"I'll throw those away. You won't have to look at any more dead plants."

"You should do that anyway. How does it not drive you nuts?" she asks.

"I've had other things on my mind," I say through gritted teeth.

She has the audacity to smirk.

"So I've been on your mind."

"Probably not more than I've been on yours. I'm sure you sit in there at night, relishing how miserable you make me."

She shrugs.

"Sometimes, yeah."

I'm dealing with a psychopath. It hits me like a flood of water that forces me out to sea. I should've taken this further sooner. I should've called the police weeks ago. I should've pushed harder, and gone back to Tim about it. I was right, she's not doing it to take care of herself. Maybe it started out as some odd attempt at that, but now she's doing it to hurt me. I have verbal proof.

What the hell have I been doing?

I feel so much more defeated right now than I've felt this entire time.

Unfortunately, I feel the tingle in my throat of an incoming cry. It's the kind that you can't will away, and it's coming in hot.

"Please," I say one more time. Without another word, I head for my front door as fast as my feet will get me there. She doesn't deserve to see me cry, I bet she'd like that too much.

I'm almost to the threshold when she steps in front of me, and our chests collide. *Hard.*

Standing this close, I can see that her nose is red from the cold, and it's almost enough to make me want to help warm it up.

I'm embarrassing myself even in my own head. She's *awful*, and yet my mind is wandering to all the different ways I could do just that.

Bad, Reya. Stop crushing on the psychopath.

She just smells so good, it's making it hard to think clearly.

"Sorry, I—" She grabs my arm, keeping me from backing away. "What are you doing?"

There's something different about this stare. She's not peering into my eyes, but her gaze is undoubtedly stuck in one place this time.

She clearly has an interest in my mouth. I take to studying hers, because it feels like I'm allowed to for a few seconds. She isn't wearing her usual lipstick, and her lips are a delicate, glossy pink.

I'd love to find out what flavor her lip balm is. I'd love to find out if they're as soft as they look.

But my common sense roots me in place. I *do* have common sense. I've never been attracted to someone that aggravates me the way she does, but I can learn to deal with it. Hell, I can be over it in a couple weeks if I try hard enough.

"I need to go inside," I tell her.

"Do you?" she asks, and her cool breath hits me so temptingly.

I step back before I do something dumb.

"What is happening right now?"

She shrugs.

"Don't know what you mean," she responds. But there's something in her tone that tells me she's full of it, as if her actions didn't already make that clear.

"I mean... we're not friendly. We don't talk," I start. "You're being *weird*. If I didn't know any better, I'd think you wanted to—"

"To what?" she interrupts.

I laugh, because it's beginning to feel especially ridiculous that the thought even occurred to me.

"To kiss me." I keep the amusement in my voice so she hears just how unserious to take the words.

The corners of her mouth curl up into a smile, but not the cheery kind. The kind that haunts my dreams, and makes me want to run and hide.

"What if that was the truth?"

I snort, more than over this. I thought I liked the sound of her voice, but not like this. Not when she's mocking me.

I step around her, hoping for my escape, but she's a surprisingly good guard for her size.

"What if?" she asks again.

"Then I'd know I was having some messed up dream. People don't just go around randomly kissing people they don't like."

"I disagree," she says.

I wait for her to go on and explain herself, but she doesn't. She just keeps on staring.

What is happening right now?

My laughter turns into a nervous, uncertain sound, but it trails off the more I study her. Not that I have any clue how good of an actress she is, but I'd almost bet that she is being completely serious.

"Why would you?"

"You've never kissed a stranger at a bar before?"

Okay, not cool if she can read my mind.

That makes this interaction so unfair.

"This isn't a bar, and neither of us have had nearly enough drinks for that."

"Kind of feels like it," she says softly.

I don't even bother questioning it, because she leans in closer to me, and it *does* kind of feel like I'm under the influence.

If I was sober, surely I'd push her away.

Right?

Her face comes closer, her intentions obvious, and I don't even flinch. I'm waiting for it, *my entire body* is waiting for it, like it's something so important. It feels like a fact that every cell in my body is aware of.

This is important.

Her lips touch mine so softly at first, and I'm surprised to feel like maybe she's nervous. She doesn't seem to me like someone that gets nervous.

The second time she does it is a little more sure. The third is even more so.

She's kissing me like she's trying to figure something out, and I'm just letting her. She can figure out whatever she wants at this point, that common sense I swear to have is lost. I might not even care if I never find it.

I put more into the kiss, pressing my lips harder against hers. I swipe my tongue against her bottom lip to find that she tastes sugary sweet. Oh, the irony.

Suddenly, she has a hand in my hair and she's gripping me with a forcefulness that lights me up from the inside out. My mouth parts, acting on pure instinct, and my brain has nothing to do with it.

She's amazing at this.

I manage not to whimper when she lets me go all too soon. Whatever she just awoke in me is not going back to bed anytime soon.

So embarrassing.

She wipes the moisture from her lips with the back of her hand, panting, and it's stupidly hot.

"Okay then, sunshine."

"Okay then?" I ask, breathless. I'm so disoriented.

"Don't get any funny ideas. I still think you're irritating," she adds.

"What the fuck?" I ask.

A smile plays at her lips, but instead of answering, she walks away.

Of course she walks away.

When she's gone and back inside her apartment, I don't know what to do. That couldn't have been real. This is the part when I wake up from a weird dream and feel weird all day, right? I'd love to wake up now and get that over with.

But I don't. I just keep standing in the same spot, catching my breath.

"What the fuck?" I whisper to myself.

On autopilot I end up in my bed, fully dressed and teeth unbrushed. I'm instinctively braced for her music to start playing, so I don't close my eyes. I just lay there, staring at my ceiling, waiting.

The music never comes, but I never fall asleep.

14

"Okay, you're going to use this spoon to measure this and put it into the bowl two times," I tell her. I'm amazed when she just listens and goes right in to do the first one. "Can I level out the top for you?"

"No, this is okay," Dahlia tells me.

Then she plops a largely overflowing tablespoon of cinnamon into the small mixing bowl, and leaves a dusty little trail of it on the counter. I guess if we're going to ignore the rules here, this is the part where it does the least harm.

She goes in for the second spoonful, and it goes more or less the same. Except when it comes to putting it in the bowl, she flings it in.

"Lean back or you're going to inhale–"

She starts coughing before I can warn her. That was a mom fail.

It's even more of a fail when she coughs right into the bowl and more of it is blown into the air. I grab her under her arms and scoop her up and away from the cloud of it.

"I like sim."

She starts coughing again, making her statement that much more hilarious.

"Cinnamon," I correct.

"I can call it sim," she insists.

I laugh at her matter-of-fact tone. Cinnamon is a hard word to nail down.

"Alright, close enough then. Do you still want to help?"

"Is it the cookie part yet?" she asks.

"So close, come here."

I wave away what may be left of the cinnamon cloud, and put her back on her stool.

I measure out the sugar, and I don't level that either. What's the point in starting now?

Her eyes light up, and she claps excitedly when I grab the bowl of the dough we mixed no more than five minutes ago.

"Finally," she whispers.

We spend the next chunk of the afternoon rolling our dough into little balls, or not-so-little. Her doing. We coat them in sugar, and lay them out on our pan. She's not thrilled that they have to sit in the fridge for an hour, but I do my best convincing her that it's worth it.

Thankfully it only takes a few minutes of impatient questioning before her attention moves to the dolls she left laying on the living room floor earlier. That's the last of the help I receive from her.

Hours later, when I'm so sick of looking at cookies that I could collapse, Autumn walks through my front door.

"It smells so good in here!" she exclaims.

I point to the newest batch that's sitting on a cooling rack.

"These ones are still warm."

She doesn't hesitate, picking one up and breaking it into two. Steam rises from the thick center, and suddenly I'm not sick of them anymore. My mouth is watering.

Dahlia comes up to hug her and swears she should have another one because she shouldn't be the only one without a cookie at this moment. I give in, handing her one of the smaller ones. She notices and makes a little face, but mercifully says nothing.

"Usually I'm the late one. You were supposed to help us with these," I chide.

She pouts.

"I know, I let Miles distract me for too long with some video game. Completely lost track of time, I'm sorry!" she says with her mouth full. A couple crumb fly out onto the ground, but I just smile to myself about it. We've got a lot of cleaning up to do anyway.

I step forward to hug her as soon as my daughter lets go.

"That's okay, I got to wrangle this little one into baking with me. Did we have fun, princess?"

Dahlia looks between the two of us and shrugs.

"Eh," she answers.

I laugh out loud, but Autumn tries to stifle her own amusement for my sake.

"You prefer cooking toy food in a toy kitchen?" Autumn asks.

"Yes! It's so easy."

I mean, that's completely true. You can't mess anything up.

She pulls Autumn by the hand to show her exactly how easy it is, and my friend is the epitome of patience as she listens and plays along. She doesn't get offended when she starts to do exactly what my daughter tells her to do, and then Dahlia changes her mind, expecting Autumn to know that without it being said. She pretends to eat everything Dahlia hands her, with an enthusiasm I'm hardly ever able to fake.

She's going to be the best mom.

Autumn hangs out until it's time for me to take Dahlia to her dad's house. The time is filled with a comfortable, quiet coexistence between the three of us. We go over the last few details of Vic's baby shower, which is coming up way too soon for my liking. Time is flying by so fast.

I enjoy having company. I soak it up while I can, because it's too often just me and my girl sitting at home most of the time. There's nothing wrong with that, but a little change of pace is always good. Seeing my best friend is always good.

When the time comes, and she's eaten five more of my cookies, I walk her down to her car. I'm a little overprotective of Autumn in her current state, so I treat her like Dahlia and make her hold onto me while going down the stairs. She laughs like I'm ridiculous, but doesn't argue.

"What was Vic up to today? I know she was busy, but she didn't say with what."

"I actually don't know, she didn't tell me either."

"Should we be suspicious?" I ask with a playful raise of my brows.

"Oh, definitely," she jokes. "The one time we don't know what she's doing must mean she's replaced us with better friends."

I scoff.

"Impossible."

"Extremely." Her phone lights up in her hand and she smiles when she looks down at it. "Oh, hold on. It's Miles."

She moves to lean back against her car, as she answers the phone. I eavesdrop a little, only because I can't go back inside yet. Not until she's in her car and driving away.

"Do I have your what?... Oh, where'd you put it?... Let me check."

The smile she points in my direction is her attempt at apologizing that she's keeping me waiting out here. I don't mind, it's a nice night. Not as cold as it could be for February.

I watch as she opens her trunk and starts looking for something. As she's occupied with it, I spot an all too familiar car pulling into its usual spot, just a few down from us.

I gasp in excitement at the timing. I want Autumn to see her, because who doesn't want to point out their crush to their best friend? I may have neglected to mention our kiss the other night, since I'm not even sure how I feel about it. I don't think I could come up with the right words.

It's not like I can have a straightforward conversation with the woman to figure it out. I don't get the feeling that she's attracted me or anything. But it had a different energy than any random kiss I've had before. Not that there have been so many, but taking Bailey for instance. That was fun and innocent, and I didn't think about it much afterwards.

This was intense in a way that refuses to let me stop thinking about it. I didn't care what Bailey thought about me, but I'm dying to know what this woman thinks. Even though it can't be anything good, I want details. I need details. It's driving me a bit nuts.

And considering how important it is that I keep my sanity, I can't let that happen again.

I close the distance between Autumn and I with two steps, and pull on her sleeve to get her attention. She mumbles at me to hold on while she opens a plastic bag, and I pull again.

"What?" she asks, moving the phone away from her face.

I point in the general direction of that other car, but my neighbor's back is already to us as she goes up the stairs. She moves so freaking fast. I sigh. Her face is so nice to look at, I wanted Autumn to know that much. Not that the rest of her isn't, because her body is sculpted perfection. I've never seen her like this, with this kind of view.

Why? Why is she the image of my dream girl when she's so mean?

It's not fair.

"Is that your neighbor? The loud one?"

I nod.

"She has great hair," she says. "Sorry, it feels like I'm not supposed to say anything nice, but that's the first thing that came to mind."

"It is great," I admit. I can't fault her for mentioning the obvious, not when I've thought the same thing so many times.

"What's that smell?"

I jump what feels like a few feet into the air at the sudden sound of that voice. She's sitting across from me at the little table, and I didn't even realize she'd shown up at all.

"Where the hell did you come from?"

I saw her go inside earlier, and her car was still here when I got back from dropping off my daughter. Maybe I somehow missed the sound of her leaving again, but I usually don't.

I'm usually listening.

"Nowhere that's your business," she says.

"You really are a ghost," I whisper, more to myself.

"Still with that?"

"Snickerdoodles."

"What?"

"The smell," I answer. "I made snickerdoodles."

"What brand?"

"*Brand*? No, I *made* them. Like, from scratch."

She hums like that evokes some real thinking on her end.

"Is your daughter home?" she asks.

"No?"

"You should get me one."

"What does—nevermind." I shake my head, confused. "Why would I do that?"

"Why not?"

"Because I didn't spend hours baking those just to hand them off to the enemy."

I watch her mouth pull up at the corners.

"'*The enemy.*' That has a nice sound to it."

"I bet it does," I say.

"I could play nice for a night if you gave me a cookie."

Her smirk is absolutely evil, and wicked, and all of the dark things in the world. Why does that entice me so much?

I give her one of my own in return.

"Nope. I'm good."

I swear there's a glint in her eye, she sits up and leans towards me over the table, until I'm forced to tilt my head up to look at her.

"Fine."

I don't understand what she's doing, or why she doesn't say more. It gives me a queasy feeling in my stomach. Like the butterflies, but worse. More aggressive.

"What is your deal?" I ask.

Her brows shoot upwards.

"My deal?"

"Yeah. I can't wrap my head around you. You torture me just to pass the time, and then *the other night* happened. Completely out of the blue. It's obviously odd."

"You think I'm torturing you and yet you kissed me back. That seems just as odd," she points out.

"I don't *think* you are, I know you are. You can't just waterboard someone and tell them they only *think* they're in pain."

"That's an awfully dramatic comparison."

I grimace at her choice of words.

"Ask anyone that knows me, and I guess they'll tell you that's exactly what I am," I whisper.

"And that hasn't made you consider taking it down a notch?"

I stand abruptly. I don't have to take this.

"You have no right to tell me to take anything down a notch, you hypocrite."

"I'd never," she says with false sincerity. "I'm only wondering why you haven't considered it on your own. Or why no one else has taken you down a peg."

"You don't know anything about my pegs," I bite out.

"I could. Are you into that?"

My eyes widen until I feel like they're going to fall out of my head.

"You are unbelievable," I gasp.

"Believe it," she says.

And just as that exact exchange pulls me into a sense of deja-vu and riles me up again–

She fucking kisses me. I hadn't even processed how close our faces were until I'm breathing her in. I can only describe my reaction as possession. Something that I don't fully have control of happens, and it's like we're still arguing. She pushes me, I push her. She grabs the back of my neck, I grab a handful of hair. We're both going hard enough to hurt each other, but it just makes me want to keep going that much more.

It's this crazy, addictive thing that I don't want to end.

Which must mean I am absolutely not myself right now. *I'm possessed.*

Somehow, our feet take us over to her front door, and I'm suddenly pushing her against it. Her shoulder blades hit it with a loud smack, and she retaliates by biting my bottom lip. I moan into her as she licks the place where I still feel the sting of her teeth. There's even the slight, coppery taste of my own blood in my mouth, and it doesn't concern me as much as it should.

I'd even be okay if she did it again.

Things move fast, and the world rushes by as I'm being pulled inside of her apartment. There are exclamation points dancing around in my head, things I'd *normally* think at a time like this.

I've never been inside, I should look around.

What will this place tell me about the woman I'm making out with?

More importantly, more prominently: *I should not feel safe being here. She's a stranger. I could end up on one of those true crime podcasts I like listening to so much.*

But all of it gets brushed aside when she grabs my breast, and squeezes like she's trying to memorize the feel of it. It's the one thing she's done that isn't bruising, and it takes my breath away.

I'd offer to take some of my clothes off, to give her better access, but I'm obviously not the leader here. I'm just enjoying the ride, tasting her tongue like it's candy. She *does* taste like candy–like a creamsicle more specifically.

How am I supposed to stop?

She gives me that answer pretty instantly when she pulls back to look into my eyes. I feel a deep satisfaction that I'm the reason for her current appearance. Flushed cheeks, and a quickly rising chest.

"That's enough," she says breathlessly.

I take a step back and put even more space between us. Not knowing my surroundings, it *of course* leads to me knocking into the corner of a side table. A chunky candle goes falling to the ground, and I brace for the sound of the glass shattering. It never comes, thanks to the dark, plush rug she has on the floor. I pick it up and put it back in its place.

"Sorry. Yeah. Okay." My words are punctuated by my own attempt to catch my breath.

I watch as she fixes her hair, flatting the top with her palms, and running her fingers through the length of it. It's hard to gauge her reasoning like this, all I want to do is stare at those swollen lips until they're on mine again.

"I'm sorry if I–" If I what? I don't know, I can't think.

I loved every second of it, but something a lot like guilt is settling in the pit of my stomach.

"Nope, it's okay." She turns away from me suddenly. "Let yourself out."

I don't get to respond before she's down the hall and walking through a door. Despite not knowing where the door leads, I'm momentarily tempted to follow after her. I can't explain why, it's not like she's someone I care about. I don't even know her.

I don't even know her *name*.

And I have no idea what just happened. At least the part after the incredible make out. The before and during will be on replay in my mind for a while.

Holy *crap*, that was hot.

I look around, hating the barrage of thoughts in my head. It's like the spirit has left my body, and I'm back in control, getting used to thinking my own thoughts.

Why would she kiss me *again*? Why would she want to stop so suddenly? I can only worry she wasn't as into it as I was. The thought crosses my mind that maybe I'm not a very good kisser, not that I've ever had any complaints.

I don't know, something tells me she was very into it. That feeling between us, that physical chemistry *had* to be felt in both parties.

Although, I have been delusionally sure of things like that in the past. I make it way too easy for people to hurt me when I sit here and convince myself I know what's going on.

What if she's in a relationship? The thought pops up so suddenly that it startles me.

It would explain why she's gone some nights.

Shit. As if life wasn't uncomfortable enough when she first moved in, this could get way worse. I knew it wasn't generally a good idea to get involved with your neighbor, considering you can't escape them.

And my neighbor in particular knows just how to make my life miserable.

My poor parents are going to be so sick of me when I move in. Their kitchen theme is all rustic, beige and brown, and everything of mine is the brightest yellow. It'll clash so bad, but I won't submit my cute kitchen towels to months of being stuffed in a storage tub in their garage. They deserve better.

Easily enough, my old bed is still there.

I do as she asked, only guessing which door is the front one because *that's* how disoriented I am. I don't know how far we moved or what direction we turned, but I make my best guess. I doubt I'll get a warm response if she comes back in here to find I'm lingering like a bad smell. Not that anything she does is ever warm.

Except for when she's sucking on my neck. Her lips are very warm.

She starts playing her music only hours later. I never really let myself believe she'd stop for good, and I was right. Whether it's fair of me to feel or not, it seems extra hurtful that she did it tonight of all nights. I can be so certain now, even more than I was, that whatever interest she does have in me is not a good thing.

I don't even have the energy to fight it by trying to sleep. I put on a pair of headphones and watch some videos on my phone while I wait for it to stop.

It takes hours as usual, until the sun comes up, and then it's quiet. My eyelids are heavy, and my back hurts from the position I've been sitting in. I stretch as best I can, and I slide back down until my head hits my pillow. My alarm gets set for nine, when I have to be awake and getting ready for work. It's sure better than nothing.

I got a whopping two hours of sleep. You feel good about that?

Her response is there as soon as I get home.

What did I say about my front door?

Get over yourself, I reply

Again she's quick to respond, because the next is waiting when I go outside to sit on the porch for a bit.

I said I'd be nice if you gave me a cookie. You chose your own fate.

Wow.

15

If someone were to ask, I wouldn't know how to tell them I ended up in my neighbor's house again. This time, in particular, her bedroom. She must have me under some kind of spell, because it doesn't occur to me that I don't want anything to do with her when I'm *actually* looking at her. There are brief moments of that reminder when I blink, but it doesn't last long enough for me to stay away.

I was determined to not let this happen again after the last week's events. She was absolutely merciless, and didn't give me one single night of reprieve. I'm grateful for my dad's home cooked meals, and their quiet neighborhood, but I'm getting so sick of not being able to come home.

I was angry. I wanted to punish her, but I couldn't come up with anything good that wouldn't either involve another person or get me into trouble. *Rejecting her* was going to be the thing.

I just didn't want to when the time came.

She seems more sure of herself today, more confident in the places she touches me. She slips my shirt off with expert smoothness, and takes her time feeling my exposed skin. It's different from any other time I've had a hookup, in the way that she's silent.

She's not complimenting how soft my skin is, or pointing out how beautiful I am.

I'm not full of myself, but there's usually *something*.

She goes in for the clasp on my bra at the same time my fingers fumble with the button on her jeans, but it's too difficult of a task with her mouth on my neck.

"Take these off," I rasp.

"I'm busy. If you want them off so badly, you can take them off."

"I'm fucking trying."

Her kisses turn into more, as she leaves little bites along my collarbone.

I'm worried about her leaving a mark, but I can't deny that it would be kind of hot if she did.

Years of lifting boxes and unloading merchandise at my job comes in handy, as I reach behind the back of her legs and lift her. She has no choice but to wrap them around me, unless she'd rather fall backwards. I take advantage of it, carrying her to the edge of the bed and leaning until she does fall.

I really like my position above her. I've always assumed I was a bottom, because I'm always on my feet during the day. It just made more sense to take it easy when it came to my nighttime activities. It might have been part of my ex, Olivia's problem with me. She always called me her 'pillow princess,' as if it were an affectionate nickname, but her tone seemed a little snarky sometimes.

The woman beneath me lifts her hips and raises her brows, and I don't need the reminder that I should get out of my head and back to the point.

It's much easier to do when her mouth is down there, and mine is up here. She pulls her shirt off, smacking me in the head in the process. No apology, obviously.

I ignore it and successfully unbutton her pants, yanking them off with very little patience. She is so fucking flawless, it takes my breath away. The room is dark, and her body is only visible by the moonlight coming in from the window. It must be a full one, because I see every line of her seriously chiseled abs. She's wearing black lace panties, and that just feels so *her*. I don't even need to know her any better to get a feel for how appropriate they are for her as a person.

"Stop gawking," she sneers.

"What would you rather I do instead?"

Her response is an eye roll, before she lifts herself up onto her elbows and gives me a look that tells me we both know exactly what I should do next.

I'm stubborn. I don't do it.

Instead I lift her bra off in a way that's probably not comfortable. I imagine it's digging into her skin a bit, but it seems like neither of us are worried when I drag my tongue over her nipple.

She lets out a delicious little gasp, and I do it again with more pressure.

"You're going to have to move that tongue elsewhere," she whimpers.

I nip at the smooth skin on the side of her breast and she whimpers again. It's the hottest sound I've ever heard.

"You think I'm feeling that generous? Towards you?"

"I thought you'd be easy to convince," she admits.

I look up at her and continue my slow torture, admiring her parted lips.

"I'm not. Actually–" I bite again– "I have a lot of reasons to get up and walk away right now."

Voicing the words causes an entire new flood of frustration. I'm mad at myself for ending up here again, but I don't have the will to go. I so badly want to take this further, I want to touch her until she forgets her own name, so my mind continues to fight itself.

She rolls her eyes at me again.

"I'm not going to beg," she snaps.

Her tone of voice gives one of the arguing sides enough ammunition to force me to lean back. I think I see the smallest hint of a pout on her face, but she gets it under control quickly and I wonder if I imagined it.

She might not beg, but something tells me she'd want to if she wasn't so stubborn.

"That's a shame. I'd love to see it."

"Kink of yours?"

"It could be." I'm open minded.

"Don't waste your time with me then," she says as she sits up.

"Okay."

I shrug as if there's no part of me pleading to continue. As if I don't care what happens here at *all*.

"Okay," she echoes.

I turn to locate my clothes, but then a thought occurs to me.

"Are you in a relationship?" I blurt out.

She laughs, and I get why it's amusing. Most people would've asked this question before things got this far.

Another thing to beat myself up over. The list is getting long.

"What if I was? How bad would you feel?"

I pretend to think about my answer deeply, putting a hand to my chin.

"It would further prove what a selfish person you are," I state. "For your partner's sake, I'd hope that *you'd* feel bad, but I'd forgive myself. I'm just the clueless other woman here."

"If you weren't clueless," she continues. "If I said that I did have a girlfriend, but then I still did this…"

She traces a finger down my jawline, before leaning into me again and pressing her lips to mine.

"You'd stop me?" she asks.

And then she kisses me again.

"Yes," I breathe.

But I let her do it again, and again. Until we're back to making out, and I'm hovering over her, and I can hardly breathe because we're inhaling each other more than we're getting air.

"You're not stopping me," she points out, breathlessly.

I take the moment to make my way down, kissing and caressing until my face is down by her hips.

"You don't have a girlfriend."

"You don't know that."

I question myself for a split second.

"You're too mean to have a girlfriend."

"What if she's mean, too? You have no idea."

"What's her name?" I ask.

"None of your business."

"Why do you want me down here so bad if you have someone else to take care of your needs?"

She hesitates once I'm so close to her entrance that my cool breath hits it. Her entire body tenses like someone who *in fact*, has not had someone's face this close to their privates in a long time.

This would be a terrible time to be wrong about my assumptions.

I blow air over her again, and watch her sharp inhale.

"Can you get to the point and stop–"

One swipe of my tongue against her clit has her choking on her words.

"Tell me you don't have a girlfriend."

"What does it even matter?" It's the closest to whining I've ever heard her. "It's not like I'd ever give you that position."

"Good, because I don't want it. What I do want is to be perfectly sure that there isn't anyone out there who'd cry their eyes out over what's happening here," I tell her.

Her hands curl into fists.

"Ugh! No, there isn't anyone! Can you just–"

I don't give her the chance to say anymore, as I resume. I don't know what comes over me, but I feel like a rabid animal. She moans when I suck her clit into my mouth, and I want her to keep doing it. I want to hear all of the possible sounds I could pull from her, so I suck harder, I lick faster. The world begins and ends with nothing but the taste of her.

Until a wave of pure stubbornness crashes over me when her hand falls on the back of my head and she begins applying pressure. I resist, pulling my face back to press against her hand.

"Are you serious?"

"Are *you* serious?" I snap back.

I have no issue with being bossed around in the bedroom. I don't mind being a little submissive, but I do mind with *her*. The dynamic is all wrong. I'm *supposed* to be punishing her, and although I clearly failed at that, it's happening on my terms. My way.

"You're already d–"

She stops with a gasp when I slide a finger inside her. Not caring if she wanted to finish that sentence, I lower my face again. Her body writhes and jolts underneath me, filling me with a deep satisfaction. There's nothing quite like having this control over someone's body.

Her breathing becomes quicker, and her hands grab at the white sheets beneath her. I pick up my pace, pressing into her faster and curling my finger in a way that I'm personally familiar with.

Part of the beauty of being with a woman is that what makes them tick is *all* more familiar.

With one final swipe of my tongue, she lets out a deep, rasping moan and every muscle in her body clenches. My finger keeps dragging the climax from her, until she's actively pulling away when it becomes too much.

She puts a hand to her chest, moving up and down with her heaving breaths.

"Damn," she whispers.

I take it as a win.

I finally get up from my position, a cocky grin on my face. I give her a few seconds to recover.

"Do you have a towel?" I ask.

She tilts her head.

"You live right next door," she says. "Go get your own towel."

Fuck me, I guess.

I use the back of my wrist to wipe my mouth. I'm going to need a shower anyway.

"You can let yourself out. Just turn the bottom lock before you close the door behind you."

Um.

I shouldn't be surprised she's shooing me away, but it's extra insulting that my face is literally still wet. That might be a record for how fast I've ever been kicked out after sex.

"Like, right this second?" She nods. "Wow. Okay. I guess I'll get out of your hair."

"Thanks."

As if my words aren't dripping with sarcasm.

I almost scoff, but stop myself. It might be a level of rude I'd never personally reach, but I have no good reason to argue to stay and hang out. I don't expect us to have any bonding time anytime soon.

It just would have been nice to have more than fifteen seconds to calm down. Would've been even nicer to have some more fun with *me* on the receiving end.

She wants to act cold and uninterested, I'm going to be even *more* cold and uninterested. I won't even wave if we pass each other on the stairs. I have to stand my ground next time. I *have* to find a way.

But first, I'm going to relive the experience I just had with my shower head in hand.

16

Dahlia skips out the front door ahead of me, and I follow after her with a smile. Her energy has been so high this morning, I feel like I've had three cups of coffee just looking at her.

We're headed to her dad's house a little earlier today, because I have Vic's baby shower to get to. I'm already running late, unsurprisingly.

I close the door, hoping she doesn't remember anything else she wants to take once we're already heading down the stairs.

"Wait, mama–" *Oh good, right before I get the door locked.*

"What did you forget?" It'll be faster if I run in and grab it, instead of letting her loose in her room again.

I start to pull it open but she tells me not to, and points.

"More junk mail."

One single word stands out on the sticky note as soon as my eyes land on it, and I snatch it off as fast as I can. I do not need her to ask me what that word means anytime soon. She seems oblivious as she walks over to the stairs and I blow out a heavy breath. That could've been an entire crisis.

I put the note in my pocket for later, and go meet my daughter where she stands with an arm raised to grab my hand.

"Absolutely not!" Vic laughs. "We are now officially done making babies."

"But you could have two of each! How cute would that be!" Amanda exclaims.

Oh, Amanda. You pushy little thing.

"If that was the goal, I'd end up with twenty of them while trying to even the number out. I have nine aunts. *Nine*," she says.

I remember just how excited Vic was to find out that Eli was a boy. The men in her family are heavily outnumbered, and she believed she was destined to contribute to those odds. Adding at least one more boy into the mix was a welcome surprise.

The baby in Amanda's arms starts to wiggle, and she smiles down at him. Little *Caleb*.

"He's probably hungry. I'll be right back," she tells us in a high pitched voice.

I'm relieved when she walks away, not because I don't *like* her, but because her pushiness knows no bounds. It's something I think most people would need a break from.

"She tried to force one of those cookies down my throat," I whisper to Vic.

She gives me apologetic eyes.

"They're good cookies?"

"I'll never find out now. I'm too traumatized to give them a chance."

Autumn walks over to us with a little plate of snacks. I see a couple of the aforementioned cookies on it and wince.

She walks quickly, keeping her eyes down, and I feel so bad that she looks so uncomfortable. Her rigid posture only relaxes when she's standing right next to the two of us and sees that we're alone.

"You okay?" Vic asks.

"I'm fine," she answers with a smile.

It's not a genuine one. We know better.

"Some people have already started to leave. I understand if you're ready to go."

Autumn shakes her head adamantly.

"No, I'm really fine. I just... maybe shouldn't walk away from you two again," she says.

I link my arm with hers, careful not to knock the food from her hands.

"Perfect. I wouldn't deal with anyone but you two either if I had it my way."

Vic playfully smacks my arm.

"You be nice."

"I'm so nice! I just can't handle that woman."

We all chuckle, but Vic scolds me some more. I'm not some mean girl that likes to stand around talking about others, it's just that I don't need a filter around my best friends.

Autumn looks my way with a small laugh, and then she gasps.

"Reya! You're one to talk about hickeys!" she whisper shouts.

I feel the blood drain from my face.

"No way," I reply. "I don't."

"You do!" She pulls my top down the smallest bit to expose what I'm assuming is a little purple bruise.

Shit. I got dressed before doing my hair and makeup, so I never saw it. I didn't even think to look.

After our little hookup last week, my neighbor decided to interrupt my night last night. I stood my ground for approximately three minutes, and then we were kissing on my porch. Again. I don't understand it in the slightest.

It started small, but she tried taking it further. I told her my daughter was asleep inside, and gestured towards my open front door. She got the message and stopped, but that *mouth* of hers didn't stop.

Hence this supposed hickey.

I was disappointed in myself, to say the least. Still am. Giving into her is becoming a trend that I might have to accept. I'll just think of some other way to get back at her, or convince her to knock her shit off.

To be fair, there wasn't any music blasting *this* week. I blame last night's weakness on that. I was in a good mood, I'd slept soundly for a week straight, and didn't have to drag Dahlia out of her own home.

I groan, and bury my face in my hands.

"We need to talk about this when we're not surrounded by potential eavesdroppers."

Which doesn't take long at all. We've already played all of the games, and Vic opened her presents. As soon as she put a hand to her stomach and started complaining about how exhausting the day had been, the place emptied out fast.

It is both hilarious and cruel that she put on the act just to get information out of me sooner.

"Bailey?" she asks, pouring herself a glass of orange juice.

I wrinkle my nose.

"No, not the bartender." I find myself relieved I haven't heard from her after handing out my number that night. "But it's worse."

"Worse? Do we know her?" Autumn asks enthusiastically.

"Not really... no. You know *of* her."

Vic waves her hand in front of me like she's waving away my nonsense.

"Don't make this a puzzle, what's her name?"

"I–" I bite my lip, preparing for their response. "I actually don't know her name."

Their jaws drop and they look at eachother, then back at me.

"Scandalous, Reya," Vic muses.

It is scandalous, it's *ridiculous*. I don't know anything about her. She could murder me and disappear, and no one in my life would have anything to go off of. Nothing other than her taste in music and the color of her hair.

Commence even more beating myself up. I'm an idiot.

"Okay, look. I know how dumb I am. I don't have any excuses, because I haven't been thinking clearly in weeks. It's just–"

"You're horny and made a mistake," Autumn says. "That's the start of a million romance novels, trust that *I* understand. And that I'm excited."

"You're *excited* that I made a huge mistake? Gee, thanks."

"No!" She assures. "I'm excited that you haven't given up on yourself entirely since everything happened with Olivia. It kind of felt like you forgot how to have that kind of fun."

"Exactly," Vic agrees. "When there wasn't a follow up after that night at the bar, I was beginning to really worry."

She moves to put the container of juice away, but I grab it from her and search for my own glass.

"It is possible to have a fulfilling life without getting laid, you know."

Autumn clears her throat.

"I believe that, but also... I'm not going to lie to you, babe. I was doing alright before Miles, but... having your itches scratched is pretty nice."

"Yeah, well," I begin with a sigh. "My neighbor isn't scratching my itches. It was the other way around."

Autumn squeals.

"What the fuck! The *neighbor*?"

"The neighbor!" Vic echoes.

I remember the note that's still in my back pocket, and blurt out my explanation as I pull it out.

"She randomly kissed me the other night, and then she did it again, and then we might have taken it even further one time," I say so fast that it all comes out in one rush of breath. "It keeps happening somehow. Like just last night, I don't even understand how."

They're at a loss for words. I hand over the note.

"We've been leaving notes since the first night she was playing her music, just aggressive little comments. Until this one."

Autumn's face turns red as soon as her eyes scan the words. Vic's smile is amused.

"Woah."

"Damn, girl."

"That's dirtier than my books."

We laugh, but I don't think she fully realizes how dirty she's making her books.

They drag every detail of information from me, until I'm tired of talking.

Me. *Tired of talking.* Doesn't usually happen.

The final result is that my friends don't like her, and I get it. I don't even like her, but there's something really helpful about hearing it from someone else. Maybe it's the push I need to tell her to fuck off. I tell them I want to, I really do, and they give me ideas. Thankfully none of them involve moving out of my apartment, because the more I entertain the idea, the more I hate it.

———eee———

I hear her coming and panic. Fight or flight kicks in and I choose flight. I stumble out of my seat, almost tripping on the slippers I had slipped off right in front of my chair. I leave my phone sitting there, despite what a terrible idea that is. It's unlocked and playing yet another true crime video. My feet don't want to listen to commands at the moment, so I decide to abandon the slippers after I manage to kick them a little further away from me.

My door isn't waiting open for me this time, and in the seconds it takes me to twist the handle, I know I'm too late. I know she's behind me.

I pause, feeling paralyzed by indecision. Acknowledge her or pretend I was already headed in? *Super* casually?

My pause is too long, and I know I lost the chance to decide without looking like a complete weirdo. I'm sure she already thinks that, but at least I'm a weirdo that gives good head.

I turn around slowly, and plant my back up against my door. She's looking at me with a wry smile.

"Missed your chance to run away from me?"

My mouth doesn't want to open to respond, so I just stare back at her.

"It's probably better that you do," she continues. "I'm a selfish bitch, after all."

"Is that your own opinion of yourself, or going off of what I've said?" I ask.

"Both."

"So you don't care that you're selfish? You're owning that?"

She shrugs.

"It is what it is."

I roll my eyes and turn back for my door before any unwanted feelings decide to pop up. They're likely to if she keeps looking at me like that, and if I keep thinking about her stupid note.

Which I *can't* stop doing. I've been thinking about it all day.

My phone chooses that moment to vibrate, and I'm not the only one that hears the loud sound against the solid table. It rattles the entire thing.

Great timing, whoever you are.

I go for it without looking over at her. Unfortunately I don't need to be looking to know that she hasn't moved, and she's still standing there watching me. I shouldn't be surprised, not given the circumstances, but I am. Surely she has better things to be doing right now.

"Poison, huh? Researching ways to get rid of me?"

I hit the pause button on the video she's referencing and press my lips into a thin line.

"I think you're more likely to be a killer between the two of us."

"I don't think so," she says thoughtfully. "It's usually the charming ones, isn't it?"

"Are you admitting to thinking I'm charming?" I ask with a roll of my eyes.

Warmth floods me, and I don't know if it's in fear or subconscious excitement that she walks over and sits down in that chair across from me. That *damned chair*, I need to get rid of that thing.

"I'm just admitting I'm not."

My legs have a mind of their own, and they make me sit. I clench my jaw, begging some part of me to have some self respect.

Hello, Reya's body. Are we listening?

Not an inch of movement, not an ounce of intention to do so.

"What do you want?" I spit with as much venom as I can muster. At least my voice still works the way I want it to.

"You know," is all she says.

"No thanks," I reply.

Good, I tell myself. *Keep that up.*

She sticks her bottom lip out in a mocking little pout.

"That's no fun."

"Seeing you never is."

"I bet you want to believe that," she says.

"I do believe that! You think I enjoy your bad attitude, and being manipulated into some weird enemies-with-benefits situation?" I shout, and hope our neighbors still have that same deafness that comes in so handy with this woman's late night concerts.

Her face falls, losing every bit of teasing. Now she's angry, and I like that. Angry is something I can handle. It's so much less complicated.

"You can't accuse me of manipulating you just because you're not happy with your own decisions. Own it," she growls. "You didn't do anything you didn't want to."

I groan, hating that her words are a partial truth. I want to blame her, but it's not her fault I'm at war with myself. Not in that way, at least. If she had never come around, there never would've been anything to argue with myself about in the first place.

"I'm not in your head, so I don't know what your game is here, but there *is* a game. You like pissing me off, and still being able to have some weird power over me."

She goes back to smirking, and I mentally berate myself for admitting to that fact.

"Yeah, maybe I do," she admits. "But I think you like your end of it too, it's just harder for you to come to terms with."

Crap, crap, crap.

I stand abruptly.

"I have to go."

She laughs softly, and it's the opposite of a warm sound.

So why do I want to hear it again?

"Do you?" she asks. "I can't help but notice the door is closed tonight."

Observant little shit.

"I know better than to confirm to a potential murderer if I'm home alone or not."

My phone vibrates again, that same rattle ringing between us. The screen is facing up, still unlocked, and my eyes fall on the notification.

Unknown number: *Thinking about that mouth of yours*

That's quite the prank text, because there's not a single person that knows anything about my mouth that wouldn't be—

I sit back down and tap on it. There's a previous one.

Unknown number: *Hey stranger. This is Bailey, remember me?*

Well, she sure waited a damn long time to reach out. Not that I was waiting for a single second, and I doubt I'm going to bother responding now.

I lock my phone, and look back up at the woman I can't seem to ignore that easily. There's something new in her expression, but I can't tell just how good or bad it is. She's skilled at keeping certain things off of her face, I could've guessed that from the first second I saw her. There has to be more going on under the surface, and now I'm possibly seeing the smallest glimpse of it in her eyes.

I'm not any more of an eye reader than I am a mind reader.

"Look," she starts as she leans back in her seat. Then she puts a finger up, and starts counting her following points. "We find each other attractive. We have easy access to each other. We could both probably use a good distraction, am I right?"

I snort.

"You find me attractive?"

Her brows pinch like the question is so unexpected.

"Yes. Have you seen yourself?"

Oh.

There are those butterflies again.

I shake my head, knocking out any ridiculous thoughts.

"Those are all beside the point. You're... *mean.* Why would I reward you for the way you've treated me thus far, by–what? Agreeing to a situationship?"

Her hands clasp in front of her, a symbol of just how strictly business this conversation is.

"Let's not even call it that. It would just be sex. We don't even have to talk to each other."

"I don't see how that benefits me."

She glances down to my phone screen with a knowing–or maybe she only *thinks* she knows something–look.

"You must see something, or you wouldn't still be sitting here," she points out.

I sigh.

"*Maybe* you have a point on the convenience of it all," I admit. "But how do I know you're going to make it worth my while?"

"I could make my case right now." My breath catches when she stands and heads for her front door. "So are you going to let me?"

I hardly even hesitate.

Of course I am.

17

Time flies and not much changes. The weather is dreary, my job is slow, and my daughter is perfect as always. I avoid Caleb, and I try to spare my parents of my presence as much as possible. I couldn't do it entirely because of *her*. Still.

Despite taking her up on her offer, and spending a lot of my free evenings at her place, she continues with her wicked ways. I've actually noticed somewhat of a pattern, that unfortunately does not align with the days my daughter is home. It's always the worst after she comes back after being gone for a night. It drives me crazy wondering where she goes that causes her to feel so angsty when she gets back.

I can't exactly ask. We don't really talk much when we're together, although I've tried. I've attempted to get to know her better, but she's given me a whole lot of nothing, so here we are.

I let myself enjoy having the release without overthinking it. She happens to be *very* good at reciprocating, not that she'll ever hear those words from my mouth, she doesn't deserve the ego boost. I'm fine keeping that opinion to myself.

Completely to myself. The girls don't know any of what's transpired since the baby shower, and I want to keep it that way for the time being. If they outright ask, that's one thing, but I think we've all been too busy for chit chat lately. Vic sends me funny videos or recipes she wants me to try, like these cranberry lemon cinnamon rolls she sent the other day. I've been drooling since.

Autumn has sent me one single photo of Elaine and Freddy curled up in a dog bed together.

That's about how things usually are between us. Not in a negative way, it's just the reality of being grown adults with our own families. We've been lucky these days, finding excuses often, but I knew a drought was coming. It just makes us that much more excited for the next time we have plans together, which I imagine will be the day Angeline arrives. Her due date is coming up, and I wait for the phone call every day.

"What are you drinking?"

"The blood of my enemies," I reply as I pass by my neighbor on my way out.

Surely she can tell I'm in a hurry, considering my hands that are overflowing with all the things I'll need for my long work shift today. I'm bringing a packed lunch, along with an extra sweater and a box of tampons.

The last one might look questionable, but it's easier if I just leave the whole thing in the bathroom at work. I'm not embarrassed for anyone to see me carrying it around either, it's just part of life.

They're all things I don't usually bring with me, so I'm feeling pretty weighed down. That, and I'm having an unusually heavy flow and some awfully sharp cramps this morning.

I look down at the cup, wishing I had added enough strawberry syrup to give it more of a red color.

"That's hot," she says.

"You would think so, wouldn't you?"

She shrugs.

"What are you doing later?"

"Aw, do you want to hang out?"

Her expression fills with blatant disgust.

"Forget I asked."

"Okay," I reply cheerily.

I'm cranky and needed an out to walk away anyway.

I'm not cranky enough that I miss the chance to check her out as I go. She's in a similar outfit to what I usually see her wearing this early in the day. A matching, slate gray workout set with skintight leggings and a cropped long sleeve top. She must be getting back from the gym, but I've never asked. I'm not sure she'd be willing to answer that anymore than anything else I've asked her.

The curves that it accentuates distract me long enough that I don't get a chance to stop her when she snatches my cup out of my hands and takes a sip through my neon pink straw.

No one comes in between me and my caffeine before work.

I'm practically snarling, but my full hands keep me from snatching it back. She goes in for another sip.

"Did you make this?" she asks. I nod. "What is it? It's delicious."

I'm not too angry to notice that she doesn't usually like to talk to me this much.

"Strawberry black tea."

She goes in for a third sip, and I grind my teeth.

"I've been ordering the wrong drinks my entire life."

"Well then go do that," I snap. "This one is mine."

She laughs at me, but hands it back.

"That's not very sunshine of you," she says, blatantly eyeing the box of tampons in my hand.

If I had the free finger, I'd flip her off. —

"Mom!"

"Oh!" She jumps up, dropping the hand lotion she'd taken from my bag. The thing is sitting open in front of her, and there are other items of mine scattered on the counter around it. "Goodness, you scared me!"

"Why are you digging through my stuff again? We talked about this," I groan.

She holds up the lotion again, and waves it in front of me.

"The scents in this stuff are not good for your skin," she chides. "And you don't have any sort of protection in here, where's that pepper spray we got for you?"

I adore my mother. I know that everything she does is with love and concern. I'm so lucky that both of my parents have always taken such good care of me, even as an adult. They both give so much, and they both accept me for every little piece of who I am. I could have it so, *so* much worse.

But my mom and I have always struggled with boundaries. She's the nosiest person I know.

I remember a *lot* of arguments from when I was a teenager. Getting my first phone was not easy, when I couldn't set it down anywhere without her picking it up to look through it. I'm well aware she wanted to check that I was being safe, but it was so hard on me at the time.

It's still hard sometimes even now, but we've made some slow progress. As far as I know, she hasn't snooped on me in a while. I'm sure the urge was building up for some time, and this was bound to happen again sooner or later.

"This is one of those things we talked about. I'm not okay with you digging through my things."

"I'm only making sure–"

"I know, I know," I interrupt. "Just ask me next time."

It's wishful thinking.

"Fine, fine. But you need to carry that spray with you!"

"I'll grab it when I get home, okay?"

I'm fibbing. I let Autumn borrow it a couple years ago, and I think she lost it in her move.

I throw everything back into my bag, and pull it onto my shoulder.

It was so much for my neighbor's good mood yesterday, because we had another unpleasant night with lots of crying. Dahlia officially doesn't like *the lady with the music*, and my heart hurts as I wish I could permanently protect her from that *lady*. I tell my mom we'll probably be back later, and I take my daughter to school.

My plans for the day consist of going to work, and trying not to snap at anyone.

It's going to be quite the challenge when I get an unsurprising, but infuriating text message on my way there.

Destiny: *Not going to make it in today.*

I don't even bother to respond. I can't keep covering for this girl.

18

*L*et me know the next time you're feeling feisty. I can work with it much better when I have the chance to get you into bed with me.

It's embarrassing how much the note turns me on.

I pound on her door, and she answers within a couple seconds with a winning smile on her face. I've never seen her look so pleased to see me, I almost wonder if that suspected twin is here standing in her place.

"I–You–" I exhale, trying to let go of this frazzled state she already has me in. She doesn't even need to try. "I need you to be careful with the notes you leave on my door. My daughter can read."

Albeit, slowly, but there's likely to be a day where I don't beat her to it in time.

"Okay," she says.

I freeze.

"Okay? That's it? You don't want to argue?"

"Oh, I always want to argue. Give me something worth arguing over," she insists.

"Perfect, I'm in the mood today!" I say, raising my voice. "Cut the shit with the music. I have been way too nice about it, but I'm done."

She pretends to look behind me, like someone should be there.

"What do you think *you* can do about it?"

"I have a running list of ideas," I tell her.

"And you've waited this long to act because..."

It's a great question, one I've been asking myself this entire time and still can't really answer. My mouth opens to give her some explanation before I've even realized what's going to come out of it.

"Because you're some sort of siren or something, that opens your mouth and makes me forget how much I really don't like you," I spit out.

Again, admitting more than I should to her about how much power she has over me.

Saying it outright makes me all worked up. I think the only other person I've been this rude to would be Caleb, but my anger towards this woman right now is overriding every feeling I've ever had towards him.

It's impressive.

"There you go again," she sighs with impatience.

"What?"

"Pretending I'm luring you in against your will or something. You could always say no to me."

I could. The pros outweigh the cons of cutting this off.

"Fine. I'm saying no," I decide. "No more."

"What a shame," she says.

And then she slams her front door in my face before I can think twice about any part of this conversation.

I hate her. I really truly do, and I wish on every star in the sky that she had never moved in here and messed up my life.

The next time I see her at the top of those stairs, I put a hand up. "Not a word."

She snickers, but listens to me and moves along.

I brace myself to go inside and grab my sleeping daughter so we can head to my parent's house.

When Dahlia is at her dad's, I take to keeping track of every minute of sleep I get. I mark the last known time before passing out, and whatever it is when I wake up. Then I do some quick math, and jot them down on sticky notes. I bought them just for this reason.

1 hour, 27 minutes.
2 hours, 52 minutes.
2 hours, 43 minutes.

3 hours, 57 minutes. That was nice of you.

Dahlia and I are playing with dolls, pretending to bake a cake— go figure— when someone starts pounding at my door. No one ever really knocks on our door, so we're startled at first.

I slowly and quietly get up, in case we need to pretend we're not home. I put a finger over my lips for extra measure, and she motions zipping hers.

I walk out of her bedroom, and through the living room to the door. It's a great thing peepholes exist, because I utilize mine. The small circular window shows me a hot redhead with her arms crossed. She looks mad.

I press my forehead to the door, deciding on my next move. She knocks again, and it rattles through my skull. Not my smartest move, considering the immediate headache.

Against my better judgment, I open the door.

And I'm attacked by pieces of paper flying at my face. When I look down at their remains on the floor, I realize they're my notes.

I smile wide.

"Problem?" I ask in my sweetest voice.

"What the hell are all these?"

I immediately shush her, and watch as it lights a fire in her. Her eyes seem ablaze with it, but as soon as she opens her mouth to fight with me, I physically shut it. I pinch her lips together.

I don't know what fuels me to do such a thing, but I pull away quickly and try to contain a laugh. That was the funniest image I've seen in a long time.

"Quiet," I scold. "My daughter is here."

"What are these?" she asks through gritted teeth. She's still pissed, but at least she respected that one wish of mine by whispering.

"Those are how many hours I've been sleeping at night," I explain, smile still in place.

"I don't care about your sleep schedule. Stop leaving things on my door."

"See… the last time you said that, you *yourself* continued to leave some things on my door so…" I pretend to think about it. "No, I'm good."

"I bet Jim would love to hear all about how you're harassing the poor girl who just moved in," she threatens.

"First of all, his name is *Tim*, have some respect. He's the only good landlord that's ever existed on this earth," I explain. "And I happen to have hours worth of video proof that you're the one harassing me every night. Want to take a bet on which one of us he'll believe? I've lived here a *long* time."

And he already knows the situation I'm in, I've just failed to follow up the way I should have. I imagine he's still waiting for the day I do hand over my evidence.

Hopefully by now he's heard some semblance of a complaint from the building's other occupants. If they were ignoring it before, surely they can't have ignored it this entire time now.

If looks could kill, I'd be done for.

"If you—"

"Want to make a truce?" she asks, breaking the moment of silence.

"A truce?" I ask in disbelief.

"Yeah. A compromise, a deal, a solution. Ever heard of any of those?"

I look her up and down as if that will help me discover what game she's playing.

Surprise, surprise: it does not.

"What did you have in mind?" I'm not giving in that easy, this has the word *suspicious* written all over it. "But watch what you say. There are some words I'm not ready to define to her."

She nods in agreement.

"You know I don't play my music only for the sake of torturing you, right? It just so happened to become a fun little bonus."

"That makes me feel better," I say with all the sarcasm I can muster.

"It's about distraction. Something to get me out of my head," she explains. "Which... you can do."

Who's admitting someone has power over them now? Wow.

"Except when I was distracting you, nothing changed." I point out.

"Keep up, I just said it was fun to torture you." She rolls her eyes. "If you'd like to continue things, I'll play nice."

I can't help it, I smirk. Then I look around to where my daughter is sitting, making sure she isn't going to sneak up on me again.

"You want to keep hooking up that bad?" I whisper.

"Don't make me take it back."

"No more music at all?" I ask. "You'll completely stop?"

She thinks about this, toying with a strand of her hair as she does.

"No, but I'll limit it, for sure. And I could start giving you a heads up."

Not that it wouldn't be helpful, but…

"You're not making it very worth my while."

"Liar," she chides.

"You just said—"

"You can't exactly distract me every night, can you?"

I sigh, getting her point.

I tell her my custody schedule, not seeing a way around it. She tells me she's often gone on Thursdays or Fridays, but it varies. I don't get an explanation, because that would be too easy.

If I'm correct in the pattern I've noticed, then we'll end up staying with my parents on Fridays or Saturdays. That could be so much worse. Having a set schedule could really be helpful here, it would take so much stress off of our plates.

And it's not like it's a hardship to be one of her distractions. It's downright fun when I'm not overthinking everything I know and *don't* know about her.

"Deal," I say. I even put my hand out to shake on it, and she takes it.

"See you Sunday," she purrs.

19

Vic's daughter is born when I'm at work. I rush around, trying to get someone to cover for me, but it's never that simple.

By the time I make it to the hospital, Vic and Angeline are asleep. They've had all of their visitors come and go. Julian is halfway unconscious himself, but awake enough to let me know I should visit another time. Probably when they're home and settled in.

I hesitate to go, wanting Vic to know I showed up. She understands my work situation, and I know she wouldn't be upset that I couldn't just leave the store unattended. It's the reality of retail management.

But I like the part that I missed, and I know it would've meant more to Vic to see me sooner. It wouldn't meant more to me to see Angeline's eyes, or hold her when she was first awake and taking everything in. Brand new babies are so special, the way you can tell just how they're trying to process what they're looking at. It's a uniquely beautiful thing, one you don't get to see often.

She won't be a mastermind or anything in a day or two, at least I don't think, but I'm still upset I missed it today.

Julian promises to pass along that I was here, and that I'm sorry. I text her to reiterate the same thing, just in case.

Every time my neighbor and I are together, I think of a new question to ask, although I rarely get a chance to actually ask them before she's ushering me out of her apartment. The ones I have snuck in usually go unanswered.

Where do you go on Thursdays or Fridays? Nowhere that's my business.

What are you going to school for? To get a higher education.

What led to you moving in here? Needing a place to live.

She's quite the locked box.

Tonight she shocked me by asking her own question.

"When did you get divorced?"

I blink at her, thinking she can't be serious.

"What makes you think I want to satisfy any of *your* curiosity?"

"Fine. If you tell me, I'll tell you when *I* got divorced."

I gape.

"You've been divorced?"

"See, I'm already giving you info. Your turn."

"I didn't think you wanted to know anything about me," I point out.

She rolls her eyes, losing her patience. I'm getting kicked out any second now.

"I'm just curious. You seem young."

"That's one way to call me immature."

"Not my preferred way. If that's what I meant, I'd say it."

I don't know her well enough to take her at her word, but it sends a rush through me anyway.

It wasn't even a compliment, Reya.

"I'd rather select the information I get in return. I have to think about it."

She sinks down in her bed, looking exasperated.

"This wasn't an open ended offer. Nothing else is on the table."

"Aren't you curious about anything else? I'm sure I've got some good, juicy details up my sleeve."

"You're pushing it," she says. "I asked *one* question. I don't even care enough to know the answer if you're going to turn it into a thing."

"You're impossible," I grumble. "It's been a few years now."

She side-eyes me.

"How old are you?" she asks.

"Twenty-seven! Ha! Now you owe me two details."

I feel victorious. Not even over my gain, but over her curiosity. She asked without even thinking.

I like knowing *Ms. Mysterious* is curious about me.

"I got divorced almost two years ago. I'm twenty-nine."

"When's your birthday?"

"Get out," she says.

"Oh, come on!"

She starts pulling the blankets out from under me, and it doesn't force me off the bed like she's hoping.

Instead I roll onto my back, pretending to look really comfortable. It's not even pretending, her mattress is so much nicer than my own. Her pillows are filled with feathers, and they're fluffier than anything I've rested my head on before. The sheets are made of something I couldn't even name, and the black comforter that's now bunched up in her arms is thick enough that I feel like I'm being cuddled by it. It might be weighted, I've always wanted one of those.

"It's a shame you won't let me pass out right here," I say with a yawn. "I'm a great person to sleep with. I don't make a sound."

She doesn't need to know about my tendency to flail my arms around, though. She'd probably deserve it if she got knocked upside the head.

"I do. Loads of sounds. Better save yourself." Her voice is monotone, bored even.

I keep asking myself why I still even have this crush on her. The only thing she does for me is sexual, and it usually takes more to hook me in.

"I've dealt with worse."

"Yeah? Ex was a bad snorer?" she asks.

"No, my neighbor's just really annoying."

"You're annoying," she snaps back. "Why are you still here? Go home!"

"Tell me your birthday and I'll go."

She glares daggers into me, and if I didn't know better, I'd say I actually felt the prick of them on my skin.

"You're going to go anyway. I don't feel like bargaining anymore."

Way to ruin my fun.

Because it is fun. I want more of this bantering, or arguing, or whatever it is. I want to sit here and fool around and get to know all the reasons why she's like *this.* I could write a couple hundred page book on why I am the way I am, but I have a feeling hers would be in the thousands.

She's in a good mood and it scares me.

"October seventeenth," she says as I approach. She's sitting in my chair, and appears to have been waiting for me.

I eye her suspiciously.

"What?"

"You wanted my birthday. October seventeenth. Be sure to get me a gift," she says.

"Okay..." I draw the word out, making it ten times as long.

She's smiling wide, too wide for my comfortability.

"No, now is the part where you tell me yours."

"July twelfth," I mutter on autopilot. If I had any sense, I would have withheld that answer in order to get more out of her. "Are you high?" I ask.

"I wish," she admits. "No, just got some good news. Feeling generous."

"What's the news?" I wholly expect her to shut me down, but she beams even brighter.

Fuck, she is so stunning that I have to close my eyes in order to not be blinded by it.

"My parents are getting divorced!" She says the words with the same tone that one might announce they won the lottery.

"That's... good?" I take a guess.

"I've been waiting years for this day." She leans back, closing her eyes, all the joy in the world still on her face.

"Do you hate your parents?"

"Just one of them."

I don't know what else to say, this is more than she's ever shared with me.

"I'm having whiplash."

She chuckles, her eyes still closed.

"Don't make it a thing. Sit down."

How can I not make it a thing? This is such a thing. Last night she was her usual closed off self, and less than twenty four hours later, I have more than I know what to do with.

"You know who I am, right?"

I have to make sure.

"Not technically. What's your name?"

My brows raise, the absurd realization that we haven't previously exchanged this information hitting me so hard. I laugh loudly.

"How have you never asked me that?"

"How have you never asked mine?"

"Good point."

She crosses her arms. "I'm Kara."

Kara. Wow. That really fits her.

It also brings up the shadow of a memory, something I don't stand a chance of remembering. She's more than likely not the first person I've ever met with that name, but I can't think of who else it was or how I'd know them.

"I'm Reya," I tell her.

She smiles again at that.

"Quite fitting for such a *ray of sunshine*."

And my breath catches in my throat.

She rolled her eyes at the last three words, but there was no real annoyance there. There was nothing negative about it at all, it was practically endearing.

There's no way she could have known that my parents have called me that since I was a kid. That hearing that nickname is the quickest way to make me feel safe and warm and—

Shit, it's finally hitting me that this might not just be a silly, forgettable crush. Somehow, even amongst all of the bullshit, I seem to have caught some feelings for this woman.

My neighbor.

Kara.

20

S he teases me with small bites to the crook of my neck and I'm instantly melting. I'd let her do anything she wanted, and I prove that fact by climbing onto her bed, and starting to undress. My shirt has buttons today, and they take an agonizingly long time to get undone.

The heat in Kara's gaze feels like it's branding my skin everywhere it goes. It's an addictive sort of burn.

I watch with rapt attention as she walks to her bedside table, opens a drawer, and pulls something out. Her body hides it from view at first, but even when she turns to face me again, she moves it behind her back

"That's not suspicious," I mutter.

"Do you trust me?" she asks.

"No," I reply quickly.

I realize it's foolish that we got this far *so many times* without trust being a factor, but I guess it must have been there on some instinctive level. I might finally trust that she's not a murderer, but I'm not sure she still isn't hiding a secret twin from me.

I've actually never asked.

Crap.

"Then why are you even here?"

"Haven't we had this conversation before? Convenience, mutual release…"

She smirks.

"You can't find that with someone you trust? I find that hard to believe. You seem…" She really hesitates to think of a word. "Likable."

My stomach does flips, and I take it for a compliment even if it wasn't really meant to be one. It's hard to say with this woman.

"I thought I was irritating."

"You misunderstand. I didn't say *I* liked you, I just think other people might."

Whatever that means.

Two seconds into overthinking it and my head starts to hurt.

I sit up, looking her in the eye.

"Look, it's pretty inconvenient that I find you so attractive, but I do. It is what it is. I'd trade you for someone that actually liked me in a heartbeat." *I'm such a liar.* "But no one that likes me has all of this going on." I gesture from her head to her toes, and it's all the explanation I need. She's perfect, and it's obvious to everyone but her.

"Sounds pretty shallow of you, sunshine. You should work on that. Maybe try out dating, find a girl with these good looks and a personality." Suddenly, she grabs the front of my shirt and pulls me in close.

"But if you're going to take my advice, do it tomorrow."

And then she kisses me hard. Hard enough that it hurts. Hard enough that I know the only thing she wants from me is *this*. Our intense, fiery chemistry. If it wasn't as good as it is, I would take her advice. I've taken a long break from trying to pursue a relationship, given my past mistakes and all. Getting hurt gets exhausting.

Apparently I'm revitalized, because I think all this woman could have to offer me is pain. I can already see what a rough, crumbling mess this could become between us.

And it's all I want anyway.

"Drop these," she demands.

Not that I've ever liked being told what to do by anyone... but I start moving. My fingers hit the button on my jeans, and in two seconds it's undone, unzipped, and they're on the ground.

I stand before her in my underwear, waiting.

She pushes me backwards so I fall onto the bed and she moves to straddle me.

I try to hold her hips in my hands, but she pushes them off. I'm starting to really believe I'll never figure her out, because where else would my hands go?

Only then do I notice what she'd been holding is now dropped onto the bed next to me. I'm staring at a glittery pink dildo.

And I never thought I'd be so excited to see one of those.

Kara's brows raise in question as she picks it up, and I can't nod quick enough. A small push of her thumb and the toy begins to vibrate.

"*Please*," I whine. There are few things I've ever wanted more than how much I want her to use it on me.

"Begging looks great on you. Do it some more," she purrs.

"You're evil."

She nods like she agrees.

"Amongst other things."

Then she gently presses it to my entrance and I lose all sense of everything. I don't care who she is, where we are, who *I* am. I do care how absolutely sinful it feels to have someone else in control of something I've used on myself too many times to count.

It's an entirely different experience.

My back arches off the bed as I try to push into it more, but she's holding it just out of the way. Just out of *me*.

"*Kara.*"

I try to open my eyes long enough to make eye contact, but hers are closed tight. Like she's getting off on this even more than I am.

She angles and slides it up until it's rubbing against my clit. My body twitches, the sensation being too much and not enough all at once.

She moves it in a circular motion, barely grazing me now. It's torturous and amazing, and I think I'm going to lose my mind for the few brief seconds when she finally applies more pressure. That pattern continues, hard and soft, back and forth, for what feels like an eternity. When I sit up as much as I can to kiss her, it's sloppy. I capture her bottom lip, sucking on it, and I could get off on the gasp that pulls from her alone.

This woman is too fucking hot.

"Say my name when you come," she says into my mouth.

I nod, unable to argue even if I wanted to.

The vibrator sinks lower again, sitting too comfortably between my lips, paused. Waiting.

I lie back down, bracing for her next move.

"Please, just—"

It presses into me further, the tip stretching me deliciously. My own wetness helps it slide in easily, but again she stops.

I let the vibration rattle through me, lighting up every single piece of me.

"Keep going," I breathe.

She leans over my body, our breasts pressing against each other. I feel her cool breath before I hear her delicate voice.

"I'm trying to be careful."

I scoff instinctively.

"You don't want to hurt me or something?"

"You haven't told me if you're into that."

Before the answer even comes to me, before I register what it is, she pushes it in further until it's reached as far as it can go. I moan so loudly, I surprise myself.

I do it again as she begins to attack at all angles. She works it in and out of me, her thumb presses to my clit, and her mouth lands on the most sensitive spot of my neck.

I'm a ticking time bomb that switched from having a few minutes to mere seconds.

I've never felt my orgasm build so violently, but that's exactly what it is. It feels like a storm raging in this very room, sweeping up all of its contents in a fierce wind.

I can almost feel it swirling around me, as I gasp my last breaths before I can't hold off any longer.

"Oh fuck, *Kara*."

I say her name with the last of the air in my lungs before the wind whips it away. I'm a woman possessed again, as my body spasms underneath her. The storm dies down, but her actions do not.

I try to gasp out the words, but I can't find them. Instead I continue to twitch, and feel, and go far past what my body was ready for.

After what seems like an eternity of trying and failing to wind down, she switches it off, and slowly pulls it out of me.

The wet sound of it is almost embarrassing, but I'm still too far gone to worry about it.

Kara throws the vibrator on the end of the bed without a care, and falls down beside me.

"Holy shit," she whispers.

"Holy crap," I echo.

We lay there for so long, chests heaving, that I let my eyes fall closed. I let myself forget where I am as exhaustion hits me full force.

I wait mere moments for her to protest, to shake me, to demand that it's time for me to go, but it doesn't come.

21

Sleeping over becomes part of our new normal, and it was way easier than I anticipated it would be. We don't cuddle, or chit chat, or anything a *couple* would do. It's still oddly comforting just to know she's next to me on those nights.

My bed has never felt so empty during the rest of them.

I let as much slip one day, and she walked right through my front door and asked me which room was mine. We've never done anything at my place before, by pure habit or what, I'm not sure.

But it's still true, because all she did was slide beneath my blanket and close her eyes.

It's been a few days of going back and forth, and now we only sleep alone when my daughter's home. I can't let myself worry about the why, or what it means for us. I'm just letting myself enjoy it.

It helps *a lot* that she hasn't played music a single night since. I don't question that, worrying that bringing it up might remind her that she does still want to be torturing me.

We fooled around in her luxurious bed last night, and then she insisted that we sleep in my underwhelming one. I thought it was too late to bother, but she dragged me back over to my own apartment.

I've noticed she sleeps better in my bed. There's a lot less tossing and turning. I wonder about all the reasons why that could be. The smells are different, the temperature is different, the feel is different. My room is messy and lived in, and hers is always clean and pristine.

I wonder which parent that trait came from. Not that I know which is which, the good or the bad. Pierre or the other.

I find myself wondering a lot. There are so many missing puzzle pieces to this woman, and I'm not even going to pretend I don't want them all.

My phone buzzes next to me, jarring me awake rather suddenly. I could've lied here and thought my thoughts for hours, probably.

I groan when I read the too-bright screen.

"Shit. My parents are going to be here any second. You have to get up."

Kara sits up quickly, but her eyes are barely able to open.

"What the fuck do you mean your parents are going to be here any second?"

I flash my phone screen at her, showing a text as evidence. Actually it's four text messages and two missed calls. This was a bad time for me to be a heavy sleeper.

"Why?" she moans. I ignore that my first instinct is to crawl under the blankets and make her really moan.

"You have to go. Seriously."

"Why can't I hide in here until they're gone?"

I laugh, loudly. It makes Kara jump.

"That's not how my parents work. They're nosy. They roam." She still doesn't move. "Come on!"

"Maybe it's fine if they find me," she says as her head slumps back against my headboard.

"I can't believe those words just came out of you." I shake my head. "But no. Please no. Please get up, and get out of my house."

I lean over her just long enough to place a quick kiss on her nose. To soften the blow maybe, but I can't help but feel like it's a wrong move. I pull back quickly, expecting the worst from her response, but she barely seems to have registered it.

She's still barely awake.

"You really know how to make a girl feel special." She throws the blankets off of her body and finally starts to move. Without pants on. "I'm not putting pants on to walk two feet outside."

"You could take off *more* clothing if that would get you moving quicker."

I know she must really be exhausted when she doesn't respond with anything dirty or sarcastic.

I see where her pants lay on the floor, and I watch her step over them as she exits my bedroom. I pick them up, figuring she'll just be irritated later when she can't find them because they're mixed in with my laundry.

I've never actually seen her repeat an outfit, so maybe I'm as-suming for no reason.

"Kara," I call to her as she reaches my front door.

She faces me as she pulls it open, and I'm frozen.

"What? I thought I was supposed to be in a hurry."

I slowly lift my hand to show her what I'm holding. Oblivious to everything else, she rolls her eyes.

"I'll come back when I've sufficiently made up for all the hours of sleep you cost me last night."

When she turns back around, she comes face to face with my smiling mother. My dad is standing a couple steps further behind, looking everywhere but at us. The paint on the walls, the tiles on the roof, the boards under his feet... *everywhere.*

Kara's feet are stuck to the floor where she stands, and although I can't see her face anymore, I know she's mortified. I was *trying* to prevent this, but she just had to waste time arguing.

I place a hand on her shoulder.

"Do you want to go back to my room and put your pants on?" I whisper.

She doesn't respond, doesn't even nod. She turns and pushes past me, only grabbing said pants from my hands.

As soon as I hear my bedroom door shut, I groan.

"What are you guys doing here?"

"I messaged you, honey."

"Was that supposed to be an explanation, because I couldn't even tell. You should take a class on how to use emojis, because they don't belong in the middle of words."

She waves a hand, dismissing what I've said.

"Life's too short. Who's your friend?"

That's a topic we're not broaching today.

"You didn't come here to talk about my friend. What's up?"

Instead of answering, she walks inside. I smile at my dad as he follows behind her.

"How ya doin', kiddo?"

"Great!" I tell him. "Only thing that would make me feel any better is knowing what this random visit is about! I have work in an hour."

"You should've planned this better, honey. Maybe you'd benefit from one of those whiteboard calendars!" my mom exclaims.

She holds her hands up like a frame over a blank space on my wall.

"I didn't plan anything, what are you talking about?"

"Well, you forgot to mention it so I can't say I'm surprised."

There's a knock at my door. *What the hell is going on?*

"Oh, good! They're not late. You should make it to work on time just fine."

"Who are *they*?" I yell, but she doesn't answer.

Instead, she does what she does best and starts opening cabinets in my kitchen, inspecting my groceries. The amount of times I've had to listen to her scold me about not buying organic, non GMO products is getting to be insane. I'm never going to change, a normal mom would have given up by now.

The knock happens again, so I guess I'm answering the door.

I wish I hadn't.

"Hi Reya!" An overly cheery Raquel greets me.

And next to her are Caleb and Dahlia.

I didn't forget this. I would've remembered if I'd planned to have all of these people show up at my apartment. Especially two of these three. I would've needed time to prepare.

"What is going on right now?"

"Family meeting," Caleb answers. That's all he says before also deciding he's going to just step past me and into my space.

I put a foot out to stop him.

"Mind explaining a few things to me? Like who's responsible for this, and why *you* are included in a *'family meeting?'*"

My dad places a hand on my shoulder, startling me.

"Don't be like that, sunshine. You kids might not have been able to work things out, but he's still family." My eyes bug out of my head. I'm ready to explain to him, and everyone else, that he's my daughter's family. The rest of us don't have to claim him. "Hi there, princess. Give grandpa a hug!"

Dahlia beams, running and jumping into his arms. I absent-mindedly start playing with her hair, while my focus is still on the couple before me.

"I still have unanswered questions?" I say it as if the particular sentence is also a question. I'm trying to emphasize that I need someone to explain what's going on.

I feel pretty confident that Caleb knows exactly what it is.

"We need to talk, so we're all sitting down to talk," he says.

"Dad, can you talk Dahlia to her room for a minute?"

"If you don't have anything nice to say–"

"I'm being so serious, Dad. Please."

I'm grateful when he only hesitates for a second before he starts to walk down the hallway. He might look a little upset, but that is the least of my concerns at the moment.

Only when I hear the familiar sound of my daughter's bedroom door closing do I turn to face my ex-husband.

I immediately poke him in the chest.

"What did you do?" I whisper scream.

"We all need to sit down and talk about this, so I made it happen."

"You made it happen by ambushing me in my own home? What the hell, Caleb? What did you tell them?"

He puts his hands up in mock surrender.

"I told them that we wanted to sit down and talk about some things."

"'We?' As in, you and me?"

One singular nod.

"You lying little snake! You didn't like my answer, so this is how you thought to change my mind?"

"Look, it wasn't the nicest thing to do but–"

I point at Raquel, a lot more aggressively than I normally would, but this is partially her fault.

"With all due respect, stay out of this."

Caleb puffs his chest out at that, and I roll my eyes. Men and their need to defend the women they think need defended. Although, Raquel does look like a wounded animal at my tone.

"Don't talk to her like that. This concerns her, that's why she's here."

"Where our daughter spends her time is not your girlfriend's concern."

My mom now steps behind me suddenly, and puts *her* hand on my shoulder.

Why is everyone treating me like I'm *the problem?*

I'm angry enough that my initial reaction is to pull away, but I realize quickly enough that I don't want to be taking this anger out on anyone but Caleb.

He's always been a big child, always stooped lower than I thought possible, but it's been a long time. Long enough that I was fooled into believing it was possible for him to have changed.

Fuck that. He had no right to recruit my parents to gang up on me. I know exactly what it's regarding to, and I don't want my six-year old to leave the country. I think that's pretty understand-able.

"Okay, I see that I was misled here." She gives him a pointed glance. "Why don't you two wait out there, and let the two of us talk?"

He looks like he wants to argue, but Raquel places a hand on his arm. "Of course," she says. "We'll wait here, not a problem."

I keep my eyes on the ground as they take a step back from the entryway, not trusting myself to look at his stupid, annoying face. I'm not typically violent, but I'm feeling that way right now.

When my mom spins me around by the shoulder, I hate that frustrated tears fill my eyes. I can't hit anything, so I guess this is the best my body could do.

"Oh, honey." She pulls me into a tight hug, and rubs soothing circles between my shoulder blades. "I'm sorry I jumped into this without questioning him. Your father and I just want to keep the peace between all of us. We don't want Dahlia to deal with family that refuses to interact with each other."

I pull away to look at her.

"I respect that, mom. I even appreciate it, but did he tell you why you're here?"

"Because you're being '*unreasonable*'—" she uses air quotes for the word— "about some vacation they want to take her on?"

"To Canada! For an entire month."

She nods, pondering.

"That is a lot," she agrees.

"Too much for her age."

She switches to shaking her head.

"I'm sorry, but I disagree with that part."

I throw my hands up, miming my head exploding.

"How is that not too much? In what world? In what way? She can't go more than few days without me, and he definitely–"

I'm interrupted by her finger in front of my lips.

"I think it's *you* that can't go a few days without *her*."

"That's true, too! So, what?" I shout.

She moves to sit down, keeping her cool. I don't think she has another setting. Even when she's driving me crazy and overstepping into my life, she's always so *calm* about it.

"Your life got turned upside down when you found out you were pregnant. You suddenly lost all your free time, and full nights of sleep, and the ability to go and do whatever you want."

I fall back onto my loveseat with a groan.

"You're not saying anything I don't know, but *mom*, I'm really happy. I don't regret having her. I don't feel like I'm missing out on anything."

"But you are," she says bluntly.

I scoff.

"I'm not! We split custody, remember? Which means that three nights a week, I get to live it up. I see my friends, I binge watch all the inappropriate TV shows I want. I take bubble baths, and get the house cleaned. And I am *so* excited to see her when it's my turn again."

"You also work most of the time."

"I don't think you understand how easy my job is."

"Reya Renee, you're being stubborn and missing my point."

I look up at her with all the teenage, angsty attitude I can muster. I kind of hope she's transported back to a time where she didn't have her own house to run off to.

She gives me a pointed finger, transporting *me* back to a time when she didn't have her own house to run off to. It's really unfair.

"Everyone needs a break. Everyone. You think you don't because you've been in survival mode. You've accepted what you got, and honestly I'm so proud of you for it, honey. You're the strongest girl I know." She drops her hand to hold mine, in that consoling way of hers. "But you deserve to have some time to yourself, time where you don't have to be on alert. And I know that alertness doesn't go away when she's with her dad, but what bad thing has ever happened to her in his care?"

I don't have an answer and she knows it.

"That doesn't mean I want to wait around for the day something bad does happen!"

She shakes her head at me, looking as disappointed as only mothers can manage.

"You'll always be waiting. No matter how much that man changes, even if he becomes the most capable father on the planet. Things happen. Accidents happen. She hurt herself the other day, didn't she? Hit her head on her little play table?"

I nod, hating that she has a point.

"And it wasn't your fault, was it?"

I shake my head.

"Okay, I get it," I say before she can continue. "But what if an accident happens, his fault or not, and she's all the way over there? And I'm here, and devastated, and dying to see her?"

"Then I'll buy your plane ticket." She reaches a hand out for me to shake, but I'm not done thinking this through.

"If I agree, she won't be here for her birthday." My voice cracks on the last word, making her pout.

"Do you honestly believe she cares if you throw her a party on the exact date? She'll be just as thrilled to do it a couple weeks early or a couple weeks late."

"I won't be!"

I know how childish the three whined words sound. I can't help myself.

"You'll get over it. There are worse things to miss, and worse reasons to miss them."

With that, she stands, flattening out any creases it caused her linen pants.

"Mom," I whine again.

"You'll get over it," she repeats. "It's an awesome opportunity for all of you. *Every. Single.* One of you. If this goes smoothly, your trust will build in him. I know how badly he has let you down, but it isn't fair to assume he's always going to. It doesn't mean his girlfriend will either, she seems like a good woman who's already helped him immensely. You'd know that if you could talk to them without letting your anger interfere."

I hate the way her little speech gets under my skin and makes me feel guilty. She's right, like usual. It's annoying. I didn't wake up this morning thinking I'd start questioning everything about myself this deeply.

I'm aware of my actions, I always have been. I just didn't care about my actions towards him, thinking it was the least he deserved.

I rarely swallow my pride enough to admit that he *has* changed over the years, and I know how much he loves our daughter. I know he wants to take care of her, and I respect that the whole point in bringing her along is to introduce her to family she might not have the chance to meet otherwise.

I assume my mother sees something change in my expression, because she opens my front door and motions them inside. When the door is shut behind them, she goes to collect the other two parties we're missing.

"We're sorry we did it this way. I was desperate."

I expected an apology to come from Raquel again, but I'm surprised when it's Caleb's voice that speaks the words.

"Desperate to take my daughter away from me?"

He sighs, and it's a sad, defeated sound. I almost feel bad about the fact that he'll have to deal with me for the rest of our lives.

"No, I'm not. You're an amazing mom, and I'd never…" He doesn't stop talking, but my ears stop hearing his words.

I'm too stuck on the fact that he complimented me. I didn't realize he thought that, I kind of assumed we both thought similar things about each other. Everytime I said he wasn't cut out to be a parent, I assumed he was saying the same of me.

I might really just be an asshole.

Dahlia comes running straight to me, and puts herself in my lap.

I kiss the top of her head, while everyone else silently watches us. The ball is in my court now that I know where they all stand.

"Have they been talking to you about this trip?"

She shakes her head. "Are we going on a trip?"

I look up to my mom, knowing her expression will help me to make this move in the right direction. I'm still not completely sold on this being the right direction, but… points have been made today.

"I guess that's up to you, beautiful girl. Your dad and Raquel are going to get on a plane and go visit some family for a while. Would you want to go with them?"

"Where's the plane going?"

"You know where Canada is, right?"

She shrugs, and I know that means she has no idea.

"It's above us on a map," I explain the best I can.

"What would we do in Canada?"

I look to Caleb to answer, and I don't miss the hope in his eyes.

"Meet some people. Play some games. Go to some cool places, eat some good food," he explains.

"Okay," she answers easily. "I wanna go."

"There's just one thing," he adds, sitting down on the couch next to us. "Your mom will stay here, so you won't see her for a few weeks."

"But I could call you every day. You could see my face on the phone," I add, suddenly sounding like I'm truly on the team that wants to convince her to do this. If anything would be her deal-breaker, it would be the lack of *me* on her vacation.

"Why don't you come, too? There's room on a plane."

I smile at her cuteness.

After a brief explanation that doesn't allow her to stress about my financial situation, she's decided she still wants to go. Unfortunately, regardless of what any of us say, she seems to think it's happening tomorrow instead of months from now. She immediately runs to her room to start packing, and Caleb goes with it, following her in there and giving her ideas.

"Shit!" I say, quickly standing. "I have to get ready for work, and get my–" I point to my bedroom door, not wanting to finish the sentence.

"Oh, yeah!" My mother exclaims. "Why don't you introduce us to your friend?"

I motion for her to stop talking, and not bring it up any further, but she's clueless.

"Oh, come on. Bring her out. We won't bite."

I roll my eyes.

"Mom, no. I don't need her to meet everyone that's currently in my house. We can set up something for another time," I lie. Kara would never.

Ignoring me, my mother pushes past me towards my bedroom door and knocks.

"Are you decent in there?" she calls out.

I run my hands down my face in disbelief. Raquel stands awkwardly by my front door, looking down at her phone. She's obviously listening, but at least she's being subtle about it.

"Mom!" I whisper harshly. "No!"

"Yes?" Kara's voice comes from behind the door, sounding unsure.

And my mother takes that as her invitation to open the door.

I am horrified. It's already been a crazy morning, and this does not need to be added to it. She should not have to meet my parents and my ex-husband right now. We're not even together!

This is probably her worst nightmare. I cringe on her behalf.

My mother looks around my bedroom with a tisk before her eyes land on Kara.

"I can't believe my daughter forced you away into such a pigsty! Reya, it's a mess in here!"

I groan, pushing past her so I can pick up last night's underwear off the floor.

I continue to whisper, not wanting to draw any further attention into this room.

"Not that you need to know this, but the mess is partially her fault, mom. Can you go? Can we do this another time?" I plead, knowing it's pointless. My mother doesn't do a thing she doesn't want to do.

"What's your name?"

Great, I'm being ignored completely. I go to close my door at least, but my dad chooses that moment to make an appearance.

"What's going on in here?" he asks casually.

"Nothing! Please dad, help me out here." I point to my mom. "This is not the time for this."

He gives me a confused look, as if he has no clue why I wouldn't want this to happen.

"Don't be rude, introduce us."

"We're not—"

"I'm Kara," she interrupts. "I live... right there." She points in the general direction of her place.

I watch the realization hit the two of them at the same time. My poor mother's face turns a bright red, and my dad is... still confused. This time I know it's because he has no idea how she went from being that girl in the apartment next to me to being a girl in my bed.

"I don't understand," he says. "Do you have a roommate? A sister or something?"

"Nope. It's just me."

He laughs loudly.

"So you're the reason we were having so many sleepovers with our girls? Now I imagine you're the reason we haven't seen them in a couple weeks."

"Yeah, I guess that's all probably true," she mumbles.

"Okay, that's enough. You met her, now you've got to go so I can get ready for work."

I resort to actually ushering them out with hands on their backs, and they pretend they're offended. Or maybe they're *actually* offended, but I don't have time to care.

"Reya Renee, what has gotten into you?" my mom asks.

I get them through the door and close it behind us before responding.

"I don't need Caleb or Dahlia to know she's staying the night," I whisper. "We're not there yet."

"Are you trying to get there?" she asks.

I sigh, attempting to let all the defeat I've felt this entire morning seep out with it.

"I don't think it's on the table. We're not serious or anything," I explain. "Is that enough now? Can you see yourselves out so I'm not any later to work than I'm already going to be?"

That would be too easy. They take a while to chat with Caleb and Raquel, and they ignore all the signs I'm giving them. Saying it outright won't work either, they're determined to act like my time and space don't matter.

After another twenty minutes, I finally fly through my room like a hurricane trying to get dressed and do my makeup. Kara laughs at me the whole time, finding every bit of it amusing. She heard our conversations, the little eavesdropper she is, but thankfully didn't have too much to say on it. I've had enough outside input for the rest of the week.

22

Kara is napping in my bed when I get home from work. Her red hair is splayed all over the place, and I watch as her chest slowly rises and falls. It's both chaotic and peaceful, and I want in on it.

As quietly as I possibly can, I slip off my shoes and slide under the covers next to her.

Apparently she wasn't very deeply asleep, because she wraps her arms around me. It's more comfortable than I knew her capable of.

"Do you want to talk about it?" she asks.

Okay, this has to be the twin.

"Not really."

"Do you want some space?"

I grab her forearm, and hug it like I'm a koala and it's a tree.

"No, please don't leave."

"Okay. I won't."

It's that painless.

It's weird, but not weird enough to keep my exhaustion at bay.

We fall asleep just like that and wake up when it's still dark out. My stomach grumbles, and I have a feeling it's been even longer since she's eaten anything.

I make us peanut butter and jelly sandwiches, and grab a bag of chips from my pantry. We move our hang out to the couch while we eat, and watch some reality competition show she's into. I watch her more than I watch what's happening in it.

She takes smile bites of her food, chews them slowly, and slightly faces away from me as she does. It makes me stress over whoever made her feel self conscious about the way she eats. Not wanting to make her anymore uncomfortable, I dart my eyes away whenever she turns her face back and hope it was fast enough for her to miss.

Her whole body seems to relax once her plate is empty. She smiles at my television, especially when a certain person pops up on the screen. She scowls when they interact with another: some douchey guy. It's cute. It's innocent. It's normal.

Everything about being around her lately has felt normal, and comfortable, and... kind of like we're in an actual relationship.

I pick up our empty plates to take to the sink, hoping it'll distract me from the unwanted idea in my head. I *don't* want that. She definitely doesn't want that. We're still not even really friends.

We just spend almost all of our free time together, even when there isn't anything sexual involved. That doesn't have to be a big deal.

I desperately wish I could talk to my friends about this. Vic and Autumn would know exactly what to say.

When I head back to the couch, she looks at me in a way that makes me feel like she can read my mind. I don't like it.

"What?" I ask suspiciously.

Her body shifts uneasily.

"I think I've overstayed my welcome," she says softly, but without moving to get up.

"No."

She smirks, and I realize I answered too fast.

But for the first time since meeting her, I don't think I'm in trouble for exposing an emotion. She doesn't look like she's ready to jump up and run out on me.

"It's something," she tries. "Maybe you're freaked out that I met your parents?"

I bite my lip, thinking about that. Is that part of what's led me down this trail of thought?

"Maybe," I admit.

And I want to admit more, I want to tell her everything in my head without worrying she's going to immediately shut down.

"Can you promise me something? That if I tell you what I'm thinking you're not going to revert to your bitchy ways?" I ask hopefully.

She laughs loudly enough that it pulls a smile onto my own face.

"My bitchy ways are always there. You just haven't gotten on my nerves much lately."

I shove her shoulder playfully.

"Is that what it is?"

"Yep. You're acting practically normal."

"Ew. How boring."

She laughs again and then holds out her pinky.

I blink at it a few times, sure I'm hallucinating. Yet somehow, the image doesn't disappear after a few seconds.

"That's a joke right? You're teasing me or something."

I continue staring in shock.

"No?"

I glance at her face, reading her expression.

"You? Are a pinky promiser?" I ask disbelievingly.

She rolls her eyes.

"Why are you making a big deal of it? Just grab my pinky."

I do as she says.

"I was going to, you just took me by surprise."

She uses our miniature hold on each other to pull me in until our bodies are flush together.

"I have plenty more surprises up my sleeve," she whispers against my ear.

I'm dizzy from the overwhelming want I feel around her. Neither of us let go for what simultaneously feels like forever and also not long enough.

"What are you waiting for?" I finally ask, out of breath somehow.

"I'm waiting for you to tell me what you're thinking."

"I'm thinking I really like this," I blurt. "Spending more time with you."

Her eyes widen, and I hope for a few seconds that it's the lead up to her telling me she feels the same way. That she's going to smile and hug and me and...

My daydreaming ends when her face falls completely. She breaks eye contact and scoots away from me.

Crap.

"You said you wouldn't," I say quickly.

It's a lie. She never actually said the words, I may have only assumed she was agreeing.

She clears her throat, taking a second to find the response she wants to go with. When her mouth finally opens to speak, she looks me in the eyes with an intensity that's not my favorite thing in the world.

"I'm not, but..." God, she looks so uncomfortable. It's really *that* hard for her, I see every ounce of the effort it takes in her expression. "I meant it when I said you'd never be my girlfriend. This isn't anything serious, you know that right?"

I nod, because I'm supposed to.

It goes against what I'm really feeling.

"Yeah, of course," I breathe.

"Okay. Good," she starts, already looking relieved. It makes me a little upset that she doesn't see right through me. "You get it, I need to make sure there isn't some ulterior motive with you telling me," she explains.

"Yep. Understood."

I mean, I tell my friends I like spending time with *them* and I'm not trying to get them to commit to me. I easily could've meant that.

She smirks, and moves to sit closer again.

I feel the relief in every single part of me.

"I like it too, but if you tell anyone I was nice enough to admit it?" She nips at my bottom lip. "There will consequences."

My first thought is that I want to know what those consequences would be. I'm tempted to find out, but who would I tell? We don't have the same friends, I have no idea who's in her circle. Whose opinion she cares about.

I can't even picture the kind of people that Kara would lean on, vent to, take advice from.

I wouldn't be all that surprised if there wasn't a single one.

23

Destiny walks in the building, and I try not to grimace. I should be glad she bothered to show up, but I find it harder every day to feel anything other than annoyed in her presence.

She walks past me with one of those polite, ingenuine smiles. I give her one in return, until she looks away.

Unfortunately she does catch the scowl it morphs into, before she looks back, *steps* back and gives my appearance a double take.

"Are you *blonde?*"

Oh God, no. Please no.

I cover the strip where I imagine my roots showing with the palm of my hand.

"You see nothing," I tell her.

"Wow. I pegged you as more of a ginger."

Not that it would be a bad thing, but I feel like the words are meant to be offensive. I'm pale, sure. I have freckles that pop out in the summertime. I see why someone could think that.

"You. See. Nothing," I repeat slowly.

She gives me the most teenage look, the kind that says *suuuu-uuuure.*

This is a tragedy. This is the worst thing. I've been so distracted that I forgot to touch up my hair. I haven't forgotten in years. Kara has really invaded a little too much of my brain.

"You," I say accusingly, when she shows up at my front door.

Kara just rolls her eyes, like my anger is nothing but an inconvenience.

It's not even real anger to be fair, but I don't appreciate her reaction either way.

"What did I do now?"

"My roots!" I swing the door open wide, and walk away. "I've never gone this long without touching up my roots."

When I hear the sound of her following behind me, I let out a fake sob. She doesn't bother asking how she's responsible, but she probably knows.

"No one can see me like this."

"But I can?" She sounds pleased about it, but she'd probably hate that I realized.

"You forced your way in, there wasn't much I could do."

I look up to watch her roll her eyes again and I smile.

"Sure I did." One of her hands lifts to pull at my curls, probably inspecting the too-bright blonde roots at the base of them. I want to pull away and hide. It should be illegal for this gorgeous woman to look upon such a mess. "Do you want some help?"

I think my heart actually skips a beat at the question.

"You want to help?"

"Don't freak out or anything. It's just that I do my own roots all the time, so I know how. It's kind of fun."

I want to kiss her. I think about how she'd react if I did, and I decide it's worth it anyway. I throw my arms around the back of her neck and pull her in for a kiss before she can argue.

Except, instead of pulling away, like I imagined she would, she presses into me. Her hands land on my hips. For a few blissful seconds, it's as if she doesn't hate acting like my girlfriend as much as she would like me to think she does.

I'm the one to pull back first, and I look up at her with all the surprise and excitement I feel.

And I could fucking melt to the floor when all she does is stare into me, full lips glistening.

I already struggle with having a filter most days, but that *look*.

"I think I–" She interrupts my sentence with a shake of her head, and then presses her lips to mine again.

"Go grab a chair," she tells me. "Where's your hair dye?"

I know why she changes the subject and I let her. I point her to what she needs and leave to get one of the chairs from my kitchen.

Kara is still in the exact same position when I get back, looking at the basket full of bottles.

"Which one?" she asks as her eyes widen.

Yeah, I lost count of how many different ones I'd collected. I use it so often that any time I see pink dye in a store, it's mine. If I see a video of someone dyeing their hair pink at home, I find out the shade and order it. It's happened a lot.

Instagram keeps showing me those videos because I keep interacting with them.

"I don't care, you can just pick one."

"But it might not match what you already have." To emphasize her point, she holds up two of them. One is a pastel, and the other is as neon as they come.

"It won't matter if you just find one with enough left in the bottle to cover my whole head."

That used to be so much easier before I let my hair start to grow out. I go through the stuff so much faster now.

"That's not how it works. You could end up with bright roots doing it that way."

"I don't think that's how it works either." At least... that's never happened to me before. "It's all pink. I don't really care if there are some varying shades on my head. It doesn't have to be perfect."

I hear the plastic bottles being moved around as she digs through them.

"I want it to be perfect," she says quietly. I wonder if she even meant for me to hear it at all, but I don't comment. Just in case. "Where's your brush?"

"Uh, it's right in front of you." I point to my hair brush, sitting on the bathroom counter. I notice things in this moment that I usually don't. Like how it's full of my bright pink hair, and stained with my dye. I should just get a new one at this point, it's been through a lot.

"No, like an applicator brush."

"Oh, pfft." I wave a hand, dismissing that. "I don't have one. I don't need it."

Kara stands abruptly, shaking her head.

"I'll be right back."

"What—where are you—" She's gone before I can ask.

What the hell?

I guess she'll be right back apparently.

I pick up my phone, scrolling through Instagram. I like most of the pictures I see, just killing time.

A cute edit of Autumn's newest book shows up on my screen. A flat lay photo taken on some sand, surrounded by flowers and seashells. The words *AVAILABLE NOW!* are sprawled across the top in a scripted font. Her social media girl is *good*, her posts never miss.

It has a whopping couple thousand likes, and hundreds of excited comments. I love to see how far she's come in the last year. Autumn used to think no one would ever read her books, and they wouldn't enjoy them if they did. I guess I wasn't worth believing when I raved about the first one, but at least she gets it now.

Kara appears with a bag in her hand, and I stare at it curiously.

"Look, I know I can be annoying, but if that's full of cleaning supplies to cover up my murder, I think we can talk this out."

She tries and fails to hide her amusement.

Throwing the bag onto my counter, she reaches in and pulls out a handful of hair clips. Then a box of gloves. A box of foils. An applicator brush.

Okay, so maybe she knows what she's doing. That's all very professional looking.

"We don't need these," she says, putting the foils back. "I just wanted to show you how seriously I take this."

"Very serious. I understand." I school my expression into the most innocent, obedient thing I can make it, until one smirk from her makes me crack.

I watch as she gets to work, rolling her sleeves up and putting on gloves. She decides on two different shades, mixing them up in a little plastic bowl. Then she turns to me, and uses the end of the brush to evenly section out my hair, and clips them up and out of her way.

Everything this woman does is hot as hell, but all of this is *really* working for me. She's so smart, and capable, and focused, and it's so fucking attractive.

I'm so distracted by her face, that I don't realize when she actually goes in to start applying the dye. The first cold swipe of the brush pulls me out of my ogling. It's not as shocking as it usually is when I plop a giant pile of dye onto my head.

Her method won't leave my scalp a neon color, so I suppose that's another positive.

"See? It's so much easier with a brush," Kara tells me.

She looks like quite the expert painting my roots.

"I don't think it's *easier*. It just looks fancier. I've never missed a spot going straight in with my hands."

"You're using so much more product that way. It's a waste."

I shrug.

"It's worth it in my opinion."

I might be lying.

I let my eyes close, something I'd never do at a hair salon. I wouldn't be able to forgive myself for falling asleep in someone's chair, it would be so embarrassing.

Falling asleep in my own bathroom? With a woman who has already seen me fall asleep in all kinds of positions? Easy.

Except I doze off for a total of five seconds before her voice pulls me awake.

"Sunshine." Her voice is soft and quiet, sending a wave of warmth through me. "I need you to tilt your chin down so I can get back here." She taps the back of my head.

I do as I'm told, trying to force my eyes to stay open.

It's not an easy feat. Her hands in my hair feel so good. From what I can tell, she's really good at this, too. I just don't have the patience to try and do it better.

It's so cute that she does. This grumpy girl that wants to pretend she can't be bothered with anything.

"Talk to me so I don't fall asleep again."

"Okay…" she trails off. The only sound in the bathroom is the rumbling of the fan. The dye I use smells really sweet, but I doubt it's the best idea to breathe it in without some ventilation. "So, Dahlia is leaving with them in a few weeks?"

I groan, hating the reminder.

"That's the last thing I want to talk about."

"Because you'll miss her?"

"Yeah, of course. I miss her whenever she's gone for a few days. This will be torture on top of the fact, that I don't trust Caleb in the slightest. His attention span is too short. Raquel better be ready to over compensate, but I don't feel confident about that either. She's never had to be responsible for a child before." I bury my face in my hands, accidentally touching my hair with the tips of my fingers. I pretend I don't notice, if only to not embarrass myself in front of Kara. "I'm terrified. I don't know how I'm going to function when they're gone."

She hums once, like she's thinking. I wouldn't be surprised if it was her only answer.

I feel her get closer, lean in towards my ear. I can't help the shiver that flies down my spine when her breath hits my neck.

"You seem like a good mom," she says quietly. "You care so much."

I know she's complimenting me, and I do feel the rush of her kind words. I also know it's because of her own mother that she felt the need to say it.

"Thank you."

She doesn't reply to that, resuming her work.

"I could really get used to you doing my hair. This was a bad idea."

"I could get used to doing your hair. You look adorable trying not to fall asleep down there."

I meet her eyes in the mirror, and her smirk doesn't drop.

It might just be me, but it seems like we're making a lot of progress today.

"You're full of nice things to say today."

"I guess I am." Suddenly her hold on my hair tightens and she pulls my head back. The dye on my head is touching her shirt, but she doesn't seem to care. "You're making it difficult not to be."

"You say that like it's a bad thing."

"I haven't decided if it is yet."

Then she lowers her mouth to mine, faster than my brain can process. By the time I register that I need to kiss her back, she's gone. She moves my head again so she can finish the task at hand, and avoids eye contact in the mirror.

"We should do something."

"I like doing things. Please explain further."

"When they go on their trip. Maybe you and I could go some-where."

I abruptly turn to face her.

"You want to go on a trip with me?"

She laughs and it's the cutest sound I'll ever hear.

"Yeah. It'll take your mind off things."

"You care about taking my mind off things? Where is Kara? What have you done with her?"

"Okay, you're pushing it," she says with a smile still on her face. "I'm done being nice today."

"That's okay, you can be mean to me. We could start in the shower in about ten minutes."

She laughs again. I am such a winner. How did I get so lucky?

Kara points to the chair.

"Sit your ass back down or I'll never finish your hair, and we'll never make it to the shower."

I'm well aware that it's confirmation she will be joining.

Dahlia and I sit on the couch, her legs are draped over my lap, and a movie she picked is playing on the screen. My eyes close and open, because I'm caught in an odd half-asleep state. I keep remembering I should scoop her up and take her to her bed, but then my eyes fall closed again.

And repeat.

It has resulted in nothing.

She moves suddenly in her sleep, kicking me in the stomach much harder than I thought she was capable of. I wince as I gently move her legs off of me without waking her. It was the reminder I needed that I also have to pee, and I'm grateful an accident wasn't just caused. The last thing I need right now is to deal with that clean up. Dahlia hasn't had any accidents in a long time, and I've really enjoyed a life where all of the pee I come across is in a toilet.

And probably her baths, but there's not much I can do to stop that. She's six. There are worse things to happen.

I pass by my front door, rubbing the sleep from my eyes.

Then I jump out of my skin when a knock sounds on it. I glance back at my daughter, making sure it didn't disrupt her. She's still out, lightly snoring and everything.

I glare at Kara when I open the door to see her face.

Before she even opens her mouth to speak, I give her shoulder a little push.

"No! Go!" I shout in a whisper.

She looks confused, and opens her mouth again. I put a finger over it and use my other to point to her door.

"Dahlia is asleep on the couch."

The realization spreads across her face.

"Shit, I'm sorry!" It's the first time I've heard her apologize for anything. "I completely lost track of my days. I'm so out of it."

Any frustration I felt is gone that quickly. She might have her cruel moments, but I know she takes my rules seriously.

"I'll go. I'm sorry," she says again.

I hold back my smile when she facepalms. It's just so... normal of her when she's always anything but.

"Don't sweat it. See you tomorrow?"

She nods her head before she starts to turn away, but a small voice has us both frozen in our tracks.

"Mama? Who is that?"

Crap.

Dahlia comes up beside me, placing a hand on my leg. It's something she always does when someone new is around. She's not hiding behind me or anything, but I can tell it gives her a little extra comfort to know I'm right there.

Kara looks like she's still ready to run, but instead she's frozen in place. She looks between the two of us, looking for some direction on what she should do next.

I sigh.

"This is our neighbor."

"The one with the scary music?"

"Yep," I tell her.

Kara doesn't even smirk.

Dahlia motions me closer to her level, so I squat down next to her. As expected, she leans right into my ear to whisper.

Unfortunately, she hasn't pinned down controlling her volume yet.

"Why is she here?"

"She was... just saying hi," I whisper back.

Dahlia waves me closer again, so I lean, trying not to lose my balance.

"She has really pretty hair."

"You can tell her that, if you want to," I chuckle. I don't bother whispering it.

The two of them make eye contact, and I watch as she assesses what to do. If she's comfortable enough to compliment the woman with the scary music.

The sentence rushes out of her so slurred that it sounds like one long word.

Kara smiles.

"Thanks. I like your hair, too."

Thank goodness kids don't hold grudges, because my daughter smiles like she just made a new best friend.

24

"Are you actually reading a book?"

I snap it shut and set it on my stomach, preparing for whatever snarky thing she's going to say about it.

"Yeah, so what?"

"I guess I'm just surprised. I've never seen you with a book before."

She actually hasn't. I avoid reading as much as possible, it gives me a headache.

"It's a rare occurrence, but I have to do it every now and then."

"Because it's good for the brain or something?"

I sit up straighter, hearing the judgment in her voice. Does she really think it would be ridiculous if that was my reason? I'm allowed to want to improve myself.

"Not really. This is more like required reading. An assignment, if you will."

"Says the woman who hasn't been in school for at least–" she starts counting on her fingers– "seven years."

I chuckle.

"A friend of mine wrote it, and I never miss the opportunity to support her. She's really good actually, I can't even complain. This is her third one, and she keeps getting better."

"What's it about?" She's on her phone, seeming uninterested, but I share anyway.

I really never miss the opportunity.

"This one is about a woman who starts hooking up with her celebrity crush every time he goes on tour. When he's in her city. It's kind of sad, actually."

Kara raises a brow.

"What could be sad about that? Sounds ideal."

She would think that. Commitment-phobe.

"Because she's emotionally unavailable, so they only talk in person. Once a year." She still doesn't get it. "That means that *all year long* they're both pining, and sad, and waiting for their next chance."

I think about not getting to see Kara for an entire year, and it's awful to even imagine. She might get on my nerves a lot of the time, but she's also fun. Interesting. Smart. Sexy.

I'm thrilled about how often we can have sex.

"I guess I'd be bummed out if I only saw you once a year," she says quietly. Almost like she didn't mean to say the words out loud. Almost like she was reading my mind.

Then she rises from her chair to stand by my side. She holds a hand out in front of me and I take it, squeezing slightly. It's as much as I'm allowing myself to say. Anything more and she'll probably go running for the hills.

Suddenly, she drops herself in my lap and I let out an *oomph* at the surprise of it. Not because she's heavy, and not because it's not comfortable.

"You've just given me way too much power," I tell her as I place a kiss on her shoulder and wrap my arms around her waist.

She faces me and bows her head, her way of asking for a kiss that she can't reach. I waste no time pressing my lips against her much softer, much plumper ones. And then I do it again.

And again.

And before I know it, we're making out right on my front porch where anyone could walk by, look up, and see.

The thought of it makes me pull away slightly, enough to giggle. When I collect myself and go back for more, she's smiling.

"What?" she asks.

"For two people who hate PDA, we're really going for it."

She laughs at that, in between more kissing.

"I can't help myself. This may become a problem."

"Doesn't sound like that much of a problem, if I'm honest."

Except that the sound of nearby tires on pavement makes us both spring into action. She quickly removes herself from my lap, I quickly wipe away the Chapstick that ended up around my lips instead of on them.

The car does nothing but drive by, being as harmless as ever. It wasn't someone we know, it wasn't someone gawking.

I don't know why I haven't told my friends about this. It just hasn't felt like there was anything to really talk about, but everyday feels a little more intense.

I haven't told Caleb, obviously, because that slimy snake decided to lie to me about his own girlfriend being around my daughter. At least what I'm doing is unavoidable, I can't keep Dahlia locked inside and away from potentially bumping into the girl next door.

Kara goes back inside for a minute, and comes back out with a folder full of papers. Homework.

She sits across from me, scrawling the occasional words on a page. I keep reading my book. It's nice.

I look up every minute or so to see how much progress she's made, and her pace is good. I don't want to interrupt and ask what exactly she's working on, but I'm impressed either way.

"You hum when you read," she says after a few minutes. "Do you realize you do that?"

"What are you talking about?" I wasn't humming. I'm too focused on the words on the page to be doing anything else.

"Exactly what I said. You hum."

"No, I don't," I say.

She puts a hand out in question.

"Okay, you're right. I lied. I haven't been sitting here for the past ten minutes listening to you or anything."

I look at her like I'm waiting for her to say she's kidding, but she's being serious. How have I never noticed that before?

I almost start to apologize, but I get the feeling I don't need to. She doesn't seem irritated or overstimulated. In fact, she looks like she could sit there and listen to me hum all day.

Kara grabs the book I was reading, snapping me out of my thoughts. It's facing down, so she starts by scanning the back.

"*If* I read this kind of thing, it might sound interesting."

"It is," I say. "You should try it out, you might realize you've been a closeted romance book lover this entire time."

She rolls her eyes and flips it over to the cover.

Then she freezes, and the energy between us shifts.

"Reya," she whispers.

"What?" I stand, something telling me to worry. The way she says my never has never sounded so vulnerable. Or scared.

I didn't know Kara could feel those things.

She doesn't respond, just continues staring at the cover. The closer I look, the more I think she's not actually seeing it. She's zoned out, her mind elsewhere.

"What? Are you good?"

She shakes her head so slightly, it's almost unnoticeable.

"You're scaring me. Can you speak, please?"

Her beautifully manicured hand holds up the book, the front cover facing my direction.

"Autumn Lane— Autumn Owens. That's your best friend?" Her voice sounds weak and strained.

I nod, confused. What the hell does Autumn have to do with anything? How does she even know her, or know that she uses a pen name?

More questions keep flying around in my head.

"Yeah? So what?"

She shakes her head again.

"So what, Kara?" I snap.

I need to know what has that look on her face. I'm not patient enough for her to simply sit there and stare and not answer me. There's a panicked, wild feeling flowing through my body, and I need her to calm it. She could easily do so, but she's not. Wondering the reason while she stays silent makes it worse and worse by the second.

She slowly puts the book down without looking up at me. If I wasn't freaking out, I'd tell her she's losing points right now. But I'm between angry and concerned, I don't know which one is more prevalent.

If she used her *words*, I might have a clue.

I watch as her lips purse to let out a slow exhale, the kind that's required when someone is stressed.

"Tell me why the hell that book is stressing you out, right now."

When she shakes her head again, I'm ready to explode. It's definitely anger that's winning.

I snatch the book off of the little table and storm around her to go back inside my apartment. I could have a very nice, very relaxing afternoon on my own. I can read my book without anyone's stubborn silence in my proximity.

Her hand reaches out to grab my wrist before I can get past her.

I pause. This is the part where she gives up and tells me, I think. It should be.

A few seconds pass. A few more.

Maybe not.

I go to pull, but then I hear her quietly speak.

"I really like you, Reya."

Oh.

That's not what I thought she was getting at.

"Did this cover make you realize that?" I lift it up and really examine it for the first time. A cartoon cover with a blonde woman and a dark-haired man. They stare after each other, but they stand apart.

It's beautiful artwork, but nothing about it would make me think of Kara.

"Your best friend is Autumn Owens," she says again, but this time it's a statement. Her voice sounds hollow.

"That is correct."

"Your best friend is dating Miles Cress."

I squint, and shift my weight to one foot. I don't like where this is going. I don't like how defeated the words sound.

"Yeah, actually. How do you know that?"

When she buries her face in her hands, I think I suddenly know. I think the only scenario in which her reaction makes sense is...

"I never asked his name," I whisper. "Your ex, I—"

"Nope. You didn't." When she looks up at me, her eyes are sad. "Miles is my ex-husband, and I'm fairly certain your best friend hates my guts."

I stagger backwards like I've been wounded.

This can't be real.

"You're kidding," I breathe.

But I know she's not kidding.

She's shaking her head aggressively, and if I didn't know any better I would think she was about to start crying.

This can not be happening.

I run inside my apartment. My fight or flight mode has been activated, and I'm choosing flight. I have to go, I have to get far away from what I just learned.

My car keys are sitting on my kitchen counter. I snatch them up and storm outside again, aiming towards the parking lot without looking in her direction.

"Wait, sunshine—I—"

"Don't call me that right now," I say as I struggle to take in air.

I stumble going down the stairs, and catch myself on the railing before I can fall. I'm being stupid, and irresponsible, and need to get my head on straight, but it all feels so impossible. Everything does.

She places a hand on my arm, pleading with me.

"I didn't know! Can't you tell I'm just as shocked as you are?"

That might be true, sure. I wouldn't know, because my mind is foggy, and everything feels wrong, and I trust nothing.

Nothing.

Autumn is my *family*. She's so important to me.

And she spent a lot of time crying on my shoulder over what this woman did to her.

"Even if, I mean..." I'm on the move again, needing to get to my car. "Do you have any idea how long I've held a grudge towards you? I've hated you for *years*. You *bullied* my best friend. You tossed her out, and gave her no choice but to live in her car." She nods, but I'm not done. "In the middle of *winter!*"

She nods along, admitting to it all. That's good at least. I already know everything, lying wouldn't help her case.

"I haven't even fully forgiven *Miles* for that yet, and he's done everything in his power to redeem himself! You've done nothing. You're not even a better person than you used to be," I point out.

She winces like my words are a physical attack, and I feel bad the second they're out. I can't help that I don't have a filter, but I can own what I say. I do own those words, as hurtful as they are.

Kara's not a better person. She still doesn't care about anyone's feelings but her own.

I thought she cared about mine, but what if it's all in my head? I fell for her suspiciously fast, and it's all been so intense. What if I want to believe she cares about me, so I've convinced myself she does?

What does that even change? Nothing.

She'll still be the person that did what she did, and acts how she acts.

It's not enough that it's not directed at me anymore. It could be, at any time.

And Autumn...oh my god, it would hurt her so bad to find out. She'd be crushed. Heartbroken. Betrayed.

"Reya, I am," she says softly as she follows after me. "I have. I mean, I'm at least learning a lot. In therapy. Because I *want* to be better. And if I wasn't so sure just how unwelcome my presence would be in either of their lives, I'd apologize. Not because I deserve forgiveness, but because she should know that *I* am the fucked up one."

The fucked up one, my thoughts repeat her words over and over.

The fucked up one. I don't have room for that in my life. I have a daughter to protect.

"I can't do this," I gasp.

"No, no, no." She's panicking now. I make the mistake of looking back at her face, and she's more distraught than I ever knew she could be capable of. "Please don't leave. Talk to me."

I plop my head against the top of my car door, and the second my face is hidden I start to cry.

"I need space. I need to think," I wheeze. "They're my friends. Both of them. They're having a baby, and they worked so hard to have–" My sentence is cut off by my own uncontrollable sobs.

She starts to rub a comforting pattern on my back, but I can't handle it.

"I need space," I repeat quietly.

I hear her sniffle, and even the realization that she's crying doesn't convince me to turn around.

"Okay," she rasps. "Okay, fine. Space. Take it."

I step back, scuffing my feet on the ground as I give myself room to open my car door. I get inside without another look or another word. I start the engine, staring out the windshield, but not seeing anything.

Maybe I need a minute before I drive away.

"You'll come back, right?" she asks, her muffled voice coming from my left. "We'll talk?"

I give one nod, and hope it's enough. I wait for her to go, but I'm too scared to check if she does.

My first instinct is to go to Autumn. To cry on her shoulder, and spill it all, but I know I can't. The timing is terrible. She has enough going on, and I can't be the one to rain on her parade. I can't tell her *this*.

My second instinct is to go to my parents, but they'll take one look at me and want to talk it all out. I'm not ready to reach into the tornado going on in my head and pull out the specific words I need. I just want to let it spin and spin until it's run its course. I'll be able to rifle through the scattered debris a little better then.

I opt for the ice cream shop.

I order a milkshake, but my stomach is in knots. I take maybe two sips as I sit in the corner and stare out the big window. Families come in and out. Couples. Friends. I tune them out the best I can, because they're all just a reminder of how overwhelmed I feel.

They probably glance at me with their peculiar looks, wondering what kind of weirdo is lurking at the far table. Not a lot of them sit inside, despite the chilly day, and I imagine I'm to blame.

Carly doesn't kick me out, ever after the sixth group to hurry out after ordering, so I imagine I'm doing her somewhat of a favor. I'm keeping it quiet.

"Hey," a soft voice comes from in front of me. My stare focuses back in, away from the dark clouds I'd be watching. Carly stands in front of me, a pitying smile on her face. "Sorry, it's closing time."

I blink. I must have been sitting here for hours.

"Thanks," I tell her. My voice is harsh and raspy from not being used, and I clear it.

She walks away with nothing else, and I'm relieved. I dig in my wallet only to find a twenty, and don't even care. I drop it in the tip jar as I leave.

25

The plan was to get home, get some sleep, and knock on her door first thing in the morning. I don't want to leave her hanging, I care about her *so* much. If I had the capacity for this conversation tonight, I'd choose to have it tonight.

I don't get to choose. She walks in behind me before I even set my bag down. Her face is red and puffy, splintering my heart into a million pieces. She still looks like an angel, I don't think there's any scenario in which her appearance would stop taking my breath away.

"Hi," I say.

She stands frozen, looking like she has something to say but isn't sure how. Exactly why I think this isn't the time to talk, but I don't have it in me to tell her to go now. Her presence makes me feel whole.

Things have changed so fast, I shock myself by even thinking the words.

Before I can bring up what my plan was, she strides towards me and wraps her arms around me. The strength with which she squeezes me is slightly alarming, but I don't care. I inhale the flowery scent of her skin, and feel like it's the first time I've been able to focus all day. Everything will be okay as long as I have this.

Her. We're going to be okay, no matter what happens or what anyone thinks. Even if we have to keep this a secret for–

"We have to stop this," she whispers.

I nod as best I can into the crook of her neck.

"I don't need space anymore, I just needed to–

"No, *this*," she says, and squeezes me tighter. "Whatever we are, we can't be it anymore."

There's a ringing in my ears. The ground feels like it caves in beneath me.

"No," I say instinctively as I pull away. Her arms take a few seconds to drop, but they do. "We can be whatever we want, it's fine."

"It's not fine," she insists. "It won't ever be, so we need to do this now. Before things get too serious, or–"

"Uh, hate to break it to you right now of all times, but it's already too serious."

Kara blinks at me a few times before shaking her head.

"You only think that."

"Who are you to say I only *think* I'm in love with you?" I ask, too loudly.

She should be able to tell by now, especially after my intense reaction earlier. How could she think I'd flip out like that if there weren't serious feelings here?

She admitted to liking me, almost as soon as I admitted to myself that I *more* than like her. I never really thought we'd be on the same page, but we're so many chapters apart. It's almost laughable.

I watch her stumble back, *still* shaking her damned head.

"You don't mean that."

"Don't tell me what I mean," I growl.

Her stubbornness is something I've grown to love about her, but not in this case. She's not allowed to put her foot down when it comes to what I feel.

I think this might be the most sure I've been. My body knows it needs her. The distance she's putting between us is already leaving an ache in my bones.

I can't do this. I can't lose her.

"What is your problem?"

She laughs, and it's a hollow, sad sound.

"I don't have a problem yet. But I will if we keep this up."

"What do you mean?"

"She's your best friend," she says quietly. "If I were to become your girlfriend or something, I'd have to see them, be around them and—" She blows out a deep, steadying exhale, and I just want to hold her again. I even try to, but she backs away further. Every inch between us hurts more and more. "I was so sure I'd never have to see him again. I can't do it."

I watch as she shudders, and my mind shoots to the worst case scenario. I'm concerned, not just for her, but for Autumn. For myself.

"What did he do, Kara?" She shakes her head, refusing to tell me. "If it's really bad, I'll never want to see him again anyway! Then it'll work out fine, no need to—"

"No, stop. Seriously, stop. I have to go."

"Why can't you just—"

"I have to go," she repeats.

I stand there in shock, in pain, as it's now her turn to run down to her car, and there's nothing I can do. I want to ignore her, I want to refuse to let her leave. But I know, deep in my gut, that I can't.

She needs to be alone right now, just like I needed it earlier.

God, I just hope that she feels as strongly as I do. If she does, there's no way this is getting in between us. It's so small of a detail. It's so easy to solve. Maybe I only go over to Autumn's place from now on, but never invite her here. Maybe she'll be so busy as a new mom that she won't have any time for me anyway.

I don't know what details the future will bring, all I know is that I want to be wherever Kara is. My stomach twists, not knowing where she's headed or when I'll see her next.

Kara disappears for five days.

I go about things as best as I can in that time, and pretend I'm fine when Caleb dropped Dahlia off that first night. I've taken her to the park, and to the mall, and to a birthday party of some cousin on Caleb's side. He offered to take her, but I'd never so easily give up time on my days. I was a little awkward around the people I don't know, but there were snacks to graze on, and Dahlia wanted to head out early anyway.

He picked her up last night, and I think I've snapped a little. I have sent Kara no less than ten text messages. I've called her at least once a day, hoping for a miracle. She has to come back at some point, because she pays rent here. Tim requires a thirty-day notice to move out, and I don't think she would be the type to ignore that.

I really hope.

I'm scared to sit outside, as much as I want the fresh air. As much as I want to see her. This is something that can't sneak up on me. My guard is down so low, and my pain is so close to the surface. I need to prepare. I need to do it when I feel ready to do it.

Yet, any plan to protect myself is thrown out the window when I hear the familiar sound. It's quieter than usual, like she's trying to go unheard.

No chance. I'd never mistake it for anything else.

I shoot up off the couch, and practically leap for my front door. Hers is just closing behind her as I reach it, and I manage to keep myself from crying the second it does. It feels like a sign I don't want. A metaphor I don't need.

I knock three times.

"Open the door, Kara."

Her response is close, right on the other side of it.

"There's no point," says her muffled voice.

I try the handle, not opposed to letting myself in without permission, but it's already locked.

"That's not true. Stop being stubborn."

She doesn't respond, so I press my ear against the door. I don't know what I'm hoping to hear, I just want *something*. I had become so used to our routine, to getting so excited every time we hung out. Every day without it has felt so empty. So wrong.

I've taken my time to process, and I've let her take hers, but this is something else. This is now her attempt to decide that we can't work through this, and I want to refuse. I want to scream and say that none of it matters, even though some of it does.

I can not believe just how small this town is.

What are the odds, *how* are the odds?

I'm seriously in love with Miles' ex-wife. I've daydreamed about getting married, and buying a house, and living happily ever after with a woman that made both him and my best friend miserable for a long time.

And maybe I'm a terrible friend, but I don't care. I don't want any of that to change the way my life has been going lately. I didn't know who Kara was when this started. I was in too deep when I found out. They would understand if I told them.

But I am definitely not telling them, not anytime soon. Getting Kara to calm down and talk to me is my main priority, and I have to make it happen before six o'clock tonight. Once Caleb drops off my baby girl, that's where my focus needs to be. For the four days we're together every week, she deserves every ounce of my attention. No relationship will ever change that.

Even when it feels fucking impossible.

———ele———

"Are you okay, mama?"

I look at her in the rearview mirror, and give her my best attempt at a smile.

"Why wouldn't I be, princess?"

"'Cause when I look like that, you always ask if I'm okay."

"But it's usually just because you're tired, huh?" My daughter nods. "I'm tired right now."

"You could take a nap," she tells me with a grin. It's a repeat of words I've said to her too many times.

She never agrees to a nap. I'm not agreeing now either, even though it sounds really nice. I'm not lying, I am tired. Tired in every way a person could possibly be.

Sometimes I hear Kara's music through the walls, although it's lower than normal. I think the only reason I hear it is because I'm *trying* to hear something.

It's torture to have her right next door. I've been hurt in breakups before, badly enough that I wanted to show up at their door and beg for the smallest scraps. Doing just that is too easy in this scenario. I've already done it once. It's taking all the self control I have not to do it again. I've always felt a rush when leaving my house, just over the possibility of seeing her. It was always so exciting. Now it's more of an anxious feeling. I'm scared of her reaction to being in my presence, but I'm also desperate for it. I need to gaze into those green eyes in the same way I need to eat food a few times a day. It's fuel.

God, it's dramatic. The only reason I haven't completely lost my mind is because my daughter needs me. I don't know how I'll survive when she's gone in a few weeks. I've been lonely before, but that's going to take the cake. Knowing it's coming is making me so tense. "Are you hungry? Should I make dinner when we get home?"

Dahlia looks at me through the mirror with so much excitement.

"Broccoli?"

"Of course!" I say with all the enthusiasm I can find.

It is pretty exciting that my child loves vegetables.

I'm convinced that no child has ever loved broccoli as much as my girl does. I've come up with some interesting ways to include it in our dinners, much to my own dismay.

I give her complete credit for the fact that I don't have scurvy.

She wiggles in her car seat, and I know if it wasn't there, she'd be jumping up and down.

What I end up making isn't that creative, just a stir fry I throw together with some things I needed to use up, and Dahlia's beloved broccoli.

It sure smells incredible, though

She runs up to her chair, where a plate of food is already sitting on the table in front of her. She's most likely going to eat around the chicken, and that will be a whole ordeal that I'll put off until she claims she's done. I can always convince her to have an extra bite or two by promising something in return. I've got ten minutes to think of what it'll be tonight.

As I pick at my own plate, not feeling very hungry, I think of Kara. Again. I wonder if she can smell our dinner from her apartment. I hope she can. I hope she wishes she was sitting here with us, and feeling terrible about avoiding me. I picture it, her having a realization so strong that she heads straight over and starts banging on my door. I picture it over and over until I convince myself it'll happen.

I wait, so patiently, for that knock.

"I'm done, mommy."

I blink, her voice pulling me out of my thoughts. Of course there isn't a knock.

"Can you do a couple more bites of chicken?"

She shakes her head, as predicted.

"Will you take a couple more bites if I let you pick a movie for us to watch tonight?"

Her eyes widen in that curious, deep thinking kind of way that only children can manage to express. If I made that face, people would just think I looked crazy.

"Okay, I'll take only two more bites," she tells me, and holds up two fingers. "But I don't know what movie yet. I have to think about it."

"Take all the time you need, princess."

26

"So?" my mother asks.

I shake my head, pulling myself from the depths of my inner turmoil.

"Sorry mom, what did you say?"

"I asked if you girls want to come over for a bit? We've finally got the play area set up in the backyard, and the sun is out and shining."

It's still barely sixty degrees outside, but if you get my daughter on a swing set? It could be a blizzard out there and she'd still be the happiest girl on the planet.

"Dahlia would love that." I glance over to where she's sitting on the floor, crayons in hand as she forcefully presses them into the paper of her coloring book. What's the fun in paying attention to the lines, anyway? "We'll get dressed and head over."

"Just the two of you?" she asks.

"Um, yeah? Since when would it–" I swear my heart stops for a couple of excruciating seconds as the realization hits me. Memories flash in my mind of that crazy morning. My mom wanted to meet her so badly, and I wanted to keep her all to myself. I regret that. I wish I had let them talk, get to know each other.

My mom always sees the best in people. She would've seen more in Kara than most people do, and now she'll never get to. She'll never understand, and no one's ever going to.

I pull the phone away from my ear long enough to let out the shaky breath that's so close to turning into a full blown sob.

I clear my throat before I speak again.

"It's just us two," I say.

The few seconds of silence on her end are loud, because that woman knows me better than I want her to.

"Okay, bug. We'll see you soon. Drive safe."

"Why don't you take the princess out to play on the swings, grandpa? We'll be right there."

Dahlia jumps up and down, and grabs on to her grandpa's hand with all the impatience in the world. He doesn't take much convincing, laughing and pretending his granddaughter is the strongest six year old on the planet as he "tries" to hold his ground. She thinks it's the best thing in the world, and I agree.

"What is that mother of yours feeding you? Those muscles are huge!"

I smile to myself as I watch them head for the back door. It's a sight that numbs the pain for sure.

"Honey," my mother starts. Before saying anything else, she walks up to me and puts her arms around me. There's something about her hug that has everything I've been trying to push down, rise to the surface. "Are you okay?"

As soon as the question is out of her mouth, I'm crying. It's the most I've cried in front of her since I was a kid, and I almost feel bad about it. She just keeps holding me, rubbing my back soothingly.

"No," I admit once I get enough air in. "No, I'm really not."

I hear my daughter squeal from outside, and it scares me into pulling back and wiping my eyes. I don't ever want her to see me like this. I want to be strong for her.

My mother, realizing what I'm doing, grabs my hand and guides me to her room. I sit on the edge of her bed, and she closes the door to ensure we won't be snuck up on.

"I've never seen you like this," she says softly.

I just nod. I've never felt like this.

"That woman? Kara?"

Even just hearing her name said makes my heart feel like it's cracking in new places. I can't handle that she exists, she's real, and she's out there somewhere and I'll never know where *ever again*. I'll be on the outside, wondering forever. I'll keep getting painfully small glimpses until her lease is up, and then I won't even have that anymore.

Hard to say which one is worse, but I'll find out.

"Yeah."

"She was the one playing the music, wasn't she?"

"Yeah."

"It's hard to see how that turned into this," my mom says.

I lean my head on her shoulder, sniffling hard.

"It's so complicated." My voice cracks on the last word, but I focus on breathing instead of crying.

Then I find the strength to tell her the story. It sounds so small when it's put into words, but I try to emphasize that it was so much bigger than just a few hookups. It felt like so much more than a few weeks.

"I get that," she says. "I've been there."

I almost ask her if it was my dad she's been there with, but it would hurt me to hear any other possible answer.

I only want to hear the version where it's fully possible that I could end up with someone like her. That this *otherworldly* pull we have to each other is for a reason. I've had enough lessons. I don't want this to be one.

I'm sobbing all over again, I've been doing it so much lately. It's starting to feel like my new normal. Autumn would be appalled.

Autumn. I wish I could talk to her like I'm talking to my mom. I wish I had the guts to confess everything, and feel positive that she would understand. That I could run to Kara with solid proof that everything is okay.

But I can't. And it's not.

27

Dahlia and I are driving home from school. She takes the bus most of the time, because I'm typically off work between the time they get on the bus, and the time she gets home. With all the stops, it takes about a half hour for her to get there, so I always beat her to the drop off spot across the street.

But today was a shockingly smooth one, and I decided to leave early. They didn't need me there, and I didn't need to be there. I haven't been much help as it is in my current state. I have enough energy to be present for my baby girl, and that's it.

"We can't hold them anymore because they're too fast. Jackson was holding the little one yesterday, and it ran out of his hands *so fast*! Mrs. Sky had to find it, and it took her *forever*. She was not happy."

"I don't blame her," I respond. "I'd be pretty grumpy if I had to go chasing down a lizard."

She laughs at that.

"Yeah, maybe I'd be grumpy too."

I glance in the rearview mirror to see her attention go out her window, and to the houses we pass. Sometimes I wonder if it bothers her that we don't have a house. She's never commented on the fact, or even said much about her dad's place when he got it. I know it's not a competition between him and I, but sometimes I still feel like I'm losing.

Until the moments when she jumps into my arms with all the excitement in the world, and I'm reminded that it's all that really matters. We have a good thing going, my daughter and I. I hope when she grows up, that's the part she remembers. Not that he had a bigger bedroom to give her.

"Is that Kara?"

My heart stops at that name.

"What do you mean, honey?"

But before she answers, I see her. It's pouring down rain, and windy to top it all off, and she's just walking on the side of the road. There isn't even a sidewalk here, her small frame in dark clothing could be easy to miss. She could easily get hurt.

What is she doing?

I know she won't be happy to see me. I know I'm heading into battle, and it won't be easy to convince her to get in.

I just have to try. There's no other option.

"Are we getting her, mama?"

"Yes, baby girl. It's not safe for her to be walking in this weather."

"Oh, yeah," she says, nodding like she knows just as much as I do. "So not safe."

I pull over, just ahead of where she's walking. Every ounce of my focus is latched onto what I can see through my mirror. She freezes when she notices my car in her periphery. I catch the moment she glances up, and realizes just what car it is.

I almost expect her to turn around, and start running in the opposite direction.

My breath catches when she instead starts forward, and only stops again when she's standing at my passenger door. I almost forget to unlock it, with how caught off guard I feel.

As soon as it clicks, she's opening the door and plopping herself down into my passenger seat.

My first instinct is to question if this is really happening. I've been missing her face, wishing I could see her, let alone be near her for so many weeks now. I think I started to convince myself it would never happen. Yet somehow, she's right here. I can smell her perfume, despite how drenched she is from the rain. It wasn't enough to rid her of the musky cherry scent.

I look away from her, hoping to hide the way tears well up in my eyes.

I can't believe that, of all things, is really making me cry. It's so ridiculous, but it makes so much sense at the same time.

From the corner of my eye, I watch her pull the door shut. Her fingers go to work angling every vent towards her body, and she turns the heat up to the max without checking to see if that was okay with me. It's more than okay, because I can hear her teeth chattering, and I know that wrapping her up in my arms isn't on the table.

"What are you doing?" I ask in a quiet voice. As if speaking too loud might make her realize just who I am, and whose car she's in.

She doesn't answer me. Her hands rub together in a desperate attempt to build enough friction to warm them.

"What happened to your car?" I ask.

She doesn't answer again.

"It's not safe to walk out there," Dahlia tells her.

"You're right. It's not," she responds.

I didn't realize my heart could break anymore that it already was, but hearing her voice does it.

I put the car in drive, and decide I need to be moving. Partially so she can't run out back into danger, and partially because I need something else to focus on.

But it's not enough to calm my churning stomach.

"Are you okay?" I try again.

Nothing.

I don't know what I'm expecting, but I keep going.

"Were you just headed home?"

She nods, and I'm relieved that I get any response at all.

"Why were you walking in the rain?" Dahlia asks the question this time, and I smile. "It's too cold."

Kara turns to face her, and the breath I hadn't realized I'd been holding rushes out of me.

"You don't like the rain?"

"No," Dahlia replies. "Well, actually sometimes I do. It's just cold when you walk in it."

"Sometimes being cold is nice. Do you like ice cream?"

"I love ice cream!"

"Ice cream makes you cold."

"Just my mouth gets cold."

They go back and forth a bit. Kara tries to find an equivalent to her walking in the rain that Dahlia will relate to. I think it's hopeless, but I listen.

If she's not going to talk to me, it's still nice to hear her.

It's excruciating, and makes me want to scream, but somehow it's also just... nice.

"Are you coming to our house again?"

I grip the steering wheel a little tighter. I bet to my daughter it feels like just yesterday she was standing in our kitchen, baking with us.

She shakes her head.

"If you come over, my mom will make you cookies."

"I bet she would." Her voice is soft.

I would make her cookies if she wanted them. I'd do anything she wanted.

I'm disappointed when our apartment building comes into view. I don't want to watch her head into her apartment, knowing I can't follow. I don't want to keep wondering what she's up to on the other side of the wall.

Probably homework. She's always doing homework. I can picture in my head just how it goes. Her hair tucked behind her ears, tapping her pencil against her chin.

Everything hurts all over again, like my previous pain has now been soaked in gasoline and set on fire. We sit in the car for a few minutes after Kara gets out.

"Why are you and Kara sad today?"

I turn towards her and smile again. It is a genuine one. She's just so observant, and smart, and kind.

"Sometimes adults don't like to talk about their feelings, even when they really should," I explain. "If you ever think that you shouldn't say how you're feeling, you can always tell me. I'm always here to support you, okay?"

"I'll always tell you."

"How are you feeling right now?"

She purses her lips to think.

"Um, I'm bored. Can we play with my toys?"

Sounds like a fun time to me. Although, anything sounds more fun than letting the woman who's currently walking away from me do it again. I have to get this under control, and move on with my life. It hurts too much to keep wishing things were different.

They *will* be different. I have too much good in my life, I will not let this pain ruin a second more of it.

28

I get home from dropping off Dahlia and immediately run to wash my face in our main bathroom. I've been trying to teach her how to wash her own face, and we play with self care like we're giving ourselves spa treatments. It's a win-win because she eats it up, giggles the whole time, and it's good for my skin. I don't do it as often as I should.

Caleb was kind enough to tell me that I had bright blue paint all over the side of my face and in my hair, after a very crafty little afternoon. Funny that my child who had been looking at me all day didn't mention it, but then again she might not have noticed. I do dye my hair pink, maybe she thought a blue face was the next normal thing for me to do.

I'm so grateful it's washable paint as I locate the strands of hair that are stuck together with it and rinse them as best I can in the sink. A normal person would probably take a whole shower, but I already did that this morning and I refuse to waste the shampoo. That stuff is not cheap when you don't want your hair color to fade within a week.

I'm startled by a noise to my left, and I glance at the wall there. It's just a wall, nothing else. I shake off what I thought I heard and go back to the task at hand.

But then I hear it again.

I step closer, straining my ears to make it out. My heart slams in my chest because I know what this wall is. I know who it must be that I'm hearing. I press my ear all the way against it, desperate for anything from her. Even if this is so out of line, if I shouldn't be eavesdropping, I don't care. I don't have the energy left to care.

Expecting to hear her voice on a phone call, or overhearing whatever she's watching, I gasp when I realize it's not either of those things. It's the heartbreaking, earth shattering sound of her crying. The woman who doesn't cry.

Not in the way that I don't cry, because I know I'm a huge baby. It doesn't take much. But Kara? She really never did, not once in the time I've known her.

I forgot just how thin the walls were until this moment. My bare back falls against the cool wall, sending a shiver through me that I ignore. It doesn't feel like anything compared to the crack that's deepening in my heart at the sound of her sobs.

All I want is to tell her that I'm here. She's spent too damn long feeling alone, and blaming herself, and I can't fucking stand that I know she's doing it now. It's the whole reason she's done this to us. The reason she broke my heart. She doesn't forgive herself for being who she is, for making mistakes, for letting fear poison all of the relationships in her life until she felt so completely unworthy.

On the surface– sure, she dumped me because she has a rocky past with one of my best friends. It was too easy of an excuse to push me away. I should've known we were walking on thin ice. Every time it hit me, just how much I was starting to care about her, I should've known.

The worst, honest truth of that, is that I probably did. But she made me feel so good that I didn't care. I would've risked it all for her. I still would.

I remember crying over Olivia, and Caleb, and even a couple of exes before them. I remember being hurt, but it never felt like this. In reality, my pride might've been hurt more than most things. With Caleb I was simply exhausted, and then I was relieved when we ended things.

I've never wanted to rip my own heart out of my chest, because I'm not strong enough to take what it's doing to me. I'm so desperate to numb the feeling, and yet I don't want it to go away. Not when it's the only thing tying us together.

That, and the pair of socks that have been sitting on my bedroom floor for the last month. It would feel too final if I picked them up. Right now, I can delude myself into thinking they're just sitting there waiting for her to come back for them.

I'll give her shit for "trashing my apartment," she'll laugh before she throws them right in my face, and I'll pretend it's the worst thing she could do. I'm not a bad actress, I could convince her I've never smelled anything more foul in my entire life. When she pretends it offends her, I'd sweep her off her feet so she falls back on the bed.

I hear her crying start up again, and throw my head down in defeat. I couldn't be more of a fool, sitting here daydreaming about a time that's likely lost forever.

A huge piece of me is aching to bang on this wall and beg her to let me in. To give me anything.

A bigger piece is aware that it's pointless. She doesn't back down when she's decided something.

The sound of her bathtub draining fills my ears. Somehow that gives me enough confidence to shout, I don't even bother to worry if it's loud enough to drown me out.

"I can't do this anymore!"

The ache dulls the smallest amount, as if I've tricked myself into thinking I've done something that's going to make a difference.

I sit there for a few more minutes, wondering if I'll get any more glimpses into her evening. It remains silent when the tub is emptied, and I know she's gone. Not just because she isn't making a sound, but because I think I'd *feel* her if she was still close by.

Soulmates have to be real, because there's no other way to explain how that works.

I finally decide to stand, now that my ass is numb from being on the hard tile floor so long. My stiff joints protest at the movement, and I let out a small groan of discomfort as I straighten.

"*Reya?*"

I freeze, sure that I've absolutely lost my mind. That, or there's a ghost in my bathroom. I did used to always say she was one.

I don't dare move, I barely breathe. I really am insane for waiting to hear it again when it was no doubt my overactive imagination.

The continuous quiet makes me snap.

"Get a grip," I whisper to myself, before my feet drag me out into the hall.

I almost trip over the sneakers I'd been too unsettled to remember to take off by my front door. I'm going to really hurt myself if I keep being such a mess. I shouldn't be trusted anywhere near shoes that aren't actually tied on my feet. They're dangerous.

I grab them to bring them over to the rack I have in the living room. Even that's a mess, not big enough to contain the mess of

Dahlia and I. I can put a lot of that blame on her, she owns way more shoes than I do, and she throws them in the general vicinity whenever she wants them off.

With nothing better to do, I sit down on the floor in front of the pile and start organizing. I find pairs and set them together neatly in front of the rack. I separate them too, putting hers on one side, and mine on the other.

One, small, sudden thud sounds at my front door and it scares me so much that the shoe in my hand is thrown towards it with all the force I have.

What the fuck?

"Reya, please. I know you're in there."

"What the fuck," I whisper. "Kara?" My voice is a desperate plea, needing this to be real.

"Yeah. Hi."

I don't want her voice to be muffled, but for some reason I just can't move. This must be what it's like to be in shock.

"Am I imagining this right now?"

"Maybe I'm the one imagining it," she answers. *"Hard to say unless you open the door."*

"I don't... What are you doing?"

"I don't know. I'm not thinking straight." Her voice cracks mid sentence, and my eyes fill with tears as if hers are contagious. *"I just need you, sunshine."*

I shake my head to myself, allowing some logical thought to break through the pain.

"You can't do this. It's not fair."

"I know it's not," is all she says.

"If I open that door, you're just going to fuck me up all over again."

"*You might be overestimating my strength there.*"

"How can I? You were strong enough to walk away from me, and you've held out this long."

"*I'm a fucking idiot,*" she whispers. "*I want a time machine.*"

"To stop yourself from ever moving in next to me?" I ask.

To prevent everything that's happened between us from happening.

I don't have it in me to wish the same.

"*No, fuck that. Meeting you is hands down the best thing that has ever happened to me. Ever,*" she emphasizes. The words make my stomach flip, and I am in agony over how much I want them to be true.

But if that were the truth, this wouldn't be where we've ended up, right? There's no way she would've done this to me.

"You might be the worst thing that's ever happened to me." I say the words so softly that she doesn't hear them. I'm not looking to hurt her, despite it all.

"*Please open the door.*"

That sentence triggers something in me that causes words to fall out of my mouth like fire from a dragon.

"That sounds really familiar, babe. How many times have I asked that of you, just to get a big fat nothing done about it? Am I supposed to just give you everything I've got, and be okay with getting nothing in return?" I shake my head, willing my voice to stay steady through the torrent of my extreme emotions. "I can't handle opening this door and knowing you're never going to open yours for me. I've played this game before, and I'm *not* going to do it with you! I deserve better."

Every fibre of my being seems to scream in protest of the words I just said. I might mean them, or at least desperately want to, but my feet are begging me to let them move towards her. My fingers itch to turn the lock. My arms are desperate to be around her.

"You're so right. You do deserve better, and I want *to be better for you."* She sniffles, and curses, and it's just then I realize that it's pouring rain out there. She's probably soaked, and this probably isn't the circumstance in which it's a nice thing. *"I thought I was doing us both a favor, but there's no universe where I could believe this is good for me. It's killing me, Reya. I fucking need you, and I'm so sorry that I didn't realize that before I hurt you like this. Before I broke your trust. I hope you know how sorry I am, even if you don't let me in. I'll understand if you need to protect your peace. I know I've been anything but a peaceful presence in your life."*

I give myself time to take it all in. She isn't going to go anywhere while I do, the sound of her voice telling me that much.

I've felt it killing me, too. Does that mean I should forgive her so casily? Giving her another chance to do this all over again is the most terrifying thought. It would be worse somehow, and I can't imagine it getting worse than this. If I'm already at the bottom of the barrel, she has the capability of burying me far beneath the earth.

I approach the door, and lean my forehead against it before I do anything rash.

"Definitely not peaceful," I agree. A small thud sounds from her side, and I have a feeling we'd look symmetrical from a side view.

"I'm so sorry," she cries.

"You're not someone I can recover from."

"What can I do? Please tell me what–"

"I don't know. I've never been so scared in my life."

And I can't tell if it's of letting you in or letting you go.

Except... I do know. It hits me as the words fly out of my mouth. Fuck it.

I flick the lock, and pull the door open faster than she can catch on. She stumbles forward, and I put a steadying hand on her arm before she can fall into me. I'm not there yet. As far as catching up to tonight's events, I'm mentally still sitting on my bathroom floor listening to her crying through the wall.

If I'm being dramatic? I'm still sitting on the porch with her giggling in my lap before everything went to shit. What I wouldn't give to go back to that moment.

"Hi," she breathes. Her lashes glisten, and streaks of tears still sit on her cheeks. The rain is falling, the wind is blowing, but it looks like the front of her was protected by her huddling against my door.

"Hi."

She nods past me, shivering.

"Can I?"

I step aside wordlessly.

My gaze tracks her as she goes to stand over a vent on the floor that's blowing out hot air. I move to turn the heat up.

"You shouldn't have been out in that weather," I scold.

"It was worth it." Our eyes lock from across the room. "I got in here."

"So, now what? You keep pretending I'm worth it until the smallest thing sets you off and sends you running?"

She winces, and I hate it. I hate feeling like I'm doing something to hurt her, but I have to remind myself that *I'm* the one who's been trying. I went crawling after her again and again while she shut me out.

"Your relationship with your best friend is not a small thing."

"Did I not stand there and tell you that I didn't have to tell her about us? I wouldn't have put you through that, not until you were ready."

"That's the problem. What if I'm never ready, and I just continue to be this secret between you two? It wouldn't end pretty."

"Why bother coming back here tonight if that's what you think."

She hangs her head.

"I want to get there. I mean–I don't *want* to. I've never been good at facing things head on, and if I had it my way, I'd avoid it all forever. But I know that's not how life works. I'm going to have to confront some shit that makes me uncomfortable, especially if that's what it takes for you to forgive me."

"I don't know if I forgive you."

She nods like my words make all the sense in the world.

"I know. I don't forgive me."

I swear the rain started pelting the window so much harder at her words. The sound of it so loud that I had to step closer to her to avoid yelling.

"What's your point? You want me to tell her now?"

"No. I mean, I want you to do whatever you want to do."

I thought I'd felt exhaustion before. I cried over the desire to sleep, or to shut my mind off. I've stood in place at work, or while cooking dinner, and wished I could drop to the ground and rest right there. I've wanted to forget my responsibilities, forget every single thing going on around me, and just check out for a while.

But I am consumed by it right now. Today has been such a roller coaster, that I can't do it anymore. The woman I love is standing in front of me, and I'm so torn between what to do about it, that my body decides for me. We're not going to do anything at all.

I wordlessly begin walking to my room, and I can feel her confusion. I'm sure if I had the energy to look up at her, I'd see that small pout of her bottom lip that is the bane of my existence.

I'm not doing anything about it tonight. She can pout. She can do anything she wants to do, but it won't change the fact that I'm going to bed.

"Reya?" Kara's cautious voice carries to me when I'm already in the other room.

I slowly pull off my clothes, piece by piece until I'm standing in my room completely naked. Underwear is too much work to pull on, but I do snag one of my big t-shirts from my closet and somehow end up with it over my head.

That's when she appears in that doorway, looking hopeless and hopeful all at once.

"Are we not going to–"

"No," I say as I lay down and pull my comforter over my shoulders.

Whoever invented and named the comforter did something right. It *is* comforting. I've always loved getting into bed at night, and feeling embraced by my pillows and blankets. It's the only thing I'm able to acknowledge right now.

I sigh contentedly, as if I have no reason not to.

I drift off almost instantly, only slightly aware of the feeling of someone climbing in the bed next to me.

29

I wake up feeling slightly less burdened than has been my usual, and shuffle through all the files tucked away in my brain to understand why before I even open my eyes.

What's going on today? It's Monday. I have a nine hour shift at work. I went grocery shopping a few days ago, so there are options for dinner if I'm up to cooking after a long day. Maybe I could throw something in my sadly underused slow cooker before I leave the house.

Note to self as soon as my eyes decide to open: Google recipes with the ingredients in my kitchen. Pretty sure I have chicken in the—

A soft snore sounds to my right and I scream, throwing my eyes open as I somehow manage to fling myself right off the side of my bed. I guess I chose to *flight* in the quick panicked second it took me to register my surroundings.

"Woah, woah, woah. What are you doing?" Kara asks.

Kara. Because she's in my bed.

She was sleeping. And snoring.

Her eyes now are slits that tell me she was as suddenly disturbed from her slumber as I was from my thoughts.

"I-I–" I get up from the floor, pulling my shirt down to cover things that probably should've been covered while my ex was in my bed. "What do you mean, what am *I* doing? What are *you* doing? Why are you here?"

Just like that, she stops squinting her eyes and I see the alarm in them before she attempts to collect herself.

"You don't remember?"

"I don't remember my own name this early in the morning. I hadn't made it past the ingredients in my—nevermind. Hold on."

I stomp away to my connected bathroom, and shut the door firmly behind me.

Okay, new task at hand. Now I'm fumbling through my internal files wondering where Kara showing up after a brutal month without her comes in.

Looking at myself in the mirror, I discover that my hair is even more sleep mussed than usual. I flatten it as best I can by running my fingers through it, until I realize it's not going to work, and grab the hairbrush sitting next to my sink.

I remember it feeling like a dream that she was on the other side of my door, crying for me like I'd cried for her every single day for the last month. Who does she think she is? I was in a weakened state last night, too tired to function. My judgment was skewed. She shouldn't be here. I should tell her to fuck off, just like she'd basically told me without words, over and over again.

I have a plan. I'm going to wash my face, brush my teeth, and have a normal little morning. Then I'm going to aggressively throw this door open, and tell her that I refuse to say a word until I have a hot cup of tea in my hands.

I'll appear unaffected, and totally badass, and like the last thing I'm going to let her do is walk back into my life this easily. It's not happening.

When my morning routine is complete, and my stomach growls, I take a deep breath in preparation of the act I'm about to put on. I've always been a good actress, and that will still be true after today. There will be no more pining, or crying, or begging on my end.

No ma'am.

She's not in my room when I emerge from the bathroom and I pause. Did I think she would actually wait around for me? That's not her style. I should've known better than that.

I can't deny that I sure did fucking hope.

With a sigh, I trudge towards the kitchen. I'll make myself a couple pieces of toast with some jelly, and face the day that I will not be in the right mindset for.

Only when my eyes land on the back of her head, her long red hair looking breathtakingly messy, do I notice that I hear the sizzling of something cooking. Or that my kitchen smells like bacon, and garlic, and something else that's sweet.

I'm hallucinating. I have been since last night, *that* or I'm stuck in a very vivid, realistic nightmare.

She turns towards me, finally realizing I'm standing here, and a small smile sits on her lips.

This can't be a nightmare. Not when that look on her face makes me feel like I can conquer anything. It makes me feel unstoppable. Powerful.

When in reality, I keep coming back to the conclusion that I am so fucking *weak* for this woman.

"Hi," she says softly. "I'm making breakfast."

"I can see that," I reply nervously. "I didn't have bacon."

I move close enough to peer over her shoulder, just to confirm with one more of my senses that it's what she's making. I never buy bacon. I love eating it, but the oil splatters when it's cooking and I can't handle that.

I've tried doing it in the oven. It's not the same.

"I ran over and got it from mine," she explains.

I look around, taking in everything else. My oven is on, and although I can't see what's inside, it smells like baked goods. My other weakness.

Yeah, my original plan? The one where I pretend I'm too cool to care? Out the fucking window. I care so much that I might be about to spontaneously explode. I put a finger to the pulse point, willing it to calm down so that doesn't happen. That would be messy.

Kara clears her throat.

"Is this... okay?"

I bite the inside of my lip to allow myself to filter my response. It's more than okay, and I'm mad about that. I should be so mad at her, I should have my guard up, but she makes me lower it so easily.

I nod. "I suppose."

"There are muffins in the oven. I'm frying eggs and making bacon. You didn't have any other breakfast food."

"I didn't have muffins, either," I point out. I have boxed cake mix, I think, but not muffins. Unless she somehow confused the two? Can't say I want red velvet cake for breakfast, but I'd eat them anyway if it made her smile some more.

Her cheeks turn a deep maroon.

"I remembered you using that book when you made them for me." She points to a baking cookbook that's not sitting in the usual place I keep it. "I hope it's okay I used up some of your ingredients. I can replace it all, I just didn't know if you were going to crave something sweet or savory so I did both. I know they don't go great together, and it's not anything fancy. I never really make breakfast, so I had to look up how to fry an egg."

Her face turns a deeper, darker shade and I balk.

What universe did I wake up inside of?

"It all sounds great," I tell her honestly. "Don't worry about anything. This is... nice of you."

She fully spins around to face me, a spatula in her hand. She points it in my direction, very matter-of-factly.

"We don't have to talk or do anything you don't want to do. I can leave as soon as this is all done." She lifts her wrist which contains her smart watch. "The muffins need four more minutes. I'm just about done with this." The spatula is used to wave a circle around my stove, gesturing to her work there. "I'll wash the dishes too, of course. Then I can be out of your hair."

I'm speechless. Who knew that was possible? I blink a few times, hoping to reset my brain function.

"You can stay and eat the food you made."

"Only if you're sure that's okay."

A nagging voice in the back of head says it shouldn't be. I should have learned enough from past experiences to say no, to stand to my ground, or to demand better.

But something about her demeanor, standing in my kitchen and making me breakfast makes me think I might not have to demand anything.

We sit in silence as we eat. I spend most of the time watching her as she avoids eye contact with me. She looks as nervous as I am, but I'm having a hard time knowing if I'm just seeing what I want to see. Because I want to see someone who's thinking up an explanation for why she ran out of my life so fucking fast, and took my heart with her. I want to see someone who really is going to do anything she can to make it better, like she said she would last night.

Wishful thinking is the worst.

The muffins are amazing. It's obvious she followed the recipe well. The bacon is a little undercooked for my liking, and the eggs don't have a drop of seasoning on them. Not that I'm going to complain. The most I've seen her eat in the morning is a power bar, or a cup of yogurt. Unless I cooked for her obviously. I did that a lot in the couple weeks before the breakup. I liked watching her go from someone that was too cool to react to such a kindness, to someone that moaned every time she took her first bite. Sometimes it was an appreciative nod in my direction, her hand covering her mouth so I couldn't see what a mess she was making as she devoured every last crumb.

"How is it?" she asks quietly.

A warm, hopeful feeling floods through me when our eyes meet.

"It was good," I say. Not exactly a lie.

"Now give me the honest answer," she pushes.

I can't help the stupid smile that ends up on my face.

"I wouldn't have eaten it if you'd done a terrible job." Her raised brows force me to continue. "Your cooking skills could use some work, but it wasn't terrible."

"Maybe tomorrow you can help me."

I don't know what to say to that, because what reason do I have for committing to doing this again? I haven't been given one yet. At least not a good one that comes from somewhere other than the feelings I fear I'll always have for her.

I must somehow have forgotten how well she knows me, because she reads most of my doubt on my face.

"I love you, Reya. I'm not going to dance around it, or pretend I'm too cold to have emotions. I won't pressure you to do anything you don't want, I just thought... I thought maybe we could start small. I want to–" She stops to huff out a breath. "Me from a few months ago wouldn't recognize me today, because all I want to do is make you smile. It's all consuming. When you picked me up yesterday, it *hurt* so bad to know I wasn't going to get one. That you could be so close, and look so crushed, and that there was nothing I could do—"

"But there was," I interrupt. "Something you could've done. There was."

"Was there? You barely let me in last night. Would a few hours earlier have made a difference?" She looks down at her plate, mostly empty now. "You smiled when you sat down, and that was the best I've felt since..."

Since she abruptly left me, without thinking about how that would affect me.

I stand from my seat.

"It would have. I've had a horrible few weeks, but something about watching you walk up those stairs after getting out of my car... it felt like the final nail in the coffin. I was literally crying my eyes out, trying to figure out the best path forward to move on. I was going to give Tim my thirty days' notice. I was going to call my mom and see if we could clear out my old bedroom."

Her eyes are glistening with unshed tears, but I'm not the reason they're really there. This is on her, all of it. The words coming out of my mouth are the result of what she did to me.

"I want so badly to make it all up to you, if that's even possible. I never wanted to hurt you like that."

I can see the sincerity behind her words. She thinks she means it. She thinks she wants to move forward.

"You did want to, or you wouldn't have. Sure, maybe you've changed your mind, but don't tell me you didn't want to hurt me. You knew what you were doing."

"It felt like I had no choice!" she shouts. "I was already scared out of my mind because of how fast you got under my skin. I thought I had walls up that would keep everyone away, and then you made them fall in a matter of weeks. And I was *glad* they fell, and that fucking terrified me. Then I find out that your *best* friend is someone I've done wrong in the past, someone who's definitely heard about my other wrongdoings from my ex-husband. Some-one who'd probably want to rip you away from me if she knew what was going on. I panicked, and—"

"And now," I interrupt. "I know that you're capable of doing it again. If one little thing scares you, and you can't talk to me about it? You run away before thinking things through? This will always go up in flames. I'm always going to get burned."

I'm crying now, and I'm filled with a bit of self-loathing for allowing her to see me so weak.

She stands from her seat, and I see the urge in her to comfort me. I raise a hand to stop her, and her face scrunches in a way that tells me she's hurting just as much as I am.

But she doesn't cry, she doesn't lose her cool. She takes a few deep breaths, keeping the space between us.

"I'm so sick of hurting people wherever I go. I thought it was easier that way, if I never gave anyone a chance. I thought if I let everyone see the worst of me, I wouldn't risk any of the good that was left." She grabs the plates from the table, and walks them over to the sink. She doesn't wash them, just leans over it with her palms on the counter. "And then you were just so... *you*. So *human*. You just let yourself exist, and you feel your emotions, and I've never met anyone who did it so perfectly before. You tore down years of protective barriers just by being yourself, it was like your superpower."

"But I didn't," I stop her. "Obviously. You found a way to build them back up in a matter of hours."

"People do stupid stuff when they're scared. I'm no different, as much as I've tried to be," she confesses.

"We could have figured it out together. We could have come up with a plan."

But you wouldn't even try.

I begged her. I let myself be the weakest, most desperate version of myself as I begged, and it got me nowhere.

"Thank you for breakfast," I add. "Don't worry about the cleanup, I just need you to go."

"I don't want to go," she says softly, turning to face me.

"I know. I never wanted you to either."

The sentence stabs another hole through my heart.

She nods, accepting that I'm not going to budge.

"We'll talk again?" she asks.

I tell her we will only to get her to leave so I can sit down on the cold floor and cry. We were barely even together. Coming from her, we strictly *weren't* together, but it felt like the worst breakup of my life anyway.

I had to grieve, and process without even really knowing her.

I don't know how to undo all of that, *because* I barely know her.

30

I 've seen what I needed to see of my life without Kara in it.

I love my life, I'm content with what's in it. Even with the aches and pains of missing her, I could probably do it just fine. Those feelings would eventually fade.

I'm just too stubborn to let them.

"We're going to get to know each other," I explain as I get comfortable on Kara's black, faux leather couch.

She looks at all of the things I've sprawled on the glass coffee table, and she's speechless. I watch her open and close her mouth a couple times, like she *wants* to give some response but doesn't know how.

Ten points to Reya.

I went to the store and grabbed all of my comfort snacks, and some I thought she might like. I don't even know her snack preferences, so that thought alone really solidified my plan to do this.

I haven't often seen what it looks like when I take her by surprise, but it's just as stunning as the rest of her looks. She wears bright blue biker shorts, and a tiny white tank top. She's not wearing a bra, and it's a miracle that I manage not to stare at her perky breasts, and the pointed nipples poking through the fabric.

Obviously I look a *little*, but I don't stare.

Her hair is sitting in a loose bun, her face is free of makeup.

"You think we don't know each other?" she whispers.

I shake my head.

"I know we don't. You know I'm naturally blonde, and you know I'm divorced, but you don't know why I've been dying my hair since I was fifteen or why my ex-husband is the person I can stand the least on this earth."

Her head slowly but surely moves in a nod, before she takes a couple of cautious steps towards me.

"I know you're a student that hates homework, and loves cheesy reality television," I continue. "But I've asked you a lot more questions than I've gotten answers for. There's more to both of us than we've gotten to show over the last couple of months."

"Do you do this with all of your girlfriends?" I see it for the attempt to be teasing that it is, but it doesn't work on me. There's vulnerability in those words.

"No," I answer honestly. "I've never felt serious enough about anyone to need this kind of conversation to happen."

She inhales a ragged breath that has me certain she's holding back tears.

"And you–" she clears her throat. "You feel serious about me? Even after everything?"

"Even after everything," I confirm softly.

It's what she needed to hear before taking a seat next to me, crossing her legs and holding onto her knees like a kid who's nervous to be at their first sleepover. In a way, that's exactly what she is. What both of us are. Just two kids figuring out how to love this intensely for the first time in their lives, and hoping the other might have some idea of what we're supposed to do.

But it's kind of beautiful that neither of us do.

Our conversation is a long one, but I don't realize just how long until I glance at my phone and see the early morning hour. It doesn't matter, it's not going to make me stop anytime soon.

I told her about Caleb and every last detail of our frustrating past.

"My parents actually separated for a couple of years when I was in elementary school. I think it was because of me, but they'd never admit it in a million years. I was a difficult kid, acting out for the fun of it. I got really good grades, and loved school, but I'd go and get suspended over the dumbest stuff."

"Like what?" Kara asks with an interested grin.

"Like pulling things out of the community garden when I thought no one was looking." I put my hands up in surrender before she can say anything. "I was *so* fascinated by carrots. It didn't matter how many of them I pulled out of the ground, it was so exciting every time!"

Her head falls back with her laughter, and I join in.

"I can't blame you there. I'd probably want to do the same."

"I haven't learned my lesson, either. If there was a garden in front of me right now, I wouldn't hesitate."

"We can be carrot vandals together," she says.

"Perfect," I agree.

My mouth is already dry, and my throat is already scratchy from all the talking I've been doing. I don't let it phase me, just feeling good about getting everything out there.

I can't remember the last time my life felt this *hopeful.* It's not that I didn't have any before Kara. I've always been hopeful that Dahlia will continue to get more and more amazing every year.

That she'll do great things. That coparenting will get easier, and I'll stop worrying every second she's not with me. Most of it has revolved around her.

She's always been such a light for me, always made me feel so much excitement for whatever the next day brings.

But she's depended on me all these years, and I've depended on... no one. Caleb tried for a couple months. My best friends have the capacity for it a few times a year, and I'm not ungrateful for that. They've helped me through a lot.

But I want this everyday. I want to end my long days of being in charge, and being needed, with someone I can need without feeling guilty. Without feeling like a burden. I want someone I can laugh and cry with every single day and know that they're happy to do it, because they're my person. I'm their person.

"Tell me about your childhood," I say cautiously.

"Oh boy," she says on a sigh. But the wall that's usually placed between us at any mention isn't there now. "What do you want to know?"

I blink away my surprise, and grab a handful of potato chips while I think. If I only get one answer out of her, what is it that I'd want?

It comes to me quickly.

"You never... explained about the scars."

Her head hangs low at that, but still no wall. It's a miraculous and curious thing, and I'm on the edge of my seat to know what drove her to that. To know if there's someone responsible.

"My depression was a lot worse when I was a teenager. My home life, mixed with puberty, and a school full of assholes was a recipe for disaster." She gives me a look that seems to ask if it's necessary to continue, and I give her an encouraging nod. I have a feeling it's the first time she's talking about any of this with someone besides her therapist, and I want her to feel the relief that comes with confiding in someone she can trust. "My parents were together, but weren't. We had two houses, and they weren't often in the same one at the same time. My mom was busy with a lot of work here, so my dad was out of town a lot. I couldn't go with him, but I tried all the time. I'd sneak into his truck with a backpack, but he always found me and told me to go back inside. I don't think he would've if he'd known back then how bad she was," she says, thoughtfully. "She had such bad anger problems. She's always been angry at *everything*, especially at me. She only ever lost it far enough to hit me once, but it's a day I'll never forget. The rest of the time she was throwing things, or hitting things, or slamming doors."

"That's horrible," I whisper. I didn't want to interrupt her, but it slipped out in my shock.

"She shattered a mirror one time, and I remember waiting and waiting for her bad luck to kick in. I was so sad when it never did, I wanted her to have some sort of consequence for the way she treated me. I told the school counselor when I was thirteen, and they sent a social worker to our house. My mom was so nice and smiley to that woman, I don't blame her for buying the act. She made her believe *silly little Kara just needed some attention*. I didn't have bruises, I wasn't being neglected as far as they could see. That's when I first got thrown into therapy, but it couldn't help me as long as I was living with her." Her voice cracks on the last word, not from emotion, but overuse. She cracks open one of the cans of Pepsi I brought us, and takes a few sips. "She wanted me to know I was a burden, a waste of space, a waste of *food*. That was a big one. I was either a pig for finishing my meals, or an ungrateful shit for not finishing them. I still struggle with eating sometimes, hearing her voice in the back of my mind."

"I hate her," I blurt out. "I hate that she got away with doing that to you."

Kara nods like she's heard the words before, but it is what it is.

It shouldn't be the way it is.

I should invent time travel to protect the younger version of this woman in front of me. Of course she's complicated, and cold, and confrontational. I'm not surprised at all that the Kara I first met was the way she was. I'd be mad at the world, and hate everyone if I'd been cursed with a mother like hers.

"She'd have me do the most random chores, clean the most random things. It was all very *Cinderella* with the wicked step-mother, except I wished I wasn't actually related to her." I reach out to hold her hand, and she clutches mine back tightly. "I only dealt with that by shutting down. If I was quiet, and stayed out of her way, I wouldn't have to face her as often. But I took that to school with me. It was easier if I didn't talk, didn't try. I had bullies didn't like that very much. What good was someone who wouldn't react? They took it pretty far in their attempt to get me to do *something*."

She wipes under her eyes, and I feel like kissing her for sharing this vulnerable piece with me. I can't imagine how hard it is to think about, let alone speak about.

"The music," she adds. "That was her fault, too. That I got used to it. She'd have men over, and things would get... noisy. I had to drown it out somehow."

"Of course you did," I say softly. "You could have just told me right away. I would've understood, and been more eager to come up with a compromise."

Her cheeks turn a darker shade, and I watch her nervously.

"About that..." she says. "I was going to. I actually--I spoke with everyone else that first week to explain. Followed up with gift cards a little later to thank them for understanding. "

My jaw drops.

"Are you fucking kidding me?" I feel residual anger rise up in me, and try to tamp it down quickly. It was such a hard time for me, and it's even harder to hear that it all could've been avoided. "Why didn't you talk to me?"

"You weren't home."

I wave my hand, insisting she explain more.

"And then you left that note, and I was feeling petty. It had been a particularly bad night, and I wasn't in a good headspace. I wanted the world to revolve around me," she says, her tone apologetic. Ashamed.

"But you got four gift cards," I realized.

Her eyes widen.

"How the hell do you know how many gift cards I bought?"

"I saw you. At the ice cream shop." The image of it comes rushing back to me, along with how appalled I was at her attitude. "You really need to be nicer to customer service workers."

She grimaces.

"Yeah, I do," she admits plainly. "I'm working on it. Not taking my emotions out on others has been a recurring topic in therapy."

I swear I love her a little more every single time she mentions therapy.

"Moving on now," she says with a nervous laugh. "I want to know how you met Autumn and... him."

A knot forms in my stomach.

"Can you tell me what he did?" I ask, scared of the answer.

She places a hand over mine, and gives me a soft smile.

"Don't panic, I don't have any devastating news about his character or anything." I instantly take a relieved breath. "He just wasn't willing to deal with me like my *husband* should have. He tried at first, I guess. Until *I* stopped trying, and he couldn't figure it out anymore. It was hard. I was really mean in my attempt to... I don't know what it was. I think I was testing him, proving further that I'm better off alone." She sighs.

"I hate the way I treated him, honestly. I try to forget it, to pretend that time in my life never happened. I know it sounds pretty pathetic, not wanting to face my own actions." Her eyes glue to mine before she speaks her last sentence. "He proved me right in a way, and I didn't want to live with that. With thinking everyone would."

I won't.

I grab her chin, and force her to face me. She doesn't get to hide from what I'm about to say.

"Kara, you are a fighter. Despite all the bullshit you've had to put up with in your life, despite all of the shitty people you've come across, you fought to keep going. You did what you *had* to do in order to keep going. I'm so fucking proud of you for that. It doesn't matter what anyone else thinks about it, or about the person you are. That just sucks for them, because they're too lazy to look any deeper. Even I'm a little guilty. You did give me plenty of reasons to write you off, to *hate* you even, at first. But thank goodness you couldn't get enough of all of this," I motion to my body, resulting in a laugh through her tears.

"I say all of that, while also acknowledging that Miles is one of my best friends, and—really sorry if you don't want to hear this—he's great for Autumn." She narrows her eyes, but nods. "As much as I wish the memory of your marriage wasn't this burden you carry with you, I'm glad it happened the way it did. If you had been meant for each other, we wouldn't have ended up here," I say.

Her head falls to my shoulder, and my head lands on hers. It's a comfortable silence.

"It still pisses me off that he made you think you weren't worth trying harder for. I promise I'll keep trying, until the day you genuinely don't want me to anymore. You just need to let me know."

"I don't think that day is going to come," she whispers.

I hope she's right.

We stay up so late, continuing to talk. I feel like I could start writing Kara's very own encyclopedia by the time she starts to yawn between her words, and the silence between our sentences grows longer and longer. She goes from sitting up to slowly sliding down and down until she's laying on her side. I do the same, just wanting to be on her level.

She gently kisses my cheek, and it's the last thing she does before falling asleep right there.

31

I'm alone when I wake up in Kara's living room. It's disorienting at first, the smell of coffee, and the chill on my exposed arms. We didn't even sleep with a blanket last night, and I assume it's because there isn't one to be found here. She might be the only person I've met that doesn't have a designated couch blanket.

I sit up, and examine the mess we left. Open bags of chips and candy that are probably stale and hard now. I instinctively reach for a chip, but think better of it before I do. That's *not* what my stomach wants first thing in the morning.

The coffee I smell does seem to be calling for me, despite my usual aversion to it. I follow it to the coffee pot sitting on her counter. There's a purple sticky note on the machine. I smile to myself.

I know it's not your thing, but I didn't have anything else. Help yourself, I'll be back soon.

Like magic, I hear her key in the door.

"Do you have any creamer?" I ask without looking her way as I pour myself a mug of the still steaming coffee.

I'd rather not tolerate the taste without some.

"In the door of the fridge," she says in a cheery voice.

Someone woke up on the right side of the couch.

I head for it, turning to give her a quick smile when I notice a bag in her hands.

"What do you have there?" I ask. But I know what it is, I recognize the red logo and the bubbly font on the bag.

"I have reason to believe you enjoy these breakfast burritos?"

Abandoning my task, I run to her and kiss her. We both only freeze for a second when realizing what I've done, but it felt right in the moment. I'm not going to regret it.

"You little stalker!" I tease. "Just how often did you watch me from that window."

"More often than I'll admit," she answers with a smirk.

Only when she sets the bag down, do I notice her other arm tucked behind her back. I pretend to peek around her, but she smirks and steps back.

"I had a really great night," she says.

"So did I."

"I just wanted to thank you. I know I probably don't deserve this second chance, but thank you for giving it to me anyway."

Then she pulls the surprise out from behind her, and holds it in front of me.

I immediately take it from her.

"You got me flowers?" I ask a little breathlessly as I study the blooms in my hand. There are carnations and daisies in the brightest yellow bouquet I've ever seen.

It's perfect. It's exactly what I would've picked out myself if I was in the habit of buying myself flowers. I never have, because I can't justify it when they'll wither away in a couple weeks.

Knowing as much doesn't make me any less happy to see them now, though. I'm giddy.

"Yeah," she says in a low voice. "These ones made me think of you. You and that stupid shirt."

"You love that shirt," I gasp.

"Both things can be true."

I shrug, wordlessly agreeing to disagree.

"This was really nice of you."

"I can be nice sometimes, contrary to popular belief."

I set the flowers down on the counter next to me, and throw my arms around her.

"I must be an outsider, because I already know that."

"I thought we already knew you were an outsider," she says.

I don't even pretend to scoff, because her own arms come up around me and she squeezes.

Hugs are so necessary, I don't know how anyone lives without them. I could never ever live without being affectionate and touchy, but I've recently realized more specifically that I can't last very long without *her* touch.

I pull away before I do something stupid, like cry or word vomit all of my current feelings. What a disaster.

"What are you doing today?"

"It really depends on what you're doing today," she says, drawing the words out slowly. "I might already be missing class."

My jaw starts to drop open, but I catch it quickly.

"You didn't have to miss class just because I fell asleep here," I exclaim. "You could've added that to your note!"

"I know I didn't have to. I wanted to spend the morning with you."

I'm a melting mess.

I rack my brain for the last time I called out of work, who's there today, and how much I'll have to do to make up for it.

I decide it's worth it, and I text my co-manager.

"My whole day just freed up."

When I look over at her, her mouth is full of breakfast burrito. My stomach growls as I remember my own, and grab it from the bag.

She shakes her head, but finishes chewing before saying anything.

"Am I a bad influence on you?"

"Maybe. But I don't care."

I dig in to my own food, and then remember the coffee I left sitting. I feel like a mess as I bounce around in her kitchen, adding creamer and putting it back. Then I take a trial sip, hate it, and go back for the creamer.

Repeat three times.

Kara silently laughs at me as she continues eating, like she has the best entertainment for her meal.

I'm sitting on Kara's lap, as we read a chapter together. I'm much slower than she is, so I feel bad for taking so long to turn the pages while she waits.

If only Autumn knew who was reading her book right now. Not only that, but enjoying it. She hasn't made a single snarky comment since we started. I may have even caught a smile or two on that beautiful face of hers.

Footsteps on the stairs below throw me out of my head. I don't know who the hell would be coming up here at this time of day on a random Tuesday? I'm not expecting anyone, and I don't think Kara would approve of our PDA level if she *was* expecting anyone.

I quickly stand, and the book falls from my hands to the dusty ground.

Ouch, sorry book.

When I look up from bending down to grab it, I see Vic standing at the top of the stairs. She's got Angeline in a front carrier on her chest, and she looks like those stairs were the workout of a lifetime.

"Who's your friend?" she asks, catching her breath.

Our close proximity is still a little suspicious. Okay, a lot suspicious, because I'm standing right in front of her, the back of my leg touching her knee.

I take a single step away.

"This is my, um–" Bad time for my brain to freeze up, but it does just that.

"Neighbor," Kara finishes.

She stands from her seat to approach Vic with an outstretched arm. They shake hands.

"Oh! That's right," she says like that's the most normal thing. Then I watch as it hits her, and her expression switches to confusion. "I forgot someone new moved in. It's nice to meet you."

Vic's a good friend, and a good actor apparently. She listened to me complain *a lot*. She is not a fan of the woman in front of her.

"You too."

Kara doesn't say more than that, considering her lack of interest in most socializing.

Vic awkwardly nods a couple times.

"Sit down, babe." I motion to the seat I wasn't occupying in the first place. "I know she's heavy."

"She fell asleep while I was walking up the stairs. She always falls asleep when I wish I could." Vic sticks her bottom lip out in a pout, but she starts smoothing down the hair on Angeline's head. Baby hair is the best. It's so soft. I'm a little jealous.

"What a little angel," I say. How appropriate, Angeline the angel.

"That's the whole point," Vic coos in a little voice that's meant for the baby. The sleeping baby who can't hear her.

Vic has the most adorable mom mode.

Kara is still standing, and I can tell she's in flight mode. When we make eye contact, I shake my head subtly. I don't want her to leave yet, and I doubt sitting here for a couple minutes is going to expose anything we don't want exposed yet.

Not that we've had that conversation, but I feel like we're on the same page.

"This is my best friend, Vic. And that's little Angeline."

She nods slowly.

"Nice to meet you."

"What was your name?" Vic asks.

"It's Karissa," she says, taking me by surprise.

I don't think, I just react.

"What the hell? That's your name?"

Before Vic looks up in confusion, I catch the roll of Kara's eyes. The sight of it makes me want to wrap her in a hug and plant kisses all over her face. I'm so attached to that attitude.

"You don't know her name?"

"She calls me by a nickname," she says quickly. For the best, so I don't blurt anything else out.

But I'm dying to know if she's lying because she's worried about Vic knowing who she is, or if I've gone the last couple months without knowing her actual name. Both answers irritate me for reasons I can't explain.

"Reya does like her nicknames. She's been trying for over a year to convince a friend of ours to call her Rey. As if her name isn't short enough already."

"I don't have to try anymore, he's leaned into it," I tell her. "I think he secretly likes that he's the only one that gets to call me that."

Vic laughs.

"Yeah, I'm sure Miles feels really special."

Kara tenses at the mention of his name, and Vic clocks it. She looks between us.

"What's your nickname?" she asks Kara.

I swear she's sweating, she's so nervous.

"Uh—"

"Babe, can you give us one minute? Sorry, be right back."

I ignore both of their shocked, uneasy expressions and yank Kara into her apartment. I accidentally slam the door behind us and wince.

"What are you doing?"

"We didn't get to go over what to do in a situation like this! You don't have to tell her your name, I can change the subject when we go back out there."

"Would she know about me? Past me?"

"She would. Our little friend group? We're talkers. All of us know everything about everything."

"Who's to say—"

There's a knock on the door right behind us. Before I even open it, I hear Vic's voice.

"If it'll save you some time, I know exactly who you are."

We both freeze.

"And if you're panicking, you can stop. I came here to see my friend, not hang out on her porch alone. Get out here."

I look to Kara to see if she has any clue of what she wants to do, but she shrugs.

"What do you mean you know who she is?" I ask through the door.

Vic throws the door open instead of answering and almost hits me with it. She looks exasperated.

"Get out here, and stop being weird."

We do as she says, stiffly shuffling outside again. I let the two of them sit, and I stand nervously near Kara's side.

Vic rolls her eyes.

"I'm going to say this one time, so hear it." She looks Kara dead in the eye. "I'm not going to crucify you for being Miles' ex-wife. There might be some explaining to do at some future point, but I don't care for it today." Her gaze lands on me. "You *absolutely* have some explaining to do, but again: not today. Fair? We good?"

The two of us quickly nod.

And then we all get swept up in conversation, like it's the least weird thing ever that she is who she is.

"Oh, please!" Vic shouts with a laugh. "Autumn is the least confrontational person we know."

It's her response to Kara seeming worried that Autumn might discover we're all doing this right now, and it's the truth. Autumn wouldn't be thrilled, but she wouldn't do anything that Kara should worry about.

"I gave her ideas to get back at Justin," I tell Kara. "She had so many opportunities, but she thought karma was doing its job just fine."

"I love her for being the bigger person, I really do."

"It's precious," I add. "But sometimes someone just needs to have their food sneezed on."

Kara's hand flies over her mouth, but I hear her laugh.

"You didn't."

"We both did," Vic says with a smirk. "Amelia kept inviting us over for dinner, being none the wiser. Between you and us? We had some things to share with her, too. I always flipped her toilet paper rolls the other way, and guess who she blamed it on?"

"I'm hoping it was Justin."

The answer is our shared grins.

It was childish, sure, but it was fun. It felt good to get a little revenge for our best friend's sake. She still has no idea, and I have been wondering if I should deliver the news of all of our little tricks as a birthday present. Maybe a cute little journal where I draw and detail them all.

She can't be mad *now*, we've been on our best behavior for months. Honestly, that family has grown on me a lot, and I feel good about it.

I feel good about it *because* of our shenanigans. Don't think I'd be able to say the same if I hadn't been the sole reason that every single one of that woman's houseplants died.

"Good for you guys."

32

"No, she didn't," I whisper in disbelief.

The flowers that had been looking like their time was coming to an end, with dry petals and stems too short after a few attempts to prolong their life, are gone.

In their place is an even more elaborate, gorgeous, *still* yellow bouquet. They have a new vase, tall and pink with textured bubbles in the glass. It's so cute.

I turn it, admiring every angle of my flowers as they spin..

I know my flowers decently enough, but there are a couple I'm unsure of. I make my way through, pulling individual stems towards my face to smell them all. I'm going to have a headache by the end, I'm sure.

When I get to the larger blooms in the center I step back with a smile on my face. I'm sure Kara didn't know. She probably couldn't tell the difference between a peony and a rose, let alone anything else. But the dahlia's are obviously my favorite.

I pluck two of them from the bunch to stick them in a smaller vase for Dahlia's room. It's so perfectly fitting.

Note to self to get the name of this florist so I can do it some other time.

Speaking of notes, I completely overlooked the fact that there's one sticking out from underneath the vase. My chest tightens at the memory of all of the aggressive little notes we used to write each other.

Spending the day with my dad, so hopefully I'll see you later tonight. Have a good day at work, gorgeous.

I fly through my store, wheeling a rack that resides in our dressing room. One that I think is a little pointless, considering most of what we carry are t-shirts and jewelry. No one is allowed to try on the jewelry, and t-shirts are a pretty simple thing to know your size in.

It might just be me, and the fact that I've always just grabbed whatever size is the biggest. There is no such thing as a shirt that's too big for me, especially because honestly—I have pretty big boobs. Who knows what size I'd be without them, but they limit a lot of what I can wear.

The t-shirt I'm currently wearing is three sizes too big, and almost reaches my knees. That fact comes in handy when I don't want to wear pants, because we're technically not supposed to wear leggings. No one can say a word as long as my butt is covered, so covered it is.

I pass by Macy, who's wearing an outfit similar to my own. It's not surprising, considering how encouraged we are to wear things we sell in store.

I know those are leggings under her big shirt, but I'm the cool manager. I'm the one that shrugs these things off, because as long as you're comfortable enough to efficiently do your job? It doesn't matter in the slightest to me.

"I can take care of those if you want," Paige tells me.

She's one of my favorites for obvious reasons.

"Really? That would be awesome. Thanks."

I leave the cart there, and give her a big smile as I walk away. I have reports to pull, and an afternoon meeting to prepare for. The less time I have to spend on the sales floor, the better.

Luckily, we're in the slower season for retail shopping. The crowds we do get are usually holding gift cards they got for Christmas, or unfortunately, trying to return something they got for Christmas. We're heavily pressured to turn those into exchanges, but teenagers are stubborn.

All the years I worked here have terrified me for what my future holds. Dahlia has a big personality now, it's going to be brutal when she's older.

I think I do a good job of showing her how customer service workers should be treated. Even when she's not around, I treat every associate, waitress, delivery driver, teacher, you name it, with the utmost respect. But it's especially amplified when I'm with her, like most things. Everything I say and do as a parent can absorbed by my kid for life, so I'm constantly thinking about what she's absorbing from me.

I sit down at my back desk, and pull up the store email.

Meeting moved forward - See you all at 1:30!

I freeze, rereading the subject line over and over. Then I check my watch.

1:07

Shit.

I have an hour less than I thought to prepare. I scan through the reasoning, something about IT working on one of our higher revenue locations. I don't see why we all have to suffer instead of letting *Paula* miss one single meeting.

Paige needs a thirty minute break, and now I have to tell her she can't go until whenever this meeting is through.

I tell her so with a pout over the radio we keep clipped on us at all times.

"Not a problem!" her cheery voice comes through.

She needs a raise.

I need a raise.

I finish ringing up a customer, and placing their things in a bag. They thank me with a smile, and I tell them to have a good day. It's a typical customer service interaction.

But as soon as they step away, I get the weirdest feeling. Like I'm being watched. I look around the small store, not spotting any other customers. I usually have a sixth sense that tells me when someone walks in without having to see or hear them, but nothing activated it while I was helping the previous person.

Weird.

I grab the shirts I'd pulled from the fitting room off the back counter, and find a couple of hangers to put them on. Paige should be back from her lunch in a few minutes, and then I finally get to leave for the day. I am exhausted. Over it. Sick of putting on my best smile, and ready to be a grump at home on my couch.

Or I could be a grump in someone else's home, on someone else's couch.

My sixth sense perks up, and I know someone's walked in without any indicators.

"Hello, welcome in!" I call the words over my shoulder without looking, as I put a shirt back in its normal spot.

If I'm lucky, this is the last customer I'll have today. Things have really slowed down, so I can probably get the store all tidied up before I head out.

"Can I speak to the manager?" a voice whispers in my ear, and I scream. I jump so hard that my shoulder slams into the chin of the voice's owner.

I turn, ready to be blabbering apologies, offering a discount, sacrificing my second born, until I lock eyes with the culprit.

Kara's hand is covering her mouth, and I'm not sure if it's to hide a smile, or as a reaction to a bitten tongue that *I just* caused. She did cause me to cause it though, so with that thought, the guilt eases slightly.

"Are you okay?"

She nods, and then I notice how alight her eyes are with amusement.

"I got you so good," she says.

Oh my God, she's so pleased with herself.

I push her shoulder in playful punishment.

"That was so bad! I could've hurt you!" Placing a hand over my racing heart, I close my eyes and hang my head dramatically. "I thought you were a customer that was seconds away from suing me."

"I really hope you don't have customers whispering in your ear."

"Not until today," I say on an exhale. "You will be a customer by the way. Seeing your face is nice and all, but I can't let you mess with my conversion."

"Conversion? What are you converting me to? This sounds like a cult." She emphasizes looking in a circle around the store, taking it all in. "Actually, that checks out. This place seems kind of culty."

I can't argue there.

Kara pushes through hangers on the rack closest to her, feigning interest in the t-shirts with band logos from the eighties.

She's a modern rock girl anyway.

"I know what you need," I say as I get an idea. I walk over to the display window in the front of the store, where a mannequin is wearing the very last of a very specific shirt.

An oversized version of the one with the yellow flowers. She shakes her head instantly.

"Absolutely not."

My mouth opens in surprise.

"But... you love this shirt."

A smile appears on her face, one of the sweetest she's ever given me, before she looks behind us. She must have been checking if the coast was clear, because the next thing I know she's grabbing my hand and lacing our fingers together.

"I love that shirt because it's yours. I wouldn't like it nearly as much if you didn't sleep in it a few nights a week."

"I sleep in lots of shirts. You always mention this one."

"Well... that one's the most like you. It's sunshiney."

I shake my head in disbelief.

"You're being way too cute right now. Can I get used to this?"

Her response to that is a wink, and I practically melt into the floor.

"Probably not," she says.

I smile anyway, because I don't think that's true. I can and I will.

I lean in to kiss her cheek, hoping it's not too much PDA, coupled with our still clasped hands. She doesn't pull away, so I take it as permission.

But I'm interrupted.

"I'm back!" Paige yells from across the store, heading out of the break room. We have radios for a reason, I don't know why she didn't make use of it.

Kara pulls away from me, but she does it gently. It's hard to be upset with that at all, considering how much progress we've made lately. Another important thing to note is that Paige knows Autumn pretty well. They went to school together. I don't expect her to know who Kara is or to put any pieces together, but better safe than sorry.

I use my radio to reply, hoping it's a subtle enough way of telling her to utilize it.

"Thanks for letting me know. Do you need anything before I head out?"

"*I need the new code for the safe.*"

Shit, that's right. I turn to Kara.

"Find something to buy. I'll be right back."

I hear her voice behind me as I quickly walk away.

"Do I have to?"

33

Kara picks out a pair of black socks with red roses embroidered around the cuff, and a couple necklaces. One with a small heart charm, and another with a yellow daisy sitting in a clear resin pendant. Neither of them really seem like her style, but she doesn't say a word as she forgoes a bag and places them in her purse.

"Are you in a hurry to head home? Or do you think we could do some shopping?"

I glance at her suspiciously.

"What are you shopping for?"

She shrugs.

"Nothing in particular. It's been a while since I came to the mall."

I clock out on the register, say my goodbyes to Paige who now has everything she needs to close up the store tonight, and walk out the door with Kara. The place is pretty packed today, which makes me a little nervous. I'm surprised *she* doesn't seem nervous. All it would take is one wrong person to spot us, and our secret won't just be ours anymore.

Clearly thinking about it way less than I am, she grabs my hand and pulls me towards the shoe store across the way. I'm terrible about buying new shoes. All of the ones I own are filthy, and falling apart.

There couldn't be a worse store for us to visit.

"Hey, Rey!" I look up to see Steven standing at his checkout counter. The store is empty, despite all of the foot traffic passing by.

I never gave him permission to call me Rey. It makes me cringe a little every time he does. I only like it when Miles calls me that.

"Hi, Stevie."

I don't think he cares for that nickname either. I guess it makes us even.

"Not working today?"

We fall into a little bit of small talk about our days, I complain about my meeting being rescheduled. I can't help but notice the whole time I speak, that his eyes are on my company.

I get it. She's everyone's type. It doesn't mean it doesn't irk me to see his heart eyes directed at her right now.

I finish my sentence, only for him to not respond because she's so distracting that he wasn't even listening to me. With our hands still locked, I turn us towards the far wall where I know the women's shoes are. If he protests, or decides to act like he was actually interested in what I had to say, I don't hear it.

"He's definitely losing points for that," I mutter.

"Losing points? What are you talking about?"

I didn't mean to say that out loud.

"Uh, nothing."

She gives me a look that I have come to learn means, *yeah, that's bullshit*. I pick up a sneaker that I would never wear. It looks oddly futuristic with its "breathable design."

Anyone with trypophobia is having a terrible day when they see these bad boys.

"I guess me and you will have to do something for my birthday. That could be fun! We could go out of town, like you mentioned a while ago? Maybe the beach or something. Do you like the beach?"

Kara grabs the shoe from my hand and puts it back on the display.

"Explain."

"Well, I really like the beach. I used to live closer to the coast as a little kid, and my dad would take us all the time. Even when it was cold and rainy."

Her nostrils flare.

"The points thing, Reya. Now."

She's lucky she's hot when she's bossy.

"You're lucky you're hot when you're bossy." I roll my eyes. "I'm not actually keeping track of numbers or anything, but sometimes when people do things I decide that they lose or gain points. If they lose enough, I act accordingly."

"Go on."

"The guys who lived in your apartment before you? They were way in the negatives. So far in fact, that Autumn had Freddy with her one day and I let him pee right in front of their door. Could've stopped him, didn't want to. I held Autumn back."

She cracks a smile.

"If you ever smell dog piss while walking into your apartment, now you know why."

I follow as she makes her way over to a pair of heels. Something I couldn't picture either of us in, but I have to admit they're pure sex. I'm already all over this woman, but if she put these on for me? We'd be stuck in her room for days.

"How many points do I have?" she asks.

"There's not an exact number, but…" I genuinely stop to think about how many times I've felt the need to subtract from the starting line. "For obvious reasons, you started low. I'd say you've just barely made your way past neutral territory."

She spins to face me so fast that it's a jumpscare. One of the black heels is now in her hand, and she lightly pokes my chest with the sharp point.

It just got so much warmer in here.

"Neutral? You mean to tell me that you've received all those orgasms from me, and I'm barely past neutral?"

She presses a little harder, although not enough to hurt. I take a step back, and she goes right with me. The heel to chest contact doesn't stop.

I'm going to have to buy these ridiculous shoes.

Two more steps and the back of my head hits the shelving behind me.

I don't care, I could catch fire and I still wouldn't break away from her stare.

Assuming someone would notice and put me out.

"I gave you just as many, which made us even."

She steps back with a smirk, and I know she got exactly what she wanted. To get me all hot and bothered when there's nothing to be done about it. Not only have we not broached anything sexual recently, but I'm not one for fooling around in public places.

On second thought, if she pulled me into a bathroom stall right now, I'd do anything she wanted.

"'Even,'" she repeats. "We'll see how long that stays true."

"Okay. What about him?" I point to guy I would've gone for back when I still giving the opposite gender a chance. His hair is black, and shiny. He has a Nirvana shirt on with dark blue jeans.

"Stop staring, his girlfriend looks like she's rip the head off anyone that breathes on him."

I'm surprised to notice she's right, I hadn't even clicked the girl standing next to him.

"Do you find him attractive?"

"No."

"Okay, what about him?" Tall. Blonde. Skinny. Has a child with him in line to get Subway.

"Not at all."

I peer over her. "Is it because he has a kid?"

"No! It's because if he had darker hair, he would look a little too much like Miles."

Miles would never wear sweats in public, but I don't tell her that.

"Good thing he doesn't have darker hair."

"I don't feel any attraction to him at all. To any of these guys."

I pause, weighing my words before they fall out.

"Do you think it might just be because you like me so much? Maybe it's not that you've switched sides, maybe I'm just so special that no one could catch your eye right now."

She fights a smile, and I can't help mine in return.

She points to a girl sitting alone on her phone.

"She's pretty. I don't know that I would run up and grab her number or anything." She looks at me. "I already like someone a lot. But I think that girls chances are still higher than any of the men in the building."

"Got it," I say as I feel myself blush.

It doesn't get old to hear her admit she likes me.

34

"**I** don't care for bars. Or most public places, really," she tells me as she's braiding her hair in front of my bathroom mirror.

She's sitting on top of the counter, having pushed all of my clutter out of the way. I heard my can of hairspray fall over and clatter against the granite. I'm hoping she'll pick it up when she's done, but not counting on it.

If she was anyone else I'd be annoyed that they're imposing on my space in such a way, but I can't bring myself to be annoyed at her these days.

"I know. I won't pressure you to go, I just figured I'd ask."

She starts humming some song I know I've heard, but can't remember. I watch as she finishes one side of her head, and looks around for something to secure it with. Before I can tell her where she can find a bag of hair ties, she opens the closest drawer and lets out an amazed little gasp.

"I haven't seen butterfly clips since I was a kid!" She clips the bottom of her braid with a bright smile. "How freaking cute!"

She is too freaking cute.

I watch as she clips the end of her braid and holds it between her fingers to study it in the mirror. A pleased expression is plastered on her face, reminding me of the day I found those clips at the store. Who doesn't appreciate a little piece of childhood nostalgia here and there? I was so excited, but I had completely forgotten I even had them until now.

Kara finishes the other side of her hair, topping it off with a matching clip.

"I should've been getting ready in here every morning. What else are you hiding from me?"

Without waiting for an answer, she hops off the counter and opens another drawer. I should be embarrassed, knowing I've never spent a second of my life organizing or decluttering anything in those drawers. A peek over her shoulder shows me that one is filled with loose cotton swabs, scrunchies, earrings, random makeup I don't use but don't have the heart to throw away.

As expected, she grows bored with that quickly, slamming it shut.

"What's there?"

I squint my eyes.

"Did you not just see?" I ask.

She smirks.

"Not in the drawer, at the *bar*. Why are you going?"

"Vic has a friend who has a thing," I poorly explain. "And she hasn't been out in a while, so I feel obligated to not miss it."

I have a feeling if I neglect to mention what the *thing* is, there's a slight chance of convincing her. I really do want to spend a night out with my friend, she deserves to have a fun night away from the house after being in baby mode for the last couple of months. I also know that she and Kara get along, *and* it'd be nice to have some extra company while she's being bombarded by all of her old yoga pals.

"I feel like you're neglecting the obvious," Kara says.

If there is something obvious, I'm missing it.

"That you don't like that kind of place? No, I get that. It's–"

"That you and Vic have a mutual friend that you might not want to see us together."

Oh.

I laugh out loud, visibly confusing the woman in front of me.

"Not a concern."

"Why? Is she not a fan of being there for her friends?"

"No, she absolutely is," I defend. I don't think Autumn would appreciate me divulging her issues to Kara of all people, so I keep it short. "Let's just say she's also not a fan of public places."

It feels like a miracle that Kara followed me out the front door, got in my car, and let me drive us here.

I'm giddy about my win,

But as soon as we step inside and I glance at the bar, I want to link arms with Kara and drag her back out the door.

I must be quite the idiot for not thinking that part through.

Somehow, like she sensed me walk in, Bailey's eyes meet mine. She doesn't look bothered to see me, but it's worse. She looks excited. I doubt her tunnel vision even allowed her to see how close Kara is standing to me.

I don't know why I feel the need to do it, but I grab her hand. That should do the trick.

Except my girlfriend— maybe I shouldn't call her that in my head, but oh well— doesn't like that at all. It's the first time I'm genuinely disappointed that she's an affection-phobe.

A look of disgust fills her face when she pulls away.

"Why would you do that?"

I sigh, playfully.

"Normal people hold hands, babe."

"Don't call me that. And don't hold my hand."

I take it one step further, and give her a pat on the ass. Not obvious enough to draw attention, but it's enough to see her ears go red.

Ugh. Such a fireball.

"If I'd known you were going to—"

"You can take your anger out on me later."

Her expression falls blank, as if there's a lag while one emotion is being flushed by another. I know it's the case when I wink at her, and any sign of irritation vanishes.

She wants me so bad.

I smile to myself as I guide her up to the bar, mentally preparing myself to pretend I don't even know who the bartender is.

And silently praying she lets me.

The same guy I recognize from the last time I was here is also back there working, so I intentionally end up on his side. He moves fast, takes our drink orders even faster. By which I mean Kara

Bailey touches my hand that's resting on the bar, and I'm a pile of fear. Things I know for a fact: I don't want to sleep with ____ again, and I really want to keep sleeping with Kara.

I don't think Kara is going to be eager about the latter if I sit here and let this other woman flirt with me.

I slowly pull my hand away, but I'm polite enough to pretend it was so I could fix my hair.

"I'm relieved of my duties in about fifteen minutes, so speak now if you want any more free soda."

I glance at my almost empty glass. I do wish it was full.

"I'll take another one. Thanks."

I don't appreciate the way her returning smile looks accomplished.

"While you're giving them out, I'll take one."

I look to her with raised brows. Kara hates soda.

Bailey's smile falters, but she nods in her direction, agreeing to grab her the drink.

For ten long minutes, I sip on my drink while Kara's sits in front of her. Untouched.

I wait until Bailey is busy on the other side of the bar before asking.

"You going to drink that?"

"No, but you can."

"It's all watered down by now, I'll pass."

She surprises me by patting my cheek. As simply as the action is, I find myself blushing.

"Sunshine's too good for a little water in her soda? Poor thing."

I roll my eyes, but there's a smile on my face.

"No, thank you." Kara's words are followed by her fakest smile.

"What?"

"I have to pee," Kara grumbles.

"Do you want me to go with you?"

She tilts her head to give me one of my favorite glares.

"I think I can handle it on my own. Why anyone wants an escort to listen to them pee is beyond me."

I chuckle.

"Got it, grumpy."

She leans in close to my ear as she stands.

"You better tell me if that pesky blonde tries anything while I'm gone."

Something about that demand *really* does it for me.

"I think I like you all possessive."

She shakes her head, like she can't believe how ridiculous I am, but I don't miss the smirk she can't keep off her face.

To no surprise, Bailey pops up in front of me the second Kara walks away.

"Is she your girlfriend?"

I don't miss the irritated way she says the last word.

"Yeah," I say, trying to keep my voice casual.

Except I realize once it leaves my mouth that it's not totally the truth, and can't decide if I should correct myself. I don't really get to decide, because Bailey sees something on my face that makes her huff a laugh.

"Are you non-exclusive or something?"

"Or something," I answer with a tight lipped smile.

"And you hate that," she observes.

"It isn't really your business, Bailey."

"It could be. You could come back without her sometime, take out your frustrations."

She has the gall to wink at me, and I want to toss my drink on her face.

Thankfully, I'm above petty fights.

I clear my throat.

"I realize I left you hanging a couple months ago, and that could be left open for interpretation, but I'm not interested," I tell her. I keep my voice as soft as I can, trying to let her down easy.

She leans in closer, *too* close. Her eyes are alight, like she's enjoying some game, or hearing a joke. You'd think I'd just said the opposite thing, like I'd dared her to try or something.

"Yeah, right."

I scoff at her.

"Yeah. Correct. I'm not."

"As soon as you're sick of being dangled along by her, you know where to find me."

Did I say I was above petty fights? I mostly meant that, but there's an exception to every rule.

"Are you really so desperate that you'll just be waiting here for me to return and hope that I'll— what? Confess how badly I actually want to be with you?"

She throws the towel she's holding down onto the counter and crosses her arms.

"Yeah. I do."

My filter leaves the room.

"Are you delusional?"

The glint in her eyes makes it seem like she knows something I don't, but I highly doubt that's true.

"Reya, no one shares a kiss like we did and moves on. Think whatever you want for the time being, but I know better. You might think you're the type to play the field, not want to settle with one person for too long. I get it. But you'll miss me at some point."

My jaw drops, unable to fathom how actually delusional she is. She really believes what she's saying.

I stand from the barstool I'm sitting on, and lay my hands flat on the counter.

She must feel like she won when I look into her eyes, but I'm so glad I'm about to burst her bubble.

"I don't have commitment issues, blondie. But you need serious help if you think I'm destined to end up with you." I point in the direction of the hallway leading to the bathroom. "If I have any say in the matter, I'm never letting that girl go. If you think our make out session was anything special, you have no fucking idea what's out there. I'm glad I ignored your texts and got to find out."

When I turn, ready to make a dramatic departure to go find Kara, I end up face to face with her.

And the smile on her face is deadly. I don't think I've ever seen her this pleased without my head between her legs.

I feel like a well trained dog, because that's exactly what the look makes me want to do. I've never hooked up in a bathroom before, but there's a first time for everything.

"Will you be my girlfriend?"

I blink.

I blink again.

It seems like the rest of the room goes quiet, but I doubt that's the case outside of the bubble that just materialized around us.

"What?"

She chuckles, making my heart flutter.

"I want you to be my girlfriend."

"O-okay," I stutter.

Her brows raise.

"Is that a yes?"

I don't hesitate, nodding vigorously. I might wake up any second now, and realize this was some dream, so I'm not looking to waste time.

Kara leans in to place a soft kiss on my cheek. Her hot breath on my face sends a shiver down my spine.

"Great," she whispers. Then, when she backs away, "Are you ready to head out?"

I nod again, still not sure how to use my words properly.

We step outside, hit by the cool fresh air of an early evening.

"Did you just say that to piss her off?"

"I mean... that was a plus," Kara admits as we approach the car.

"So... no?" I ask, needing confirmation.

"I might be a bitch, but no. I'm not enough of a bitch to ask you to be my girlfriend just to piss someone else off."

It's nice to hear her say it.

35

I slowly open my eyes. Confusion is the first emotion to break through my sleeping mind. Then my heart rate picks up, my blood starts to boil. Oh, this too familiar feeling that I had assumed wasn't coming back.

I sat up in bed so quickly that it made me lightheaded. One glance to my nightstand, and the shaking photo frame made me not care.

"Oh, no you don't!" I yell, sure I'm the only one that can hear me.

Before I know it, I'm running out my door. I don't even throw my slippers on, and all I'm wearing is an oversized shirt and my underwear.

I aggressively bang on her door, seven times before it opens before me.

"You are not pulling this again. You can't just—" I'm stopped short by the realization that she's laughing at me. Deep, uncontrollable laughter that has her hunched over with one hand on her knee and the other in a fist in front of her open mouth. "What the fuck?" I ask, but some of my anger has turned into astonishment, causing the words to sound less hostile.

She can't stop laughing long enough to answer me. Between shaking her head, and fanning her face, she's really going through it with this laugh.

And I let go of an even bigger piece of that anger because… her laugh is the most beautiful sound I've ever heard, and it's so rare. Maybe she chuckles at my sarcasm here and there, or I receive a titter in return for my bad jokes. I'm smiling before I can stop myself, aware that I should stop myself.

Her music is still going, and my body still aches to be in my bed asleep right now.

"You evil woman, why are you laughing right now?"

She fans her face, an attempt to dry the tears that her laughter caused.

"It's just like old times," she says in a high pitched, amused voice. Then she surprises me by invading my space and wrapping her arms around me. I don't waste a single second returning the hug, and enjoying the way she feels in my arms. "I called you, but your phone must have been on silent. This was the only other way I could think to get you over here."

I slightly shake my head, and I know she feels it while my face is buried in her neck.

"I am not a fan of your methods." I place a kiss to her smooth skin. "But I'm here. What's up?"

She pulls out of our embrace to take my hand and pull me inside. She walks backwards, her gaze locked on mine while she goes, a smile still pulling at her lips. She outstretches a hand to hit the power button on the speaker that has been used to torture me way too many times.

"I just didn't want to sleep alone."

Something about that sentence, that small piece of vulnerability that I didn't have to fight tooth and nail for... it's everything to me. I pull her closer again, and press my mouth to hers sweetly.

I really hope I don't ever have to say goodbye to moments like these again. I want all of them, always.

"Let's get to sleep then."

We walk hand in hand to her bedroom, and then I help her out of her pants until we both have the same amount of clothes on. She's still smiling at me, like my being here is the best thing to happen to her.

I've forgotten all about the rage I felt when I was first woken up. If she hadn't done that, I'd still be oblivious and unaware of just how cute she is tonight. It would've been a tragedy for me to miss.

We climb into her bed, and our arms go right back to being around each other.

"You look way too happy to be my girlfriend. What did you do with her?"

"You make me happy, you idiot. Don't ruin it."

"Is that what it is? Not that you take pleasure from ruining my sleep schedule? Just like old times?"

She laughs breathily, and my arms tighten around her.

"I love you so much," I whisper.

"I thought I was an evil woman," she teases.

"Both of those things can be true at the same time."

Her head tilts up, and she captures my lips in a kiss that's filled with heat, and emotion. All of the things she put off telling me for so long. Every word I pried from her, and every little thing about herself that she shared with me willingly. The unfiltered joy that we got here, after how brutal and complicated our path has been.

"I love you so much, sunshine."

"I love you, too," I say, already dozing off.

Until a thought occurs to me that I should have brought up before now.

"Wait, what is with the music? You never told me?"

"Oh... long story. Not worth telling."

I sit up, facing her with my most determined look.

"We've got all the time in the world. Tell me why you tortured me for so long."

She lean in to kiss my cheek, surprising me.

"You sure you want to know?" Kara asks.

"Yes, I'm sure!"

She chuckles.

"I used to have to block out the sound of my mother's... night-time activities. By the time I moved out, I was so used to doing it that I couldn't sleep without it. It made anxious that I'd something I didn't want to hear whenever it was silent."

I sit with that for a minute, filled with a combination of horror and sadness. I couldn't begin to imagine how bad things must have been for her to blast the music at her preferred volume.

I don't have the heart to ask what age that started.

"That's awful," I say, at a loss for any more than that.

She pulls me in again, squeezing.

"Not as awful as me keeping you and Dahlia up at night. Sorry, again, by the way."

"I actually don't think you apologized before."

"Better late than never," she mumbles into my shoulder.

When I end up with a longer weekend that normal, it's never *really* a weekend. I always end up on the phone with an employee, or texting an employee, or running to the store for an employee.

I wasn't having it this weekend. Fate allowed me three days without being on the schedule, and I wanted to really experience those three days without an inconvenience popping up on that phone screen. Dahlia and I stayed in most of the time anyway, only going on a brief drive to get some ice cream and coming back. We played games, read books, watched some of her favorite movies. It was perfection.

The cherry on top was propping my front door open, and sitting outside with Kara every night. We didn't do anything but talk, but it was all I needed. It was comfortable, and silly, and at times a little deep. We talked about life as only children, and what kind of vacations our families used to go on, and what snacks we used to eat so much of that we can't stand them anymore.

Her answer was popcorn, to my dismay.

I love everything about, even the *experience*. It's so convenient to throw the bag in the microwave for a couple minutes, plop it into a bowl and cover in salt. Then the smell of it when you leave the room and come back? It really works for me.

Apparently it makes her nauseous now, after too many late night cravings as a teenager. It's heartbreaking.

The weekend with two of my favorite humans revived me in a way I didn't even know I needed.

I wake up feeling like myself again, refreshed, and ready for anything. I almost question if I even need to make a fun, fruity tea this morning, but decide *of course* I should. I might not need the help, but it sure isn't going to hurt anything.

When I pick up my phone to turn off my alarm, it almost feels wrong. I wish I didn't need to rely on it for anything day to day so I could go even more days without it. I sigh as I press a button on the screen and plop it back down next to me.

Then I worry I hit the wrong button and lift it to my face again.

So many notifications stare back at me. More than I think I've ever had on my phone at one time.

Definitely more than I've ever had from Autumn and Miles at one time.

Oh crap.

"He's amazing. He's perfect. I love him," I coo.

Riley's little baby hand is grabbing onto my shirt so tight that I find myself impressed with his strength.

Autumn and Miles are looking down at him too, completely enraptured. I'd feel suffocated by their inability to stand more than a foot away from me if I didn't entirely understand. I'm holding their whole world in my hands, it's hard to take a step back.

"I'm really sorry again, you guys. I really should have checked my phone."

It's at least my twentieth time saying those words, but the first in person. I won't forgive myself for not knowing my new little bestie was born three days before I found out.

Three. Entire. Days.

As much as my phone can drive me nuts, I'm never going more than a couple minutes without checking it ever again.

They share a look that I can't decipher before responding.

"No, it's fine," Autumn says softly. "Things happen."

Miles nods in agreement with her, but he stays silent.

I know they want to say more. I know I disappointed them, at the very least. Hell, *I* want to say more, but I refrain for the sake of not trying to drive them absolutely mad. They'll have plenty of that coming up.

"Wook at this wittle beanie," I say, directed back at their son. "How do they even make them so small?"

We fawn over all the little pieces, Autumn even steps away for a second to grab a pack of his socks. *Baby socks*, those are really something else. Just the sight of them makes me emotional, thinking back on the days when my girl had clothes so small I couldn't handle it.

It feels like I merely had time to blink, and now I can't handle how big they are.

36

I hug my girl tight, breathing in air that I'm going to go crazy missing. I can't believe it's happening right now, and for a long moment I regret giving in. I regret agreeing to this, and not holding my ground. This is insanity. Just the thought of living life like normal without her feels so wrong.

It won't be normal, I guess. I'll be on vacation myself, but that doesn't mean I'm not going to feel Dahlia's absence so hard.

"We'll call every single day," Caleb's quiet voice comes from somewhere in front of us. "Multiple times if that's what you need, seriously. If you want to wake me up in the middle of the night to prove to you that she's still alive and well, I'll answer and show you her sleeping face."

The words twist something in my heart, and it makes me feel... grateful. I can't remember the last time I felt that way about my ex-husband.

"Thank you," I whisper. I lean away to look at Dahlia's face and give her my best smile. "You're going to have so much fun, aren't you?"

"Are planes fun?"

"They can be," I say honestly. I don't personally think so, but some people feel that way. I think. "You get to relax, and eat snacks, and watch movies."

"And you're not getting on the plane with us?" she asks. We've already explained this a few times, but I don't blame her for needing one last confirmation.

"Not this time, but you'll have your dad and Raquel. I think they'll make pretty good company."

I meet Caleb's eyes and an appreciative smile pulls at his lips.

Dahlia suddenly jolts in my arms.

"I don't have my gloves!"

"Oh my goodness, you better go find them!" I say as I set her on the ground. She doesn't waste a single second running back into the house and down to her room. It's a disaster in there after getting her packed and ready. The amount of things that I haven't seen her wear in the last year that she *needed* to find before she left was... a lot.

The gloves shouldn't be buried too far, she wore them to school every day this last winter.

There are a few seconds of uncomfortable silence that follows her absence, but not as uncomfortable as it normally is. I like the feeling of this progress we've made.

"You okay?" he asks.

I blow out a quick, pained laugh.

"How can I be? I'm going to miss her so much." I'm mortified when my voice cracks on the last word. Not enough to shut up, though. "I'm just glad I won't be stuck here the whole time. This apartment feels really empty when she's gone."

"I know the feeling. It was the biggest downside of getting the house. Way too much space to have by myself."

I've never thought about it that way, not for him. I thought he loved being his spoiled self, and basking in all the things his family's money brought him. But what's a big house without someone to share it with? Even the worst of people get lonely.

Not that I think he's the worst. Not really.

"Is Raquel going to move in?"

"It's something we've talked about, of course. I would really like that, but we wanted to handle one thing at a time. This trip became the priority."

I nod in response, and accept the fact that my daughter practically has a step-mom now. I'm not worried about feeling replaced, it's just different. I think things are going to move pretty fast in their lives, and it'll be an adjustment for all of us.

Dahlia comes back out, running past me to hand her gloves to her dad.

"Can you keep these so they don't get lost?"

"I sure can," he says as he takes them from her and tucks them into his coat pocket. "Are you ready to go?"

"Yes, yes, yes," she responds. She jumps up and down in between the words, and it's so cute that I have to dab at the corner of my eyes. I want to get through this without giving her any reason to worry. I really do want her to have the best time, and it won't happen if she knows I'm as sad as I am.

"Have a great time, princess!"

"I will," she shouts back.

I scoop her up to hug her again, as tight as possible while still letting her breathe. She giggles, but squirms to be put back down. I'm making a fuss. She doesn't really understand why yet.

"I'll miss you so much."

"I'll miss you too, mama."

Yep, I'm crying. I don't even think she knows what it's like to really miss someone, but she's going to find out.

Raquel and Caleb both give me awkward hugs and promises that she'll be taken care of. That she'll have fun. That this is all worth it.

I cry harder, but Dahlia is too excited to notice. I'm relieved when she takes Raquel's hand and they start down the stairs without looking my way again.

"Sorry," I apologize to Caleb for whatever reason. "I told myself I'd keep it together, but I'm freaking out."

He hugs me again, but the weirdest part is that I *let* him hug me again. I even squeeze him back a little tighter.

"I promise she'll be safe, and we will call you every single day so you can see her face."

I nod a few times, not trusting my voice.

"Thank you, Reya."

I nod again.

"Call me before your flight leaves."

"It's at five in the morning," he says.

"I know. I'll be awake."

"Okay. Of course."

"Thank you, Caleb."

He smiles and leaves, and I can still hear my daughter's cheery voice from down in the parking lot.

I don't bother going back into my own apartment, I walk straight through Kara's front door.

"Are you okay?" she asks me as I fall into her arms and bury my face in her neck.

"I don't want to step a single foot in my apartment until she's back."

There's a problem with that. We leave in two days and we're only going to be gone for a few. That leaves a lot of days for moping around.

"Oh no," she teases. "If only you had a girlfriend with an apartment of her own that loved having you around all the time."

"You love having me around *all the time*? I thought you'd be missing your late night rock concerts by now."

She playfully slaps at my shoulder, and I laugh as I squeeze her harder.

37

The air is knocked right out of my lungs when we step off the path that leads to the beach. I've been here before, I've seen the ocean, but there's something about this piece of the ocean and this time of day. The sun is reflecting off of the sea in golden waves, water gently splashes onto rocks in the distance.

"It's gorgeous," I whisper.

"I needed this so badly," Kara sighs. I look over to see her facing up towards the sky with her eyes closed. Soaking in the sun like the tanned goddess she is.

She's always glowing, but there's something that shines brighter about her here. This is her element. This is what it looks like to see someone who usually carries so much weight on their shoulders finally be able to drop it off and fling it into the ocean.

"Race you to the water," I say.

She looks over at me and smirks.

"Count of three?"

"One, two–" I run, kicking up as much sand behind me as possible.

I hear the beautiful ring of her laughter as she follows behind me, and then the sound of her spitting out the sand that's flying into the air.

"You monster!"

My heavy steps slow as they splash into the shore, soaking through my shoes. The shocking cold water is a welcome sensation.

Kara sloshes up next to me, and sucks air through her teeth as the water reaches her ankles.

"Gah, that's cold!"

"It's perfect."

"You're perfect," she replies quickly.

I lean over to kiss her, grateful that the beach is crowded with onlookers. I want to kiss her, and hold her hand, and look into her eyes, without worrying about any ugly looks from anyone who might not want to see it.

We do all of the above. We hold hands as we kick water back and forth at each other. When my feet finally go so numb that they feel like they're being stabbed with hundreds of tiny needles, I move back onto dry sand and rip off my shoes and socks. There are shells and rocks everywhere, and I take to looking through them for the prettiest ones. Something I've done since I was a kid. I think my parents still have jars and jars full of them in a storage closet somewhere.

I pick up every single one that's colorful or shiny enough to stand out, and stick them in the pocket of my sweatshirt. Kara walks alongside me silently, only picking up the occasional rock to skip across the water when the tide pulls back. I clap and cheer as she goes. Her high score of the day is nine total skips, and I won't be getting over that anytime soon.

Boulders eventually block our path and force us to turn back around. I suppose we could keep going if we felt like a big swim around them to the beach on the other side, but it's a little too windy to have to continue on our way in drenched clothes.

Neither of us complain about our overworked legs. I can't remember the last time I took this many steps. I zig zag from the water and back to the sand, over and over. She keeps following, either watching me or watching the waves that are now gorgeously illuminated by an almost setting sun. The foaming waves go from white to a shimmering gold.

It's so mesmerizing, I feel like I'm meditating. I can't remember the last time I felt so present somewhere, and not like my mind was miles away.

"You look like you don't have a worry in the world," Kara murmurs as she watches my steps. "I like it."

"Me too." I look over at her, taking in the way the wind whips her hair around. It would drive me nuts, the way it swats at her face and hinders her view.

She does nothing, acts as if it's not happening.

"The worries still exist, but they are blissfully quiet right now."

"It's about time they piped down. I'll have to bring you to the beach every time they take over."

I smile.

"Good plan. Where should I take you when yours get too loud?"

She hums in thought, and starts walking out towards the water. Further into the water. Her leggings become more and more soaked, and I *wish* that wasn't destined to also happen to me. She puts her hand out, asking me to meet her where she is, and of course I go. Wet pants or not, I'll follow her anywhere.

I pull my pant legs up as far as they'll go before making my way to her. She intertwines her fingers with mine before dropping her head to my shoulder.

"You could take me anywhere. It's not any specific place, it's you."

Before I can appreciate the sweetness of her words, she's flicking water at my face and then covering her own.

Little does she know, she just started a war. I use both hands and arms to shove as much water as I can her way. She shouts as the wave of it drenches the front of her.

"I take back every cute thing I said!"

I move to do it again, burying my hands in the water, but she grabs my wrists to stop me. We're chest to chest, both uncomfortably cold in a way our closeness is no match against.

But I love it.

We're a giggling mess as she holds onto me tightly, moving her grasp down to my hands. I feel more alive than ever as the wind rushes past us, rocky sand pokes at our feet, and salt water sticks our palms together.

We crash down onto the bed in our hotel room. My legs are sore and overworked, my skin is sunburnt. The warm, windy day sucked out every ounce of my energy, and now there's nothing that could get me off of this bed any time soon.

"What a day," I sigh contentedly.

"Let's just stay here and never deal with anyone else again," Kara says.

I look over to see her laying on her side with her eyes shut, and strands of her wind-knotted hair falling across her cheek.

"I could get behind that, but... I do have some other people I'd kind of miss."

"Can't relate," she replies softly.

I reach out to tuck those strands behind her ear, but I don't pull it away. Instead I let myself hold her face, and feel her warm cheek against my palm.

"Do you really hate everyone? Or is it just easier to pretend you do?"She freezes, probably feeling a little taken aback. If she doesn't want to go there after our peaceful day, she doesn't have to. I won't pry.

But now that I know my chances of getting answers to my questions are much higher, I'm not going to stop myself from asking them.

"It's not that I hate everyone," she admits. "I mean, mostly. I just don't think there's much of a chance that they won't let me down. That *they* won't hate *me*."

"So you don't want to let anyone figure out how they feel about you?" I ask. "You probably don't need me to tell you, but you're a blast to be around. If you let people see more of what I see, they wouldn't."

"They did. Why do you think I'm like this?"

"Yeah, but kids are ruthless. No one in high school cares about anyone more than themselves, it's not a good reason to–"

Hey eyes fly open as she interrupts me.

"It's not only the kids back in high school. Everyone has always wanted me to change, but that's always been *their* problem. My whole life I've heard people try to tell me why I'm like this, whether they blame it on my depression or assume I have some other mental setback. I've always known they were wrong. I feel fine, I'm just content with less than other people think I should be content with."

"I can understand that."

She sighs.

"But can you? Because I'm not going to change. I don't want to change anything about myself to make anyone else's life simpler. It's why no relationship has ever worked out for me. It's why my marriage was such a disaster."

"So Miles wanted you to be someone you aren't?"

"Not necessarily. We were young and stupid when we first started dating, and I didn't even know who I was. We learned that much together, and I still get so angry sometimes that it took that many years of learning for us to figure out we weren't compatible," she says.

"Was that it, you weren't compatible? Or could he just not accept the person you were?" I ask.

"I think you're assuming that he was in the wrong, and *should've* accepted things, but that's not true. If I knew enough to give him a disclaimer at the start of it all, he would've known it wasn't going to work out between us. We would've broken up before we got married, and before I got comfortable enough to let the facade slip. If anything it's all my fault for not having that disclaimer ready."

I shake my head as I sit up. This can't be said lying down. She must agree, because she moves to sit up against the headboard.

"It's not your fault. You said it yourself, you were young. You didn't know any better." She doesn't have a response to that so I continue. "Did you have any relationships before him?"

"I mean... kind of. Nothing serious, just a couple of random high school boyfriends. Don't think either of them tolerated me more than a couple of months."

"They both dumped you?"

"Everyone's dumped me. I've never been the dumper, despite what my cold, hard exterior might lead you to believe."

"I thought your divorce was mutual?"

She shrugs.

"By the end, yes, but he's the one that initially brought it up. Like I said, I'm content with less. It got to a point where he started to leave me alone. We stopped sleeping together, stopped eating together. And it was... fine. I mean, I wasn't thriving or anything, but I was comfortable enough to accept my life for what it was. I would've gone on like that for another eight years. Another eighty, honestly."

"That makes me so sad to think about." So sad, in fact, that I struggle to clear the lump in my throat.

She's so deserving of love, and joy, and it's criminal that she's only just getting it now.

"It shouldn't. I was fine. I'm fine now. Everything happened the way it was supposed to."

I trace delicate lines down her bare arm, and watch the goosebumps that raise in the aftermath.

"So do you think... Do you think you were supposed to end up moving in next to me and shaking up my life?"

I look up at her face to find her staring at the ceiling. I couldn't begin to read her expression, it's as blank as it's ever been.

"Probably," she whispers.

"Well, I've received the disclaimer," I say.

She finally looks down at me.

"And?"

If I didn't know any better, I'd think she sounded hopeful.

"I'm okay with whatever you're okay with. I don't need any-thing from you that you're not willing to give."

"That'll change." She says the words like they're a fact.

"What do you need me to do to prove it?"

"Stick around, I guess."

My lips spread in the widest possible smile.

"So, you want me to stick around?"

She doesn't hesitate.

"Yes."

And that little word, that little piece of vulnerability that might seem so unimportant to anyone else? It just reaffirms what I already knew. I'm absolutely sticking around.

❧

"What a view! Are you guys at the top of a mountain?" I ask, flabbergasted.

I hear various voices in the background, a couple of them laugh-ing at my surprise.

"Yeah, it's really big," Dahlia says. "We were walking so much, and my legs are too tired to walk anymore."

"Well it's a good thing your dad doesn't mind carrying you around. That would make my legs *so* tired." Something about that makes her giggle. "How are you guys even calling me? You have service up there?"

"I'm as surprised about it as you are," Caleb replies. "I took some pictures to send you, but this is way cooler."

He flips the camera to show me the mountains surrounding them and I gasp. Early afternoon sunlight covers the world around them in a golden, shimmering warmth. It looks so peaceful that I could actually cry, and I'm not even experiencing it in person. There are miles and miles visible from their vantage point, and every inch of it is breathtaking.

Note to self to stop being lazy and see more of the world.

Which is exactly what I'm doing, but even after this. When Dahlia is home I want to be able to experience things like this with her.

In a perfect world, I picture all of us going on a trip together. Kara too. Maybe even my friends and their partners, and their kids. That would be so good for Dahlia, but it would also be good for me. Therapeutic even.

With tears in my eyes I thank him for showing me.

"Happy to," he replies, and I believe him. "Where are you at the moment? That's not your place."

"A hotel. On the beach." I go to the window so I can show him my beautiful view.

"That looks nice! Look Lia, your mom is at the ocean!"

She beams at the phone, and coos about how pretty the water looks. We talk about planning our own beach getaway when she's home, but her attention doesn't stay on me for long. I don't blame her, she has too much to take in over there.

I thank Caleb again. He tells me to have a fun time and I tell them to be safe. It's the first time I don't feel all that doubtful that she is safe with him.

38

"Did you know they had a little chapel here?" I laugh. "Seems like such a random place, this isn't Vegas or anything."

"I had no idea. I wonder how long it's been there."

Although, the faded pink paint on the outside tells us it wasn't all that new.

"Would you ever consider getting married in a place like that?" The question makes me think of another one I don't have the answer to. "Where did you get married before?"

"I don't know," she answers like she's considering that. "And it was at a park. Our parents, a couple friends, nothing fancy. What about you?"

"At his parent's lake house. Huge backyard overlooking the water. I hate to say it, but it was kind of perfect."

"Everything but the groom?"

I give her finger guns.

"Bingo."

We walk past the building, taking in its details. Our destination is the taco truck across the street, but something about it draws me in. As hungry as I was, I feel like making a stop to go inside and see what it's all about.

Kara gives me a side glance and a smirk.

"Something funny about this?" I ask, knowing the answer.

It is kind of funny, the way we're two divorced women that fell in love walking past a dingy, old chapel. It feels like a silly sign from the universe, reminding us where we've been.

Or something poetic like that.

"Would *you* ever consider it?" she asks me.

As she does, a woman steps out of the large, open double door in the front. Twice our age, twice as cheery. As far as I can tell, she wasn't getting married today. Maybe she owns it, or works there. She's humming along as she strolls down the couple steps out front, and I can't keep myself from staring. It helps that she doesn't notice, as she walks around the side. A green hose sits on the ground, coiled like a snake. It might as well be the most entertaining thing I see as we get closer and closer, the sidewalk leading right by her.

She turns it on, and begins spraying some nearby bushes, and her cheery demeanor never dulls.

To my surprise, when we're close enough to notice, she smiles and waves. I wave back, Kara refrains.

"Would you?" she presses.

"Probably. Yeah." I don't even know why I say it, but it feels right coming out of my mouth. Maybe it's just the trance I'm caught in, some weird magical spell that makes the place seem so captivating.

"To me?"

I stop walking and face her.

"You're asking if I'd marry you?"

I can't be sure how I was able to ask that much, can people talk when their hearts completely stop beating? Because that's what feels like is going on.

She has to shield the sun from her face when she faces me, and the way her eyes crinkle is pure perfection. Like when she laughs at me. It lights me up.

"What if I was? What would you say?"

A few beats pass before I wrap my head around it.

"I'd say that's crazy."

How could I say anything else?

She shifts her weight from one leg to another.

"Everything's always changing, and it's always out of my control, and I feel so alone with all of it," she starts. It feels like her eyes are staring straight into my soul. "But I don't when I'm with you, and it... It makes me feel like I never want to lose this."

Holy shit.

I feel the same way about her. Of course I never want to lose her. I've experienced a taste of it once before, and I can live without that feeling for the rest of my life.

But getting married again? Now?

"That's like... I don't know, Kara. That's a lot. I've been divorced once already."

"So have I, remember? Do you think I'd even broach the subject if I wasn't a million percent sure about you?" she asks.

"You're being so serious?" I breathe.

"I am," she says. "I can't believe I am, but this moment just feels like *something*. Like why else would this just be in our path while trying to find some tacos?"

"You sound like you believe in fate."

"I have to now. I moved in next to you."

The words reach my ears, and I run up to hug her. Her arms don't even take very long to wrap around me in return, and then she's kissing my head.

"I love you. A lot," she whispers.

I'm scared. I think it would be weird if I wasn't, but I trust her. Maybe I'm a fool for it, and maybe one day I'll regret not being more apprehensive.

But life is short.

With that running through my head, I tell my worries to fuck off, and I grab the back of her neck.

"Okay."

She immediately leans back, and her eyes bulge when they meet mine.

"Seriously? You'll marry me?"

"I totally will."

With those words, she's all I see, leaving kisses all over my face, my head, my neck. I giggle at her enthusiasm and feel my heart somehow expand to fit all of the love I have for her.

"I'm so in love with you, how is this even possible?"

If anyone knew how it was possible, it wouldn't feel so special.

"I'm going to love you forever."

When you spontaneously decide to get married while on vacation away from home, you do it at the courthouse, and it costs more than you'd think it would.

The woman we saw watering her plants was Connie. Her and her husband have owned the place for almost twenty years, after spontaneously getting married there themselves. When they found out it was for sale, it felt like *fate*.

They love love.

And she didn't even flinch at the fact that we're two women, so that seemed like another good sign.

We had to run to the courthouse to get a marriage license, *after* we ate obviously. I'd hate to do too much on and empty stomach. We signed some things, and paid a fee to wave their usual waiting period. By the time that was done, we still had an hour before the time we arranged with Connie to be back.

We were feeling even more grateful for small beach towns, when we passed by an antique shop on the way back.

"What if one of these is haunted?" I asked Kara as we browsed the large jewelry case on the far side of the shop. I'd never seen so many unique pieces of jewelry.

"I could make it work," she replied.

She got a side eye in response to that, but I kept my lips sealed.

I just silently hoped we got some ghost free rings.

After the shortest and sweetest ceremony I've ever witnessed, I was Kara's wife. The rings on our fingers reflected each other's birthstone, and the amazement that we found them felt like yet *another* positive sign.

There wasn't a single doubt in my mind by the time we made it back to the hotel room, hand in hand, giggling like we didn't have a care in the world. We kissed until our mouths went numb, and then we used other means to feel closer to each other.

Why is it a million times hotter to watch someone have an orgasm when they're wearing a wedding ring that you're responsible for putting there?

"Best sex of my life," I gasp, falling back against the covers. "Have you been holding out on me?"

I lean in to kiss her again before she can respond, eliciting sweet laughter that tilts her head back and away from me.

"Yeah, sorry. You had to unlock this level."

"Worth it, I guess," I say.

I drape an arm over her and pull her into me. She buries her face in hair.

"I can't believe you're my wife."

"It's going to take some getting used to," I agree.

Not to mention when we head home and have to face our new reality with our loved ones. I feel a panic rise in me when Autumn's face flashes in my mind, but I can't go there right now. This day is not going to end on that kind of note.

We will cross that bridge when we get to it.

39

The day after our ceremony, Kara woke up with a purpose. She shot out of bed, and rattled off half the details of a plan. Which I was still half asleep for. Missed the plan entirely.

I only woke up once I heard the door slam closed, and barely squinted my eyes open to make out the shape of her holding something. Food.

She went out for breakfast sandwiches.

I am in love with her.

I also happen to be a bit frustrated with her, because she really rushed me to eat and get ready. Vacations are meant for sleeping in, and I deserved that much after the previous twenty-four hours.

When I pried for an explanation, I was met with a sneaky little expression that told me I'd have to find out the hard way.

And it *was* hard. I don't do enough hiking.

I stand there at the base of that waterfall, and I just feel. I relish the tiny freezing pricks of the water that land on my cheeks, and the wind that numbs them. My hair flows wildly around me, something I've never let it do. I've always tied it up or tucked it behind an ear, but it's feels amazing. It's so freeing.

"You look so happy," she whispers. Almost like she didn't mean to say it out loud.

"I am." I reach a hand out for her, and know I don't have to reach far before she takes it and steps beside me. "Close your eyes."

We stand there in silence for so long. Maybe a few minutes, maybe twenty. It's hard to tell. I only open my eyes because my teeth start to chatter. I see hers doing the same, but beside that... she looks so at peace.

"I'm so glad I married you."

She slowly opens her eyes to gaze over at me.

"So am I."

"I think this is karma for all the times I've shown up unannounced at someone's house."

Her laugh is muffled by the pillow, and I can tell that the ringing doorbell isn't bothering her nearly as much as it's bothering me. Probably because wherever she's still hanging out in dreamland isn't somewhere she needs to worry about the repercussions of getting married and not telling a single soul.

I drag myself out of bed, fueled by panic when the ringing doesn't relent. It must be someone that gives a damn about me if they're trying this hard to get me to the front door.

I take a deep breath and decide that whoever it is: I don't have to tell them anything today. I could avoid doing this one on one and throw a dinner party or something. Maybe I'll bake a cake that'll be so delicious it distracts everyone from the news.

Happy taste buds, happy emotions. Hopefully.

Autumn stands at my front door, her brows scrunched in what seems to be concern. *Shit.*

I never ignore her, and definitely never for this long. It wasn't even intentional, things just got away from me for a while. All I want to do when I pick up my phone lately is find out what my daughter is up to.

"Rey," she says like she's relieved. "I thought I was going to have to call the police or something."

"That's extreme," I say in an attempt to sound casual. "Sorry, babe. I was sleeping."

"Have you been sleeping for the last couple months? Honestly, what the hell?"

I laugh, pretending I don't notice that she's not happy.

"I know, I've been so distracted lately. I haven't really been socializing."

"Or going to work?" she asks, raising her voice. "There was some new girl working that told me you haven't been there in a while. What's going on?"

"I went on vacation, did I not tell you? It's okay, Autumn. I promise everything is fine. I just needed a break. It's been really nice to take a step back."

Her shoulders drop, relaxing at that.

"Where did you go?"

"Just to the coast for a few days."

"When are you going back to work?"

"Such an interrogation," I joke. Kind of. I'm too tired to be answering all these questions. "Next week."

"How'd you afford that?"

I scratch at my jaw, hating that I'm getting frustrated with her right now. I just wasn't ready for this. I wish she could come back tomorrow or the next day and worry about me.

"I had the vacation time."

"What the fuck is that?"

I look down quickly, nervous there's a bug on something. I start swatting without seeing anything.

"What?" I'm a little frantic. "What is *what*?"

She stops me by grabbing my hand.

My heart ceases to beat when the realization hits me.

"Why is there a ring on this finger?" Her voice is deathly calm. I don't know what emotion is fueling it, but it's big. *This* is big, and I am terrified.

"Um... It is..." I hate my brain for failing to fill in the blank. I don't want to lie, but I really don't want to tell the truth. Not yet.

Her head snaps up, and my reaction time to the responsible sound is much more delayed.

My bedroom door opens.

Autumn can't see it from where she stands, but I can when I turn my head. Kara is frozen in place, realizing I've got someone standing at the front door. It's too late. It's clear that I'm not alone, and when you combine that fact with the ring on my hand...

Why didn't I think to take it off?

"I don't like this." Autumn takes a step back, dropping my hand, and my heart sinks. "I'm not going to beg you to tell me what's going on, but if that—"she points to my hand again—"is what I think it is..." There's no end to the sentence, because I know. I know how fucked up it is, and how much it's got to hurt her that I'd keep it to myself.

I hear shuffling to my right, and turn to see Kara making her way over. I can't shake my head fast enough, but it doesn't matter. The gesture exposes me enough, there's no doubt I want to be keeping something from Autumn when I make it. Kara doesn't see me anyway, keeping her eyes down until she's standing next to me.

Until she's *right* next to me in the doorway. Right where Autumn can see her. She's not even wearing pants, just one of my big shirts.

My friend's face looks so pained as her hand flies up to cover her mouth.

She takes a step backwards, and I take one forward.

"Can we just talk about—"

"This is some joke, right?" I hear the emotion in her words, and I watch as her eyes start to shine. "What the hell, Rey? What did I do to deserve this?"

I was ready to apologize profusely, but the last sentence stops me. What did she do to deserve this? As if the choices I've made on behalf of my own emotions, my own happiness, are an attack on her?

I must be misunderstanding, because she's never been that self-ish.

"Are you serious?" Kara asks, and I know it's only going to make this worse. Autumn doesn't want to hear from her right now. What needs to happen is for the two of us to come back together another day and talk about all of this.

It's a lot, and I fucked up, and I'm willing to admit it.

"I'm so serious. I can't believe you." She looks at me the entire time, acting as if Kara hadn't said a word.

She sounds so wounded, that it tears me up inside. I instinctively want to comfort her, but I can't believe she's acting like my relationship is something being *done* to her.

I gape.

"Come on, Autumn. This isn't about you. Kara makes me happy. We love each other, and–"

"Stop. Please."

It's like I'm watching her heart break further and further, but that's how I feel. I'm not going to act like I'm guilty for being this disgustingly, happily in love. She'll get over it if she would take a second to see it for what it is.

I don't even know how much I care if she does. My emotions are high, and I'll probably feel differently tomorrow, but right now... I don't care at all.

I can tell she wants to say more, but she holds it in. Whatever it is.

"You should leave," I tell her.

She shakes her head.

"Why would you n—"

"I want you to leave right now. I didn't want to have this conversation today."

Her head drops in what I assume is defeat. My limbs ache with the urge to hug her, but I stay still. Painfully still, like a damned statue.

She hesitates for a few seconds, but she does it. She leaves without another word, or another look my way.

Arms wrap around me from behind.

"I'm so sorry, sunshine."

My head falls back onto Kara's shoulder.

"Wow," I whisper. I don't know what other words there are to say. Trying to come up with some just sounds exhausting.

Being back in bed sounds so appealing, and Kara must see it on my face. She guides me back to my room, and my head is hitting my pillow before I know it.

"I'm here if you need anything."

The last thing I'm aware of before falling back asleep is the soft kiss she places on my cheek.

How could *this* upset someone that cares about me so much?

"We have to figure out how to tell people. I don't want to take this ring off, but I can't go back to work with it on. I don't want my coworkers to figure it out before we tell the important ones."

"Who do you want to tell first?" she asks before opening up my junk drawer and pulling out a pad of paper that should look all too familiar. We smile at each other before she clicks a pen and encourages me to answer.

I guess we're getting organized.

"My parents. They'll be cool about it, I think. *Definitely* surprised, maybe a little disappointed they weren't there to see it, but I don't think they'll be upset."

She writes it down.

"I'm glad. That's one less terrifying conversation for us to have."

"Who do you want to tell first?"

"No one, but I guess I have to tell my parents too. They won't be happy. It's going to go terribly."

I rest a hand on her shoulder.

"You want to give me a heads up on what to expect?"

We've already established that her mom isn't a good person, but I want to be as prepared as I can possibly be. My wife takes a steadying breath before diving in.

"On top of all her other endearing qualities, she's very traditional. Actually—traditional isn't the right word. She's hateful. Believes marriage should only be between a man and a woman." Her eyes scan my face like she's waiting for me to be scared, but it won't happen. I've dealt with plenty of shit over the years, even while I was with Caleb. My appearance has always made people believe I wasn't straight, before I even knew myself. "I remember when same sex marriage was legalized, and she went into a rage. Went on about how that didn't mean she'd have to work with any of them, and that she hoped there wasn't a real estate agent in town that would because, 'they're lifestyle shouldn't be enabled like that.'"

She gestures with air quotes for the last part, and I hold back a wince.

I need to give my mom the biggest hug the next time I see her. It's not like I wasn't aware how lucky I am to have her, but I'm finding new evidence every day.

"What about your dad?" I ask quietly.

Kara shrugs. "He's always been scared to disagree with her, despite whatever he actually thinks. Such a peacekeeper. I don't think I know his opinion on anything."

"Why don't we tell them separately? We can talk to Pierre first, and hope he handles it better than she will."

Kara leans in and presses a kiss to my lips.

"I don't know, but we can try." Another soft kiss. "Thank you."

40

Pierre takes it so well. Apparently all he needed was to put some divorce papers into play in order to gain his own opinion, because he's ecstatic that his daughter is happily married. He hugs me so many times I lose count, and he insists on paying for the dinner we invited him to. He offers to do it again, says the three of us *must* get together often.

If my dad went years without genuinely smiling at me, and then turned into this overnight? It would be overwhelming in the best way, and that's exactly how my wife is feeling.

Kara is lit from within, more alive than I think I've ever seen her. I can't fully imagine being as strong as she's been, or what it's like for her to feel like things are finally working out for the better.

I'm thinking we should have told her mom first, and saved the best for last, but it's too late now. I'm scared. I was nervous about meeting with him, but I'm terrified of Colleen.

Rightfully so.

The woman before us is doing the most aggressive pacing I've ever seen in my life. Her red stilettos tap harshly against her polished, white tiled floors.

We're sitting at a counter, in a kitchen that looks like it has never been used despite its size. Baking would be so much easier for me if I had this much counter space, I'm drooling at the thought.

It's the only thing I like about this mini-mansion. It's cold and void of any color or *life*. Amelia should be allowed inside, she could make it feel a lot less like a prison. Or an insane asylum, because I'm definitely going insane just looking at the tall, bare walls.

"You're getting it annulled. I'll take you myself," Colleen states once she's standing in place.

Kara scoffs a laugh.

"No. We're not doing that."

"Yes, you are. You simple minded, girl." The sentence feels like a gut punch and it wasn't even directed at me. *Who talks like that?* "I'm not going to have you embarrass me anymore than you already have. This–" she gestures between us– "is not happening."

"You must have missed the memo *years* ago, but I've made it pretty obvious that I don't care about embarrassing you."

"Of course you don't, you've always been absurdly ungrateful," she says with a roll of her eyes. I hate to even think it, to compare the two of them at all, but that's exactly where Kara gets it. "This is too far. When you got divorced, I did my best to look the other way and let you navigate things. It was challenging for me, I could not believe you screwed up such a good thing like that."

"It wasn't a good thing," Kara says through gritted teeth. "Separating *was* the good part."

"Stop speaking to me like that! You walked into my house to speak with me, and you'll do it with respect," she demands.

"Do something that makes you worthy of my respect first."

There is fear deep in my bones at the way the words make Colleen seethe. The temperature in the room feels like it goes up ten degrees. I'm starting to sweat, and panic, and it's not pretty.

"I raised you! I don't know how you turned out like this, but–"

"You did not! You showed up a couple times a month to tell me what a disappointment I was. Stop with the bullshit."

"If that's how you feel, then maybe you shouldn't have been so pathet–"

"Okay, we're done here," I decide sternly.

I can't just sit here and watch them argue and insult each other. I can't just let this monster of a woman talk to my wife like that.

"No one is talking to you, you can leave at any time," Colleen says without even glancing my way.

"My *wife* isn't going anywhere without me," Kara shouts. Her mom winces when she says it, and that makes Kara smile for the first time since we walked in. "That's what she is, and will continue to be. We're married, and you can deal with it or not. I don't care. You should be grateful I even decided to tell you!"

Colleen clasps her hands together in front of her, and quickly slips on a mask of poise and calm. It gives me whiplash, it's so sudden. No wonder she's successful at what she does, she can *act*. Well.

"I wish you hadn't," she says with false sweetness. "I wish I had no idea that my daughter decided to make a mockery of marriage by playing house with some random woman. Don't come crying to me when you have two divorces under your belt, because I won't be acknowledging that this one exists."

It's rich coming from someone that's in the midst of a divorce.

Kara stands abruptly, and I follow suit, almost falling off the seat in the process. Thankfully, she's there with a steadying hand on my arm.

Steadying *me,* when I should be doing that for her.

She's needed it her entire life, and never had anyone to hold her up.

I promise in that moment, even stronger than I did the day we got married, to make sure she feels it for the rest of her life.

"I don't have to acknowledge you exist at all, thanks for the ammunition to finally let me take that step," Kara says, mocking Colleen's previous tone.

Her mother doesn't respond, turning away from us towards a large staircase behind her. Seeming unbothered, or like it's a relief to hear those words.

"You shouldn't have been allowed to be a parent," I call after her. "You have no idea what an incredible person she became without any of your help, but I *want* you to know. I want it to haunt you."

I swear I see her steps falter for a fraction of a second, but I don't care. I lace my fingers with Kara's and we head out together. She'll have my parents now too, and they're going to love her enough to make Colleen a distant memory.

41

I knock on Autumn's door with a gentle hand, not knowing if I should be disappointed or relieved that Miles' car isn't in their driveway.

Autumn opens it slowly, and in her arms is a swaddled bundle. Baby boy is fast asleep, and she sways in place to keep it that way.

"Hey, babe," I say with a newfound shyness.

"Hi."

She's not happy to see me, that much is clear.

I blow out a steadying breath, and twist the ring on my finger. It's a habit I've picked up doing a lot lately, especially when I'm nervous. Even though I couldn't be more nervous right now, I force myself to drop my hands to my sides. It might be kind of a rude reminder, given the situation. I should've taken it off before coming here, but yet again, I didn't think that through.

"I'm sorry it's her. I know that must be so hard on you, but we really do have something special. It was never—"

"Okay, stop." She puts her free hand out to emphasize her words. "That's what you're apologizing for?"

I look around like I'll find something to clear up my confusion, but there's nothing.

"Yeah?"

Autumn shakes her head, and I'm in shock that she manages to look so disappointed. It's not something I've ever really seen on her, and definitely not directed at me.

"It was never about it being Kara. I'm upset that I have to even explain that." I widen my eyes in an impatient attempt at encouraging her to keep talking. "Don't you know that I get that part? Wanting to be with someone even if the people around you won't be happy about it? Doesn't that sound familiar?" She pauses as if waiting for me to confirm, but I have a feeling it's rhetorical.

"My first thought wasn't that you betrayed me by being with her, it was that you told me *nothing*," she explains. Her voice cracks on the last word.

My face falls. My stomach twists into a knot.

"That's what hurt. I'd understand if you needed time to process, to think of what to say to me. It's a lot. I'd understand if I'd found out months ago, but what am I supposed to think now? You snuck around. I talked to Vic, I know you wanted her to keep quiet, and not just for a couple days or a couple weeks. I've been cut out of your life for *months*. Think about the fit you'd be throwing if I had a secret relationship I didn't tell you about for so long." She shakes her head, looking so defeated that it physically hurts. "And then got *married*. Imagine if I got *married* and didn't tell you? You would never forgive me."

"Autumn, I…"

Words fail me. She's somewhat wrong, and somewhat right. I can't even believe how backwards I had it. I was so focused on who Kara was to Autumn, that I barely gave the other details a passing thought.

"Crap, of course. It's just been this huge whirlwind, and the time has really gotten away from me," I confess.

What was months for everyone else, felt like a few days for me.

The most gigantic roller coaster of a few days, but still.

"You couldn't even answer your phone? That's how much *time got away from you*? Vic had to go collect you when I was in the hospital! I really tried to play it cool, but that sucked," she tells me. "I was crying to my boyfriend on what should've been the happiest night of my life, because you barely made time for us."

I take a small, sad step closer to her, wishing I could magically pull that hurt away.

"I made you cry?" I ask, my voice hoarse.

She nods, not meeting my eyes.

"Look, I'm exhausted. I need to try and sleep while he is, so..." She trails off, letting me fill in the blanks.

"Autumn, I'm really sorry."

She nods like she believes me, but the tense air between us doesn't lighten up.

"I know you think I forgive too easily, that I'm too nice to people. Well, here you go, Reya. I don't feel like being nice right now."

And she closes the door in my face.

Not a slam, that's still not her style, no matter how hurt she is.

When I finally walk away, I'm feeling a million times worse. I showed up thinking I could talk some sense into her over an assumption I was making, but I was so wrong. I was so stupidly wrong.

I've never been more annoyed with myself, because for as much as I want to talk to her right now? As much as I want us to make up, and hug, and have a normal conversation? Hell, as much as I'd love to just see her smile?

The ache that comes with it is the least I deserve for so easily pushing her out of my mind for my own convenience.

I've been a shitty friend.

It doesn't take me long to come up with a new plan. A few days of sitting in self pity really gives a girl plenty of opportunities to brainstorm.

And plenty of opportunities to kick that self pitying attitude.

Autumn and I have been friends too long to bullshit. I apologized, I know I messed up, and now's the part where we just need to move forward. After talking Kara's ears off about what to do that night when I got home, she agreed with me. We're too grown to let this come between us. I miss my best friend, and I'm doing something about it.

Better late than never.

I texted her a couple of times, called her too. No answer, of course.

So I'm doing the next best thing.

Except when I walk through Amelia's front door, I have a moment of regret. Everyone stares at me like I've grown an extra head on my shoulders, instead of the usual smiles I'm used to getting. I mean... I'm usually the life of the party here. I'm not a fan of this change.

"Why are you here?" Autumn asks, her voice cold and distant. So unlike her.

Amelia looks between us, visibly concerned. Miles, Sam, and Justin keep their heads down. Vic is nowhere to be seen, which makes my confidence slightly falter. It would have been nice to have one person on my side.

If she's even on my side right now. I can't confirm that much.

"I was invited."

Not directly, but it was discussed in our group chat. They probably forgot I was a part of it, considering how rarely it gets used. The last time it was active was the day Autumn went into labor, and it was a bunch of hectic, all caps communication about the details.

I felt horrible when I noticed. I reread them all just to let the level of how bad I messed up sink in even further. I deserved it.

Today was the first time the chat's been used since then, and I jumped at the chance to be face to face with her.

I didn't have another choice, really.

Amelia mouths over to her, something about that chat. Autumn's head falls into her hands and she sighs. I choose to ignore it, taking a seat at my usual spot, right across from her.

"This smells delicious, Ames."

She nods in thanks, but it's unsure. She's done a lot wrong by Autumn, and wants to make sure she's playing her cards right. She wants her to know who's side she's on, whose she'll always choose.

The tension is so thick, I could drown in it. Everyone's quiet, everyone's uncomfortable. It really makes me feel like I ruined what was a perfectly fine night a few seconds ago.

I don't want that to be true. I had no intention of ruining anything when I decided to be here.

"I don't want any drama right now," Autumn finally looks up to tell me.

"Neither do I."

"Then why are you here?"

I'm silent for a few seconds, thinking through the least dramatic way to answer the question.

It must be a few seconds too many, because Miles clears his throat.

I watch as she turns to him, they make eye contact, and her face softens. He's always had that effect on her, but so did I. For all the years she didn't have him, it was me and Vic that helped her let her guard down.

"I think you should leave, Reya. I'm not ready to talk about it. I just want to have a nice, relaxing night." Her voice is kinder, but it doesn't ease the blow.

I scoff.

"You're not ready."

A quick shake of her head.

"When will you be ready? Just so I have a general idea of when you'll start responding to my messages."

"I don't know," she says.

The rest of the table is quiet, trying their hardest to pretend this isn't interesting them. It doesn't work, I know everyone loves an argument when they're not a part of it.

It's actually kind of pissing me off.

Maybe they should be a part of it.

"For all the shit you've been through with the rest of the people in this room, you didn't feel the need to punish any of them. Why me? Why your best friend?"

"I'm not–"

"I forgot to exclude Sam, of course." I wink at the man himself. "But the rest of them? You'd rather have a little dinner and chat with the guy who cheated on you, and the woman who implied for months that you were going to ruin her family? That you weren't good enough for them? Do you remember all of that, because I can't forget it."

Amelia gasps.

"Dude," Justin whispers. He sounds offended, but I'm not wrong. He should be offended. Offended by the reminder of what a shitty person he can be.

"Reya." It's Miles that says my name in warning. So protective.

"Have I not suffered enough? What, do you need something bad to happen to me so you can tell yourself that karma did its thing? You can't just avoid every inconvenient thing that comes your way. Some of them," I point to my chest, "won't let you. I'm *sorry*, Autumn. I hid something huge from you, I made stupid assumptions. It wasn't okay, but I can't go back in time and take any of it back."

Her eyes squeeze shut as she blows out a sharp breath.

"I don't want anything bad to happen to you," she says so very quietly. "I'm *hurt*. I'm tired. I'm overwhelmed. While you've been dwelling on this–" she motions between us– "I haven't had a free few seconds to process anything. I have a newborn that's cluster feeding, and keeping me up all night, every night. I know it's been a few years, but you must remember what that's like?" She allows no room for arguments. Her tone is sharp and to the point, and *of course* she knows I remember what that's like.

When she pauses, I think maybe it isn't a rhetorical question. Maybe I'm supposed to agree, tell her, but then she points at the man next to her.

"And aren't you two supposed to be besties now, *Rey*? You have nothing to say to him about all this? It's not my ex-wife you're fucking."

"Damn," is Justin's commentary to that.

I have another D word in mind whenever he opens his annoying mouth.

I level a glare at him.

Miles puts a hand on his girlfriend's shoulder.

"You understand why my priority is the way Autumn's feeling, right? I figured whatever there is for us to hash out can wait until after that's sorted," I tell him.

He looks between us, like he's not sure what thing he might say will upset which person.

"There's nothing to hash out. It's... weird, but everyone's got a person, right? If she's yours, then I can deal with it."

Because he found his person when everyone was telling him they *wouldn't* deal with it.

Why the hell does he have to be so likable?

"Great." My eyes land back on Autumn. "That part is settled. Of course I remember how hard it was when I first had Dahlia. I know you're exhausted, but I don't–"

"I think that you have an easier time working through things in your head, Rey." Miles gives me a tight smile. "Every word you say, every ounce of pressure you put on her to get over it is making things worse right now."

I'm silent for the first time since I sat down. I feel everyone looking at me, but now I refuse to meet any of those stares.

"Isn't that hypocritical?" I ask Miles. "Of all people that have pressured her to get over something, you're probably at the top of that list."

"Okay," Autumn clears her throat. "You're reaching, because this isn't going the way you want it to. I love you, I'm always going to love you, but you have to give me space. This isn't negotiable."

Her eyes bore into mine, and I notice what a massively, thick wall is behind them tonight. There's nothing I can do.

I'm sure I look like a child when I do it, but I stand abruptly and huff.

I obviously don't like the idea of space from her, which seems ridiculous now. I should've realized that during all the time I was so caught up with Kara. I realize that I've been giving Autumn space for months, and it's immature of me to demand her presence now that it's a better time for me.

I never claimed to be mature. Not once in my life have I ever said those words or expected anyone to believe them.

"Fine. Have a good night," I tell the table sharply. Then I head for the door.

I hear a chair pull out behind me, but I don't look back to see who it is. It's more than likely Autumn excusing herself to go cry in the bathroom, and my heart feels like it shatters a million times more at the thought.

I stomp all the way to my car, and as soon as my hand touches the handle I hear my name called behind me. It's Miles.

"I'm sorry," I say on a much needed exhale. I was too stressed to breathe in there. "I know you didn't do anything wrong, and you're not a hypocrite, and you guys don't need this on top of being new parents." The words rush out of me, desperation seeping through every one.

He nods, looking down at his feet that he's scuffling on the driveway. Watching him gather his thoughts fills me with so much gratitude. He's this worked up, he cares *this* much about her, and she deserves that.

They deserve each other.

"She'd do anything for you, Rey."

"I know."

"She thinks you don't know that," he says.

I let myself fall back against my car door with a little thud.

"And I'm pretty irritated with myself over that fact, don't you worry."

He walks over to stand next to me and does the same. I glance over to see an expected smile spread across his face.

"Surely not what you want to hear, but I'm so proud of her right now," he says, beaming.

"As you should be, but... why?" I ask.

"For standing her ground. Knowing what she needs right now and not backing down from it."

I don't know why, but that's what makes me start crying. I look up at the starry sky to clear the blurriness in my eyes.

"I am, too. She's gotten a lot better at that." I elbow his arm. "I'll give you some credit for helping her in that regard."

Out of the corner of my eye, I see him shake his head.

"It was all her."

"Someone's circumstances do a lot for their capabilities. You changed her circumstances and made her feel more capable," I tell him.

I couldn't do that.

"Stop sounding smart."

"My bad. I'll go back to being ditzy and ridiculous."

He laughs, and steps away.

"I should go back in, but I can't resist telling you," he starts. "You're like a little sister to me, Rey. I don't want to see you get hurt."

I roll my eyes.

"Please don't assume things aren't going to end well."

He puts his hands up in surrender.

"I'm not assuming. I'm just a little worried, naturally. It's hard to imagine the two of you... your two personalities..." He shuts his mouth tightly. "I'll stop. Sorry."

"The personality you saw, and the one I see are completely different," I say quietly. "I changed her circumstances."

He nods understandingly– *thoughtfully*– before saying good night and turning to go back in.

42

Weeks pass. Kara meets my parents, and *loves* them. I've never seen her so cheery as when my mom gets her talking, and *wow*, do the two of them *talk*.

Twice now, I've woken up to Kara on the phone just to find out that's who is on the other end. *Twice now*, my wife has been the one to let me know that we're going to my parent's house for dinner.

It's kind of nice to not have to organize it all myself. I've given her so many points for it.

Dahlia came home a week ago, and we've been doing a lot to make up for the lost time. I got to see a million pictures and videos, and I got to hear all about the family she met while she was up there. A small piece of me is jealous, wishing I could meet all the people that put these huge smiles on her face. She misses them already, and asks me when she can go back, but I know she's glad to be home too.

Such a big vacation took a lot out of my little girl. We'll go to the park for less than an hour and she's yawning and ready for a nap. Must be all that hiking they did.

She's willingly napped most days since she got back, and it blows my mind every single time. I couldn't keep myself from joining her either, we both need to catch up on some sleep after the crazy rollercoaster our summer's have been.

I kept her with me for a couple extra days, thanks to Caleb's understanding. Our normal schedule was not enough, but it's really never enough. I'll never stop missing her when we're apart.

If I could avoid my other responsibilities and pretend I didn't have a job, I absolutely would.

Kara hangs out with us for a few hours each night. For some reason, Dahlia has decided that Kara needs to do all of the arts and crafts the world has ever heard of. They made cards for nearly everyone my daughters knows, which is a *lot*. I think her entire school was on the list.

Friendship bracelets, finger painting, homemade play dough, you name it. And Kara hasn't looked sick of any of it.

But she needs a daily nap just as much as the rest of us, that's for sure. I move around my living room, picking up the paper scraps the two of them left all over the place during last night's collage making. I can't even be upset about the mess, they fell asleep leaning on each other, stacks of magazines still in their laps. It was precious, I totally snagged a photo. The boards of the front porch creak outside, and I wait for Kara to let herself in. She was out dropping off resumes, wanting to add a part time job to her plate after the blow up with her mom. Apparently fighting like this is their norm, but it's never stopped her mom from helping to financially support her until now. Pierre does everything he can, but he doesn't have the same means as Colleen, and Kara doesn't want to stress him out.

The way she put it was very respectable. She was grateful for the time she had to focus on school without having to work, but it was about time anyway. It had been a thought in her head for a while already. When she doesn't walk right in, I imagine she went inside her own apartment first. She does still live there, but she hardly ever spends time there when it's just me at home. I should have figured she might need to grab something, or even have a moment of alone time. Things have changed so fast, I should check in and—

A knock sounds at my door, making me jump.

"Since when do you knock?" I call out as I bend down to pick up one final scrap. I think I've finally got all the pieces that my vacuum would struggle to suck up.

"Since I know you weren't expecting me," a voice comes from behind me.

Not Kara.

Autumn.

I drop everything I just picked up and run to hug her. I don't even think, I don't even worry that maybe she still wants nothing to do with me. I've thought about her every day since the last time we spoke, and it's hurt more and more every time.

I've needed this hug for too damn long.

She returns it, and I feel her chuckle.

The relief that floods through me is enough that I'd probably collapse if she wasn't squeezing me so tight.

"I missed you."

"I missed you too, Rey."

She pulls away first, but I grab her hand in the process and pull her to the couch. I'm not going to trust my legs to do their job for this conversation, the couch is safer. Less possibility of a head injury when I'm sitting on it.

"Are we good?" I ask. I can't ease into it, it's all I want to know.

She laughs at me again.

"We are," she says.

She looks at me

"I've never had anything close to what you and Miles have. You're addicted to each other, you know there's nothing he could do that would make you stop loving him, and vice versa. I thought it wasn't possible for me to find. I thought I was destined to keep dating women that would never really understand. I've *never* felt understood. Not until her."

She blinks a few times, clearly processing.

"That's really..." Autumn clears her throat. "Your relationship is really there?"

"It is. I know that's shocking because I've usually told you every dirty detail by this point, but I think that helped us in a way. She's more of a private, reserved person. Taking time to figure our relationship out with anyone knowing anything or interfering was the right step for us. I'm sorry it hurt you as much as it did." I take a step closer, reaching for her hand. I breathe the biggest sigh of relief when she lets me. "I see why you needed some time. I'm sorry I wasn't ready to give that to you at first. I just love you so much, babe. It was hard to know I couldn't come knocking whenever I missed you."

She nods, clearly having made some peace with all of it.

"Obviously I've been a little extra emotional lately," she starts with a sniffle. "I'm surprised by how all of this hormonal turmoil has made me angry more than sad. And I *was* angry that you didn't come knocking any sooner. It made me feel like with everything changing for all of us, that maybe you couldn't be bothered to stick around for this chapter of my life as a new mom. It was lonely."

I shake my head, only in disappointment for myself.

"I know that feeling, and I shouldn't have been so distracted that I forgot about it and let you deal alone. I completely regret that part."

"I know you do. I'm not angry anymore." She gives me a tight lipped smile, but for the first time in months I know it's not my fault she's holding back. There is a dam inside her, ready to pour out of her eyes at one wrong move, and she's desperately trying to keep it back. "It's so weird that you're married to Kara."

We both laugh at that, because it is really weird. The odds of it are kind of crazy.

"I know," I say. "She's good to me, Autumn. I promise."

"I know," she agrees. "You've been through too much by now to settle for just anyone. She better keep it up."

"I can let her know that if she breaks my heart she has to go through you."

Another loud, surprised laugh.

"Because I'm so *scary*."

"I wouldn't want to mess with you."

"Good!"

She pulls me by the hand into another hug that is so well needed. I squeeze her tight, and she squeezes me back. It's just another thing in my life that finally feels right again. One of the last puzzle pieces.

"I love you, Rey."

"I've been letting it slide," I admit. "But I only gave Miles permission to call me that."

She jokingly shoves me away with a scoff.

"It felt wrong coming out of my mouth, but I thought I was being nice!"

We laugh some more, and I apologize some more, and we catch up on the craziness of these huge chapters in our lives getting started this year.

I hold baby Riley, and he wiggles the whole time in the way that only babies do. I look into his gray-blue eyes and wonder if they'll turn into Autumn's hazel, or Miles' brown.

Then I apologize some more for not being there when he was born. I'll let him hold it against me, in the half-serious way that my friends hold things against me. Not with residual anger, but just as a reminder that I can be a little shit.

And Riley will do it just like that, because we *are* going to be friends. I'm looking forward to the day when he's old enough for me to get on his every last nerve.

43

"You ready?" I ask her, squeezing her hand.

I made it as clear as I possibly could that she didn't have to come to this. There will always be other birthdays, and other celebrations, but she said she was ready. If I've learned anything from this woman in the last few months we've been together, it's that I trust her to know herself. If she says she can handle it, she can.

It just makes me admire her strength and resilience that much more.

She also really likes Vic, which helps. If it was Autumn's party, there would be some hesitation there. I don't think she dislikes my other friend, but she hasn't yet forgiven herself for their shared past. I think it's too hard, because she looks at her and sees a version of herself that she wants to move past. Sometimes I feel bad that my connection to them won't allow her to shove it all away, but I suppose it's healthier to face it. I'll be here to help her the whole way, however long it takes her.

Kara only looks mildly panicked when she nods.

"Sure. Let's do this."

I prepped everyone else, too. I wanted to avoid any awkward conversations, or attempts to feel her out. She doesn't need to be prodded like a zoo animal, and I will swat away anyone that makes her feel that way.

We step out of the car, and I watch her as she looks up at Vic's two-story house, covered in large windows, and deep green details. Her jaw drops, just slightly.

"Isn't it gorgeous?" I ask.

"Is Vic loaded?" she asks in return.

I laugh, surprise at her astonishment. It's not any bigger than the one her mother lives in.

"Kind of."

The door opens before we get to it, and Vic steps out in a beautiful blue, floral dress. She smiles so sincerely when she sees us, that my body has the sudden urge to produce tears. I clear my throat before I go in to hug her.

"Happy birthday, babe!" I kiss her cheek when I pull away. "You are *stunning*! This dress is everything."

At that, she feels around the sides of the dress and slips her hands inside the fabric.

"It has pockets!"

"It's a ten out of ten from me," I say.

Then I gently grab Kara's hand and pull her a little closer.

Vic doesn't give a second of hesitation before going in to hug her.

"Thank you for coming!" she tells her. "I love your outfit."

Kara slips her hands into the pockets on her skirt and gives a little wave to show them off. Vic lets out an amazed laugh.

"I need one!"

They make more small talk, telling each other where they shop, and I step past Vic to go inside. Everyone's in the living room, and they all turn to stare at me when I walk in.

"*Play it cool*," I mouth to the room.

Lacey and Wyatt, a couple of Miles' friends, look just fine. They're maybe a little confused, which makes sense if no one has filled them in yet. Julian is his normal self, his ever-calm demeanor in place.

Autumn looks way too nervous, and my heart sinks for a minute. She's another person that told me she was ready for this, but now I'm worried she only told me what I wanted to hear. Before I can ask if she's okay, Kara steps up beside me. She gives the room an awkward wave, and it's returned by everyone but Autumn and Miles. He looks pretty uncomfortable too now that I actually look.

Crap.

Well, there's no going back now.

"Let's get you two some drinks," Vic says cheerily from behind us.

My beloved icebreaker.

Kara takes my hand as we turn to follow her into the kitchen. Only once we're hidden behind a wall do I lift hers to kiss the back of it.

"You're amazing," I whisper. "You're a star."

She scoffs under her breath.

"I love you, but tone it down a notch. I'm not freaking out, it's okay."

I wouldn't say all of the worry falls off my shoulders, but at least a few pebbles of it tumble down.

"We have margaritas, juice, water, and–obviously–Pepsi." Vic gestures to the counter full of things with a flourish, and I giggle.

"How is a girl to choose?"

Without another word, she goes to hand me a can of Pepsi, but I shake my head.

"You kidding me? I need a *drink*." I tug on Kara. "What are you thinking?"

"A margarita sounds nice."

"Strawberry, blackberry, or peach?"

If this was a cartoon, I'd have heart eyes at our options.

"Blackberry," I answer with confidence.

"Strawberry *and* peach sound enticing," Kara offers.

Vic finds her own glass on another counter and shoves it towards my wife.

"That's exactly what I made. Try it!"

As she sips from the large glass, Miles walks in behind her and I freeze on instinct. I love everyone in this kitchen more than I have words for, but I will get fiercely protective over my wife if I need to.

Please don't give me a reason, I try to telepathically tell him. *Please play nice.*

"Hey," he says quietly.

Kara startles a little, and I think the liquid goes down the wrong pipe because she starts to cough into her hand. I take the drink from the other and hand it back to Vic.

"You okay?"

She holds her chest and laughs.

"Yeah, all good."

"I... need a refill," Miles tells Vic with a shake of his glass.

"How does strawberry and peach sound?"

"Delicious," he says.

Vic steps up to her ingredients in front of the blender, and we stand there in a briefly uncomfortable silence.

Kara surprises me by breaking it.

"Can you show me how? You shouldn't have to make *all* the drinks on your birthday."

Vic beams.

"I'd love to show you! None of them ever ask," she says and points in mine and Miles' direction.

"I make plenty of things for you, drinks just aren't my specialty. I don't know what this guy's excuse is." I go to playfully poke him with my elbow, but then I notice the look on his face.

He's basically flabbergasted, and it makes me feel like I'm winning inside. *That's* why I want her to spend more time with them. Not because she has anything to prove, not that either of us do, but it feels good to know that there's a change in her. A positive change, that's obvious to everyone else too.

I bet he can't imagine a time she'd offer to help anyone with anyone.

"You're staring," I whisper.

"You're a wizard," he says back, not as quietly.

"I didn't do anything. I just fell in love with her, and she's done all the rest."

He puts an arm around my shoulders and squeezes me into a side hug.

"I'm glad you're happy, Rey."

"Me too, Cress."

He pulls away and shakes his head.

"It took you this long to give me a nickname, and that's the best you could do?" he asks with mock offense.

I sigh.

"I'll keep trying then. Your name is just too short."

"Then call me by my name like the rest of the world."

"Nope! Too easy," I declare. "Happy belated birthday, by the way."

"What'd you get me?"

"Another year of irreplaceable friendship," I say cheerfully.

Kara turns back to us with a soft smile, and her hands full.

She gives one to Miles first, and he accepts it with a nod.

"Thanks."

"Sure," she replies. Then she hands me the other and gives me a knowing look. "I'll make yours, I just have to rinse the blender. Do you want to try mine?"

I shake my head.

"I'll rinse it. You two should catch up."

They both laugh a little uncomfortably, but they accept the set up for what it is.

I try to eavesdrop over the sound of the sink, but I can't gather much. They ask each other how they've been, and then nothing. Just the sound of water hitting the plastic blended I pout to myself, but I'm sure my wife will tell me everything later.

Vic leans into me.

"Smart."

"Hopefully."

The night carries on smoother than I could've imagined. I check in on Kara at regular intervals, but she doesn't seem to be struggling at all. Her and Autumn don't interact much, but they're polite when our board games force them to talk to each other.

I'm counting it as progress.

Wyatt, with less of a filter than I have, decides to ask the room if they think it's super weird that Miles' ex is here with his friend.

Yeah, he's plastered. Everyone just laughs him off, thankfully. It's not long after that when we call it a night, and Vic tells us all to get out of her house so she can take her husband upstairs.

She's pretty drunk, too.

As we walk towards our cars in cool autumn air, we give simple goodbyes. Kara gives Miles a quick nod, and he returns it the same way. I don't expect them to ever be best friends or anything. I couldn't imagine them smiling or hugging in greeting, but this is still good. This works.

If I had it my way, Miles would know exactly what the problem was with their marriage, but it doesn't matter. It's not about me, and if Kara wants to keep that to herself, then so be it. That's her prerogative.

I'll let everyone think she was this big, bad villain, while I enjoy what a sensitive little softie she is behind closed doors.

"You look like you want to say something sweet," she tells me with a sneer.

"It can wait," I respond, having mercy on her.

Not too much, though, as I place a wet kiss on her cheek. I giggle as she wipes it away, but that's all she does.

Oh, progress indeed.

Acknowledgements

First off, I want to start by saying that my mental health was not well during the time I wrote this book. It's instinct to say I don't know how I got it done, but I do know. I know that every single person on this list has helped me in ways they'll never fully understand. Ways I can't find all the correct words for as I type this up at four in the morning.

I suppose I could start by acknowledging the person that Kara was originally inspired by in Years Between You. I had no idea I'd be turning her into a love interest, let alone a main character. The real Kara was horrible to me, but you know what? Every person that's ever hurt us has a story, and a reason, and I hope this book has helped you realize it as much as it's helped me realize it.

Now to all the gushing.

Dominik, my dear husband, *wow*. Someone give this man an award for all of the late night meltdowns he had to deal with. I couldn't have gotten through a single second of it without you. Thanks for believing in me no matter what. You help me believe in myself, even when it feels impossible.

Alex Kettell, you beautiful human being. Thank you for continuing to check in on me, even when I always had the same answer: I'm stressed. Thanks for making me feel like a real author, one worthy of a dedicated reader like you. And thanks for being a real friend, despite the distance between us. Book besties for the restie. (Insert all the cheesy emojis here.) I love you.

Erica Grimes, you are brilliant. The details you notice are incredible. I can't wait for the day you have your own book published, because I know it'll be perfect. I appreciate you more than words can even say. I'm so glad to have a friend and fellow writer in you.

Ashley Orton, how are you real?! Thank you for suggesting my book to everyone you even *suspect* might be a reader. Thank you for supporting me and always having something kind to say. It has helped so much just to know you're always rooting for me. I also can't wait for the day I get to read a book with your name on the front cover, you're going to do amazing things.

Delaney Schwantes. Delaney, Delaney, Delaney. I dedicated this whole book to you, because I'm always looking for ways to show you how much I love and appreciate you. The only thing that would make you a better cheerleader is if we handed you some pompoms. I can't thank you enough for embracing every version of me you meet, because you have met a *lot* of them. We're all very grateful for you.